THE STORE

Knight Isaacson

The chapters are all designed to fulfil the required "guess who" game. It abounds in power plays and sex. It's great fun if you like to play the game (for a game it surely is). —*Joan Crawford*

Tearing away the glittering façade of the world's most famous and prestigious department store, Knight Isaacson's novel reveals the shocking power struggle and sexual decadence that lie beneath.

Knight Isaacson's knowledge of the fashion industry is based on a long career in retail merchandising in New York, London, and the West Coast. He has also written for the Broadway stage, motion pictures, and television.

AUTHOR'S ACKNOWLEDGMENT

To Greg Gunther for his invaluable help in proofreading, wit, punctuation, grace, spelling, patience, and only agreeing with us on pay day.

An especial toast of appreciation to Ann Pearle and Natalie Ray— your images and prose always create exactly the right magic. Thank you and love you both.

THE STORE

Knight Isaacson

A STAR BOOK
published by
W. H. ALLEN

A Star Book
Published in 1976
by W. H. Allen & Co. Ltd.
A division of Howard & Wyndham Ltd.
44 Hill Street, London W1X 8LB

First published in Great Britain by
W. H. Allen & Co. Ltd.

Copyright © 1974 Knight Isaacson

Printed in Great Britain by
Richard Clay (The Chaucer Press), Ltd., Bungay, Suffolk

ISBN 0 352 39840 X

This book is
gratefully dedicated to
'1052'

Lehson's

MEDITERRANEAN GALA

Tomorrow at 9:30 A.M., and for these next two weeks, Tulsa City escapes to the enchantment of the Mediterranean. Come with us on an odyssey to the sun-washed white stucco island of Mykonos. View the uninhibited colors of San Remo's flower carts, and the most fascinating bazaar of boutiques this side of Marrakesh in our Gift Casbah. Have a fling on the French Riviera for your cruise casuals. Shop the Costa Brava for shoes — and stop by the bench of our own Spanish cobbler. Discover the silks of Samarkand, the jewels of a potentate, the fabulous creations in the Persian Fantasy of our couture collection.

An event so far-reaching, so fashion-influential, you won't want to miss a minute of it, starting with the ribbon-cutting (Mesa Street entrance) when His Excellency, Count Ramon Villanueva y Portolo, Spain's Ambassador to the United States, joins our Mayor Herman Cupp. Tomorrow, 9:30 A.M., accompanied by the U.S. Marine Drum and Bugle Corps in concert.

Tuesday, October 4 Morgan Moore, dean of American couture, will personally present his gala fall collection in the Persian Fantasy Room, fourth floor.

Wednesday, October 5 Unveiling of the unique $100,000 mink Tabriz rug. Fur Salon on four.

Luncheon fashions will feature original cruise wear flown from the Riviera via Air France, Blue Grotto restaurant, fifth floor.

Thursday, October 6 Juan Felipe, America's own creator of Latin sophistication, in person with his holiday collection. Regency Room, fourth floor.

Theatre Centre, opening night charity for the new Centre of Performing Arts, 8:30 P.M. *Lysistrata*, adapted by Quentin Kimball, with a Greek chorus from Athens.

Friday, October 7 Ceil Bordon's personal appearance in our Cosmetics Shop for the unveiling of her new fragrance "La Mediterranea."

Gari Reichman, fashion's daring young man, brings his latest collection — a wave of resort ideas.

Saturday, October 8 Children's fashion show, fifth floor, 10:30 A.M.

The Gourmet Shop (Grand Street) featuring a gorgeous gluttony of Portuguese wines, Greek cheeses, French bread, Spanish olives, Italian pastas and Persian sweetmeats.

Sunday, October 9 All downtown theaters will feature this year's entries in the Cannes Film Festival.

World Premiere of Leonard Bindman's *Mediterranean Suite in B* (commissioned by Lehson's), Tulsa City Symphony Hall, 8:00 P.M.

Monday, October 10 Visit "The Casbah," — Lehson's gift Mecca, main floor.

Tulsa City Museum of Fine Arts loan exhibition of Greek antiquities. Charity party to benefit the museum.

Tuesday, October 11 Aaron Seton, in person, with his singularly unique and aristocratic gown collection. Couture Salon on four.

First American viewing of exact replicas of the Persian Crown jewels. Fine jewelry, fourth floor.

Wednesday, October 12 In person, Heymano, eminent designer of French couture and recipient of this year's "AL" award. Persian Fantasy Room, fourth floor.

Thursday, October 13 Meet America's own Alice Short and see her stunning dresses in the Regency Room.

Friday, October 14 Consult Ceil Bordon, in person, in cosmetics.

Visit Monte Carlo Casino where the odds are stacked in favor of the gentlemen, Men's Department, first floor.

Saturday, October 15 Last day to cruise through Lehson's world of the Mediterranean, entire store.

Gala Ball and presentation of the Annual Lehson "AL" Fashion Awards. Formal attire — Grand Ballroom Tulsa City Royal. Charity to benefit the Tulsa City Retarded Children's Clinic.

AND COMPANY

Founded in 1899
TULSA CITY, OKLAHOMA, U.S.A.

Abraham Lehson	Chairman Emeritus and Founder
Stella Lehson-Manchester	President and Chief Executive Officer
Edna Hope Lehson	Executive V.P. (Store Operations)
Lyla Lehson-Reid	Couture Director
Eugene Boardman	V.P. General Merchandise Manager
William Warren Bethel	V.P. Director of Public Relations
Frank Preston	V.P. Chairman of New York and Foreign Office
Walter Culbertson	V.P. Merchandise Manager Moderate Apparel
(position vacant)	V.P. Merchandise Manager Better Apparel
Sonia Angelini	V.P. Fashion Director
Milton Fine	Director of Personnel
Della Blye	Director of Advertising
Carl Zane Guest	Director of Display
Eleanor Long	Executive Secretary to the President

LEHSON'S AND COMPANY
"Taste Can Never Be Compromised"

SUNDAY, OCTOBER 2

Stella Lehson-Manchester stood naked in front of a three-way mirror, her firm body salted with tiny beads of lanolized water. She stepped from the sunken marble tub and continued to examine herself in the trio of glasses, before toweling down.

Wet and bare, her medium height and well-proportioned figure, with those surprisingly firm breasts, reflected the active, vital woman who commanded the nation's most famous fashion department store, Lehson's and Company.

The store, which bore her name, was more than fifteen years her senior. That now famous building had begun as a small, elegant shop on a dusty side street in an emerging Tulsa City when Victoria was still on Britain's throne. It had grown in the ensuing years in an orderly, yet haphazard fashion into the present conglomeration of thirty-six separate departments that formed the now overwhelming Lehson's and Company structure, which dominated the corner of Mesa and Grand, the hub of the new bustling downtown area.

Her forty-eight-year-old body belied its years. It had been well taken care of, like the store, and seemed to grow more elegant with passing time. It had never been a spectacular body, again like the store, but serviceable with a patina of chic that could be called 'handsome'. And, like the store, her body was totally owned by Stella. Customers might come and go, but their intrusions were invited, permitted—never against her will. The analogy between several hundred thousand square feet of bricks and mortar and a still perfectly maintained human figure was never lost on Stella.

In an almost mystical duality, Stella became the store and the store was indeed Stella Lehson-Manchester.

Stella leisurely finished her toilette, slipped into a heavy silk kimono and applied light makeup to her face. She smoothed her eyebrows and put a trace of pale lipstick on her mouth. She checked her triple image, smiled that even to herself she seemed taller and more im-

9

pressive now that she was dressed, was satisfied and left the massive bathroom. In the upstairs hall, Stella rearranged the two dozen freshly cut chrysanthemums that sprayed out from an exquisite pale yellow Ming vase on the hall table. Her eye approved of the arrangement, flanked on either side by rare Tang horses and went down the wide stairs to the morning room for her late Sunday breakfast. The meeting of the executives from the store wouldn't be taking place until after lunch, so Stella had several hours to check the *Tulsa City News* and the *New York Times* for all the fashion advertisements. Her maid smiled as Stella entered the room. Stella returned the smile.

'Good morning, Martha. Isn't it a lovely day?'

'Yes, Miss Stella, it certainly is.'

The maid held the chair for her and Stella nodded a thank you. Martha poured a large cup of steaming tea and went back into the kitchen for the breakfast, as Stella turned to page three of the *News* and the store's full-page ad.

She approved of the printed ad, as she had in rough copy form, but hoped the day would not be too far off when full-color ads were economically feasible in newspaper advertising. She faintly heard the telephone ringing in the kitchen. Martha brought in the breakfast tray and Meg, the cook, carried in a phone, which she plugged into the socket near the table.

'Good morning, Meg.'

''T' would be better if they let you alone for one Sunday. It's that Mr. Preston of yours. From New York, no less.'

'Thank you, Meg. Good morning, Frank, or is it afternoon there?'

'One-thirty and raining for a change.'

'Well?'

'Just left Amos Barron. It's official now. The State Department has formally approved of your nomination as ambassador to a European nation . . . which one hasn't been decided.'

'Good. Now what happens?'

'The President will make his recommendation, the Senate confirms and you take a refresher course at Berlitz.'

'Frank, I really can't thank you enough. Now that it's all happening, I'm so excited. When do you feel it will be official?'

'Amos has promised the President will make his decision in two weeks. Senate confirmation, in your case, will be a rubber-stamp routine.'

'Wouldn't it be marvelous if we could announce it at the gala?'

'Exactly what I had in mind. The press coverage would be maximum.'

'Dear Frank, you are something special.'

'Indeed I am. Anything else?'

'Not that I can think of. Have a perfectly marvelous day.'

'In this weather? Okay, Stella, I'll talk with you tomorrow.'

'Good-bye, Frank, and thank you again.'

'Yes, good-bye.'

Even though it was Sunday, the closed store was busy with activity as the top executives made their way from the employees entrance up to the fifth floor executive offices. Everyone from the display department was putting the final, finishing touches on the prefabricated décor that had been brought in as the store closed Saturday, turning the giant complex into various reproductions of Mediterranean locales. The largest exhibition company in the Southwest had been manufacturing the major units for the interior and exterior of the store and their work crews were still mounting, nailing and erecting the walls and ceilings. It was a kind of organized chaos and the edgy, high-strung temperaments of Lehson's creative personnel clashed and grated against the technicians' sober mechanicality and stoic industry.

The various senior executives, as they made their way up in the freight elevator, comprised as successful and eclectic a group of merchandising professionals as could be found in any major department store in the world. Lehson's had won them away from the most famous stores in America with more money, more power and prestige than the competition could offer. Their expertise helped mold and define the Lehson image into the shining mercantile star that it was.

The first to make the elevator trip to the executive offices were Eugene Boardman and William Bethel.

Eugene Boardman, vice-president and general merchandise manager, had been lured to Tulsa City from Chicago. In the Lake Michigan metropolis he had turned a creaking giant of a department store into the smoothest running, most profitable retail operation in the entire Midwest. Boardman's manner and method were conservative—sometimes rigid—and his superior pecuniary abilities were based on this pragmatic foundation. A balding man, sixtyish, impeccably tailored and well-manicured, Boardman's grey patriarchal image was as respected in the world of financial management as it was in the retail community.

William Warren Bethel, vice-president and director of public relations, dressed with the same subtle, colorful flair that marked his combined talents as a high-class entrepreneur and dignified oracle for the store that had created more merchandising firsts than any of its competition. He carried his tall, rangy, loose frame with more youthful energy than other men in their late thirties. Bethel was solidly attractive to both sexes (a must in the fashion business) and like most superior promoters, smitten with a wanderlust. Bethel had moved from his initial successes in the Pacific Northwest to Lehson's, not so much for the money—which was considerable—as for the excitement of the challenge. His sterling marketing and image-building talents were given full reign, and his success at Lehson's was unqualified.

Boardman spoke first.

'How's the wife, Bill?' He pressed the button for the fifth floor.

Bethel shook his head and half-smiled. 'Tina is going through one of her "trying" times, Eugene. Like all exquisitely volatile packages, she combusts on whim. It can be wearing—especially before a fortnight. How's Mary?'

'Excellent, as always. One comment though, if I may?'

'Of course.'

'You and Tina should think about having children. Not only are they the cement of marriage, making it complete; but, and I'm sure you know this, for some hormonal reason a woman becomes more of a woman after childbirth, more domesticated, settled down.'

'You think so?' replied Bethel with a lick of facetiousness.

'I know it. It worked for Mary and me.'

Boardman and Bethel left the elevator on the fifth floor and made directly to Stella Lehson's office, which also served as the executive board room. Her private secretary, Eleanor Long, was there to meet them. Their copies of the afternoon's agenda were ready and they strolled into the large, art-appointed office to await the others.

Edna Hope Lehson, executive vice-president and head of store operations, came up in the elevator alone. Edna, a trim, no-nonsense woman of fifty-three, was the oldest of the three Lehson sisters. The eccentricities and flair of the fashion genre had missed her, though she was highly efficient and effective in a job that usually was held by a man. Edna ran a tight, trim ship and she was as dedicated to her area of store responsibility as either of her sisters. She had driven in this afternoon from her Circle 'O' Ranch, twenty-four miles to the south of Tulsa City, where she maintained a highly successful farm of thoroughbred horses for both breeding and racing. Edna's colors had finished in the winner's circle of the world's best racetracks and bloodlines from her stock coursed through champions in twelve of the world's finest stables.

Eleanor Long greeted her with the deference due to the eldest Lehson.

'Good afternoon, Miss Edna. Mr. Boardman and Bill Bethel have already gone in.'

'Is Miss Stella here yet?'

'No, but I know she's left her home.'

'Coffee?'

'Yes, inside the office.'

'Good.'

Walter Culbertson, vice-president and merchandise manager of moderate-priced apparel, was getting out of his car when Lyla Lehson-Reid drove up in her sleek Porsche convertible. He waited for her and they walked into the store together. Even as coworkers they made a strange sight. Lyla, at thirty-six, was the most beautiful of the Lehson sisters and her position as director of couture was the perfect position for her talents. Lyla was a genuine arbiter of good taste and her expertise in the salons of Europe, New York and Beverly Hills had helped maintain the store's image over the years. It was often said of Lyla, and correctly so, that even if she had not been a Lehson, she would still have gotten the job. She was that good. Lyla had divorced Neal Reid seven years ago and their separation was an amiable parting. Reid preferred the tennis courts and fairways of America, while Lyla preferred the bedrooms of young men everywhere. Walter Culbertson could be most charitably described as looking like an overturned ashtray in an unmade bed. He constantly had a cigarette dangling from his mouth and was usually covered with its ashes. He not only chewed gum incessantly, but often cracked it—to the chagrin of the ladies present. He was unkempt, totally ruthless, eager for even more authority and power, and always kept his eye on tomorrow and the advantages it might hold for him. Walter was an anachronism at Lehson's—he worked for himself, while everyone else worked for the store. He would put the screws on a clothing manufacturer whenever possible and maintained the highest profit picture of any floor in the store. He was distasteful to Stella and her executives, but no one could deny the money he made for them all. He was common, avaricious and damned good in his job.

'Hi, Lyla. Lousy way to screw up a Sunday.'

'Always last-minute instructions from the general before a fashion gala.'

'Big deal. My floor's ready.'

'Only because you do less to enter the spirit of our little galas than anyone else. Admit it.'

'Look, volume is my business and volume can't be bothered with all these chi-chi trimmings. It's a lotta crap if you ask me. We should start thinking about going discount pretty soon and stop all this fooling around with a bunch of fag designers who usually end up on the sale rack.'

'Darling, you are talking about some of my dearest friends.'

'Screw 'em.'

'Most of them would adore it. Shall we go up?'

Della Blye, advertising director, slammed her station wagon to a stop, switched off the ignition, scratched her left breast and got out of the car. Della's solidly compact, wiry frame always vibrated energetically. She looked around, spotted Edna's sedan and strode into the employees' entrance. Della had been a captain in the WAFs, handling the recruitment promotion. When World War II had ended, she realized that the service offered little career for her highly exploitable talents and she gravitated into retail advertising. Her excellent work for a large dress shop in Atlanta had come to Stella's attention years back and she had been lured to Tulsa City with the one thing she wanted—a larger advertising budget and a relatively free hand to hawk the wares of the country's most famous store. She still walked like a WAF officer and barked commands to the staff of artists and copy writers who toiled so diligently for her. She was genuinely respected, though her manner was distant and her social life almost nonexistent. Like everyone else in the higher echelons of Lehson's corporate structure, Della Blye was professional, tops in her field and tough. She didn't go directly to the freight elevator, but stopped to see how the display workers were progressing with their job. Overseeing the store staff, as well as the workers from the outside exhibition company, was Carl Zane Guest, Lehson's display director.

'Hey, C.Z.! You going to the meeting or not?' Della asked.

Carl turned away from the two men hanging a modern Greek seascape on the whitewashed false wall that had transformed the costume jewelry section into a Mykonos taverna.

'If it isn't Captain Blye. Dahling, I've only been here since five. I guarantee you I shall not survive another year like this! Idiot! That picture is supposed to hang *straight*. Up. Up on the left. You, dahling, the one with the Neanderthal eyebrows, that's your side. There . . . that's better. Come on, Della, I can't stand any more of this. Let's go up.'

Carl joined her and they were heading towards the elevator when Stella Lehson appeared and joined them.

'Miz Stella, have you any gin in that office of yours? I'm dying.'

'So soon, C.Z.? I just finished breakfast.'

'Dahling, some of us have been toiling in your Mediterranean vineyards since predawn. I don't need a clock to tell it's cocktail time.'

'I think we can rustle you up a martini. The ad looked just fine, Della.'

'Thanks.'

'It's your best gala campaign so far.'

'The concept's good. It's easy to make ads when you've got something to talk about.'

'Mr. Bethel is going to have trouble topping himself next year. C.Z., you *will* be ready when the store opens tomorrow, won't you?'

'I'll be ready. Whether the store will be is another matter.'

'Come up and we'll get you your cocktail.'

'At least I'll expire placid.'

Sonia Angelini was last to arrive. Sonia was fashion director. Half Italian and half Moroccan, she had been a top model for Claubert when he was Paris's reigning couturier. Stella had admired her chic and awareness; it took little but a high salary to bring her to Lehson's. From model, Sonia had progressed to her current job and Lehson's could boast the best, most exotic fashion coordinator in the nation. Her strange accent highlighted the fashion shows and her unerring good taste turned many a sorry creation into an instant sale by the addition of the right hat, shoes or scarf. Sonia was sphinxlike in appearance and manner and seemed to exude an impenetrable air of mystery. No one knew too much about her, but Stella knew how well she did her job and that made everything else superfluous.

They all sat around the Chippendale library table that served Stella as a desk and conference site. Edna nursed her cup of black coffee, while Carl Guest was beginning to unwind with his dry martini. Eleanor Long sat beside Stella, her tape machine recording the proceedings. Even in the comparative calm of a Sunday afternoon, the sense of urgency that permeates any large department store was present. The aggregate salaries of those assembled was well in excess of four hundred thousand dollars a year. That much professionalism in one room created its own energy. Stella Lehson dominated the meeting quietly with the tacit approval of her executives and sisters. The Chair was hers by right.

'Any comments on the ad?'

There were none. This was the highest form of approval. Della Blye relaxed.

'We've gone over everything and all the unforeseen problems should be covered. I hope the crises will be minimal this year.'

C.Z. hissed a stream of blue smoke from his black Balkan Sobranie cigarette and commented to no one in particular, 'It'll be as calm as a bitch elephant in heat.'

'Thank you, Carl, for your graphic confidence.'

Stella went quickly through the agenda of the upcoming two weeks. Every contingency, every possible problem, every facet of the operation for the Mediterranean gala was detailed and assigned to one of the people present. No general on the eve of a major battle had more organization than the Lehson high command. Nothing was left to chance. No minute detail had been left out. Still, they all knew that problems would arise. They always did. Some would be handled routinely. Others, the larger ones, would respond to the rationale of gut instinct. The cataclysmic ones—and they always occurred—would somehow be corrected. The outsiders, the customers, never knew that the fantasy world they shopped in was as computerized and planned as a Disneyland presentation. The last item for consideration this afternoon was the agenda for the visiting dignitaries who spiced the two-week sales spree with their personal appearances.

'We have to make a slight change in Princess Judith's itinerary, Bill.'

'She's still coming, isn't she?'

'Yes, of course, but she won't be here for the whole two weeks.'

'Too bad, she's quite a draw.'

'I spoke with her last night. She'll be here for the ribbon-cutting tomorrow morning and through Saturday. Then she's flying back to Boston to spend some time with her family . . .'

From Carl Guest: 'How regally dull.'

'The Princess was born regally dull, C.Z. May I continue?'

'May I have another 'tini?'

'Of course.'

'Then you may continue.'

'She has promised to return, however, a few days before the ball. Bill? Any problem in switching your more important appearances to three days next week and two days the final week?'

'No problem.'

'Good. I've also made a change in Heymano's schedule. In thinking it over, I feel keeping him here for the entire two weeks might dissipate his value.'

Lyla said, 'Oh, Stell, Heymano is this year's lion. The award and all. I could use him for a month, let alone two weeks.'

'Granted, but your lion tends to roar a bit when kept too confined. No, I've thought it over and feel it's best for everyone concerned to bring him in for just the last week. Bill?'

'I agree. God knows he's talented, but away from Paris he can also be a problem.'

Walter Culbertson cracked his gum and spat out, 'Two days would be plenty for that freak. He's trouble.'

Lyla sighed, 'Walter, Heymano is a personal friend. There will be no problems, I assure you.'

'Look, Lyla,' Culbertson continued, 'Heymano's not your ordinary homegrown variety of faggot, y'know. I've heard he becomes an animal when he gets horny.'

Carl Guest murmured, 'No one who went down on the *Andrea Doria* can be all bad.'

Lyla laughed. Stella smiled. Culbertson cracked his gum and dropped a cigarette ash on his trousers. Eugene Boardman leaned forward and said, 'May I remind you, Walter, that Señor Heymano's visit is costing the store a great deal of money. To recoup something more than publicity, I feel he should be with us for the entire fortnight.'

'It isn't going to help anybody's image if he turns Tulsa City into the Sodom of the Southwest.'

Boardman insisted. 'I've spoken to his manager, who'll be with him, and am assured that the visit will be everything the store would wish for. He will be controlled.'

There was a pause. They all looked towards Stella for the decision.

'Thank you all for your thoughts, and you Mr. Culbertson for your concern. Heymano is being honored by the store for his genius in fashion. Part of our courtesy to him and his associate while they're our guests is to see he is protected, even from himself. I'm confident Lehson's is up to that assignment. Two weeks, however, might prove a strain. Two days is economically unsound. One week should prove a reasonable compromise. Are we agreed?'

Eleanor Long handed Stella a handwritten memo sheet. A single word was on it. A name. 'Frankel'.

Stella glanced at it and slid the memo into her folder of notes. 'Which brings me to something that has nothing to do with this year's gala. As you know, since the death of Sylvan Moss, the store has been looking for a suitable replacement as merchandise manager of better apparel. Miss Lyla has stepped in, in the interim, but it is impossible for any one person to handle two such important divisions. I must add though, that under the circumstances, Lyla, you've done an amazing job.'

'Thanks, Stella, but do me a favor and find someone else in a hurry. I'm running low on tranquilizers.'

'I think Mr. Boardman may have solved our problem. Do any of you know Joshua Frankel?'

They all looked round at one another. Lyla was the first to speak. 'Merchandises fine apparel for Alleff's in New York, doesn't he?'

'That's right.'

'Of course. I've seen him in Alice Short's showroom a few times.' She smiled and her eyelids lowered. 'He's definitely worth considering.'

Boardman spoke directly. 'His figures with Alleff's are exceptional. In my opinion he's turned their profit picture around single-handedly.'

'There is only one problem . . . Mr. Frankel is reluctant to leave New York. He believes his future in merchandising is in the East.'

'I've spoken to him,' Boardman continued, 'and he's agreed to fly here for a few days to look over the operation.'

Stella went on, 'And it's our job to change his opinion of this vital American area. Mr. Frankel is a young man with a fine potential. I believe Lehson's is the proper environment for that future to be realized. If there are no objections, I believe we should pursue and encourage him during his stay. We must all be extremely positive in getting Mr. Frankel to join us.'

Lyla toyed with her pencil and remembered back to seeing the virile Josh Frankel three months ago. She said softly, 'He can join me anytime he wants.'

Stella's eyes hardened for just an instant as she flicked a direct glance at her younger sister.

Lyla Lehson blushed slightly beneath her makeup. Stella's put-down, unnoticed by the other executives, stoked the latent rage that always lay in the pit of her stomach. It welled up instantly and enveloped her, but the years of practice in keeping it hidden allowed only the tinge of a blush to betray her inner emotion.

Stella realized her seemingly innocent glance had triggered the response she wanted and changed the subject.

'I have one final announcement that I'd like to make. We are through with the agenda, aren't we?'

Eleanor Long nodded.

'But before I do, are there any other bits of business anyone would like to bring up?'

Carl Guest was starting his third martini.

'Miz Stella?'

'Yes, Carl.'

He inserted another Balkan Sobranie cigarette into an art deco cloisonné holder and lit it. 'I'm a smidge worried about the look of the epicure department.'

Boardman answered for her, 'It looks the way it always has.'

Carl blew an incongruous smoke ring across the table. 'Exactly. I feel it's time for a change. It's becoming a teeny-weeny bit delicatessen, if you ask me.'

Stella allowed herself a smile. 'Carl, is this really the time to discuss our food store?'

'As good as any. I just want to put a little sparkle in the loaves and fishes, if no one has any objections.'

'I assume you've estimated costs?' Boardman habitually objected to any expenditure that hadn't been cleared by himself.

'I feel we can do a creditable job for about thirty thousand.'

Boardman sat up. 'This is a matter for the planning committee. It meets next month. I'll pencil you in for a hearing.'

'Next month? I'll be on holiday.'

'Still, this isn't the time for it, Carl.'

'Very well, Miz Stella. But don't start complaining to me when the customers start referring to your epicure department as tongue in chic.'

'Carl, I'll make the recommendation for you.' Stella closed the folder in front of her and sat back. 'Eleanor, you can turn off the recording machine.' She savored for a moment the incredible luxury of knowing that what she would say would be a minor bombshell. She looked lightly at Edna. Edna, the spinster, direct, no-nonsense, professional, this well-groomed, unemotional executive was her older sister. What was it in her that had turned the quiet girl into an automaton of regularity? They had never talked closely; even when, as children, Edna had held out the hand of a semimaternal sister. Stella had rejected the advice early and Edna had withdrawn, never to offer it again. She had grown to young womanhood solemn and correct. She accepted her obligation to the store and quickly found a niche where she would function to optimum effect. Their father had been pleased, of course, but store operations were just so much necessary sinew. Fashion. Innovation. Promotion. These were the vitals of the growing store. He had accepted Edna, then ignored her. She grew to what she now was. The old man had been a trifle jarred when she started the Circle 'O' Ranch, but said nothing. Raising horses, even thoroughbreds, was a far cry from the frills and furbelows of the Lehson image. Still, Edna had made her hobby pay, pay right from the beginning. That was in the family image and the fact was accepted. Stella wondered if the old man had ever thought about why Edna had never married. Probably not. The old man never spent much time thinking about anyone or anything that wasn't vitally connected with the store. She wondered if he had ever heard about Edna's attachment to the succession of masculine women who had worked at the store over the years. If he had, he would have dismissed it as 'her business'. His was guiding the destiny of Lehson's.

Her eyes moved next to Lyla. The baby. So pretty. So smart. So desperately yearning for love. Whereas Edna had rejected the concept of family affection and molded a rigid world of her own design, little Lyla had sought a human bond to hold on to at an early age. Lyla had been told she was loved. Unfortunately, she had never felt it. The words were insufficient, so she looked elsewhere for that elusive magic she knew she needed to complete her life. The family was delighted when she had become engaged to Neal Reid. He was strong, handsome to a fault, thoroughly engaging and doted on the Modigliani beauty of the youngest Lehson. Their wedding was the highlight of the social season and had meshed the proud Jewish family into the WASP machinery of the Oklahoma establishment. The Reids were rich and rich was enough. Poor Lyla, Stella thought, her strong, athletic groom had been a dud in bed. The pent-up fury of ravenous affection that spilled out of Lyla overwhelmed the trickle of kindness that Reid used for love. He was soon swamped by her demands and, exhausted, took to the tennis courts and fairways to regain his equilibrium. They separated as they were joined and an even hungrier Lyla began to haunt other places for some fleeting fulfillment. Her encounters were legion. Her satisfaction nil. They had divorced without rancor and remained friends, but Lyla's appetites grew along with the suppressed rage at never being fed what she desired. Stella was unable to give Lyla anything but a sense of place. Discipline and a firm guideline in business decorum would have to do. It was all Stella had. It wasn't nearly enough for the starving sister.

How would Boardman take the news? The cold, methodical, rightly important accountant who wanted nothing more than the power to create even more millions for the family.

Unkempt Walter Culbertson? His ambition and greed were so effective that he didn't even need the veneer of social polish. Culbertson, gum cracking and chain smoking, could wring a profit out of a corpse. Nothing stood in his way. His ego was his ambition and his ambition was everything. Never discount Culbertson in the success stakes. He was a born winner.

Bill Bethel came into focus next. Dear Bill. A creative mind second to none. Imaginative, too genuinely nice to be true and a great guy to boot. If there were any flaws, outside of the disaster of his married life, it would be his worship of the successful promotion over the long-range life of the project. Still, that was a minor fault and one that was being corrected as the seasons came and were milked of their potential. Bill deserved even bigger things and Stella knew he would get them. If only he hadn't fallen for such an astonishingly beautiful and equally astonishing stupid girl.

Carl Guest sat next in her line of vision. Poor, unhappy, brilliant C.Z., the best display director in the business. All façade, like his displays, but a caustic wit that cut through the sham of fashion. He saw it for what it was, even though he didn't know it. Carl was an oracle of merchandising, proclaiming the transience and shallowness of selling people things they did not need, but always with flair and élan. His epigram of himself was right on the target: 'Basic hack with pearls.'

Only Josh Frankel—and he would join the store, Stella never questioned that fact for a moment—was absent to hear her that sunny Sunday afternoon. Mr. Frankel, somewhere on Long Island with his wife and little children, never dreaming of the wonder and prestige that Stella Lehson would soon hand him. Enjoy yourself today, Mr. Frankel, for on the morrow you taste the addictive elixir of power. And, Mr. Frankel, remember that Miss Stella owns the cup.

'My dear friends and fellow workers,' Stella began and then stopped. 'I'm afraid I'm starting this off like a campaign speech. I'm sorry.' She smiled and continued, 'For once in my career, I'm a little lost at how to tell you something.' Everyone in the room caught the ring of import and listened intently. 'I really wish I could be casual about what I'm going to say, but I can't, so please bear with me for a moment. You all know that Lehson's has been my life. I'm proud of the store. Proud of my part in helping make my father's dream a reality. Proud of my sisters, of all of you here who are so instrumental in maintaining what's been built. But, the time has come when I must look beyond the store.'

The words that told them there was something besides Lehson's rang untrue to the listeners. They were all inhabitants of a special planet called Lehson's in a constellation named Retailing and to imagine anything or anywhere else was unthinkable.

'And in looking beyond, it must be a vision of something that will do honor to the store. Now honor is an old-fashioned word and to some an outmoded virtue, but you all know that here at Lehson's civic responsibility has gone hand in glove with marketing. We have woven the store into the very fiber of the city and the state. Della's handsome ad of this morning is testimony to how far we have gone to become an integral part of this community. How influential we have become in the world's markets. There is no modesty . . . Lehson's is the most famous store in the world today and that is a fact. Our Christmas catalogue is a best seller that ranks with Pulitzer Prize winners' works. Our image is unassailable and our customers are friends. We have become very big, by being very personal. We have never lost sight of our motto, which is as true today as when my father wrote it more than sixty years ago, 'Taste can never be compromised.' Now, I feel, is the time to move to another sphere. I have been told this morning that the President of the United States is considering my appointment as ambassador to a major European nation. If that honor should be offered, I shall accept. In accepting, I shall of course have to leave the store.'

They were genuinely stunned. Too stunned to even offer congratulations. Stella looked around, her attitude benign in the moment, and continued.

'Since we at Lehson's have always prided ourselves on planning ahead I am taking this opportunity to have you all think into the immediate future about who shall replace me in this chair. I realize, as you all must, that it is a far cry from being considered for such high office to actually moving into an embassy, but as people who do think a year ahead we must consider the remote possibility that this might occur.'

Stella looked around again and saw the momentary shock of what she had told them start to give way to private thoughts. Ambition, and its corollary, power, emerged and their eyes mirrored their thoughts.

'It goes without saying that what I've just said must remain in this room. It is more than a rumor, and I would sincerely welcome such an appointment, but idle gossip just might affect the President's decision in a negative way. After all, his wife is a valued customer. In conclusion, I want you all to think about what I've said and I want you to come to me with any thoughts you might have or ideas on how to maintain the continuity that we have established. In any event, I thank you all for what you've done and for what I know you will continue to do—no matter what happens.' She rose. 'This is a rather dramatic and possibly auspicious beginning to our annual fashion event. I know we shall all work hard to see that 1964's Mediterranean gala is the most successful and memorable one we have ever had.'

Bill Bethel stood and started the applause. He was genuine. As Edna rose to join him and the others, she thought, 'The pretentious bitch. She actually believes all that shit.'

They were all around Stella, congratulating her, laughing, savoring the news. Their emotion was open, only their thoughts were private. Edna knew that if she betrayed the slightest affection, Stella would puncture it with some comment like, 'Now Edna, you're worrying needlessly. We would never embarrass you with the presidency. Besides, we wouldn't want to lose the store's decidedly feminine image.'

Lyla didn't cry, though Carl Guest did. He had reached the zenith of his career in retailing as well as the end of his third martini and was thrilled at the prospect of perhaps redecorating some foreign embassy. Lyla reined her fury and kissed her sister on the cheek. As they embraced, Lyla caught her reflection in the mirror on the wall. Midthirties, damned attractive, sensational figure, looking good enough to make anybody's best-dressed list and yet, so frustrated she could scream. She was charming, more than intelligent, warm, capable of great friendship, every plus virtue and still an empty life. A void. A cypher. Zero in the living department. She didn't want the damned chair. Stella knew that and wouldn't give it to her even if she did. Oh yes, make no mistake about it, Lyla girl, it is definitely Stella's to give. Why the goddamn hell did she feel so frustrated? Almost to the point of panic. Why? Why was it that in moments of triumph, someone else's, she felt so completely empty and alone? Lyla's worm of despair began to crawl inside her. She had to get out of this room. This bloody successful, impersonal room. Find someone. Today of all todays there must be someone. Anyone.

'Oh Stell, I'm so damned happy for you. God, honey, you've certainly earned it.'

'Thanks, Lyla, but it's far from settled.'

'Fat chance. If I know you, big sister, it's as sure as next season's sale rack. Must dash, but really—it's just great.'

And she was gone. Walter Culbertson shook Stella's hand and paid her his highest compliment—he took out his chewing gum and extinguished the cigarette. 'You'll make one helluva lady ambassador, Miss Stella.'

'Thank you, Mr. Culbertson.'

'Say, when are you going to start calling me Walter?'

'Why Mr. Culbertson, who knows better than I that someone at the top must maintain a certain amount of reserve. You had better get used to it.'

Culbertson beamed inside, but held no illusions about the chair. He would have to work for it, since it would never be given to him. It was too late and too obvious to alter his physical image, so as he left, he began the plot to capture the seat of power away from what he rightly considered the only competition. Boardman and Bill Bethel.

Bethel kissed her warmly and Stella enjoyed it. Della Blye shook her hand and hoped no one would succeed Stella who would start interfering with the advertising department. Carl wiped his now red eyes, gave her a peck on the cheek and swept out with the others. Boardman was the last to leave. He stood for a moment and held both her hands in his.

'Dear Stella, what can I say? I'm so proud for you. For the store. It goes without saying that you can count on me for everything in the future as you have in the past. There'll be no problem with Frankel. The gala will be even more successful than we've planned. And, you will probably be made ambassador to the Court of St. James. It should be an eventful night.'

'Eugene, you are genuinely enthusiastic. I've never seen you like this.'

'Now Stella, even merchandise managers have very human sides.'

'Mine certainly does. It should stand him in good stead. Do give my love to Mary, and again, thank you.'

'You're welcome. Until tomorrow then.'

'Until tomorrow.'

As Boardman closed the door behind him, Stella sat back into the chair and turned to Eleanor Long, smiling.

Eleanor blinked her moist eyes and turned to her employer.

'Will I be going with you, Miss Stella?'

'That is a problem, Eleanor. You are invaluable to me here and would continue to be for my successor, so that is a real consideration. Still, I don't know how I could get along in some foreign embassy without your faithful and competent guidance.'

'I'd like to be with you, Miss Stella, but you know I shall do whatever you decide.'

'Oh Eleanor, I do wish you were twins. It would make it all so much simpler.'

'I'm sorry, Miss Stella, just an only child. Will you be stopping by Mr. Abe's this afternoon?'

'Oh yes. Father will be delighted at the news.'

'He's well?'

'As well as can be expected. Our Sunday afternoon meetings together do him a world of good, or so the doctors tell me.'

'Shall I call down now for your car?'

'Yes, Eleanor. And Eleanor. . . ?'

'Yes, Miss Stella?'

'Thank you again.'

'Shall I follow you in my wagon?'

'No, Della, get in beside me. I'll drive you in, tomorrow morning.'

'Check.'

Della Blye slid into the seat of Edna's sedan and slammed the door. The powerful car moved easily out of the executive parking area and on to the almost deserted downtown streets.

'Good ad, Del, not too frilly.'

'Yeah. Quite a little bombshell she threw.'

'Big deal.'

'Will you take the chair?'

'Hell no! But you should've asked, will she give it to me.'

'Jeez, Edna, you're the eldest and you've got as much stock as she has. You can take it if you want.'

'Maybe, but I don't want. Besides, my colder-than-steel sibling votes the old man's shares. Give her control.'

'Then why don't you get your ass outta the store? You know you'd rather be at the ranch anyway.'

'No, Del, not all the time. I'm still a Lehson and that store's as much in my blood as it is in hers. Besides, I'm the best operations director around and you know it.'

'I do that. I'd just like it better if we had more time to ourselves.'

Edna ran her tongue between her lips. 'Do you now? Well. I saw that new stud, Praxsis, service a little filly this morning and Della, it was really something to see. Jesus K-rist! What a performance.'

'Let's hurry, Edna, step on the damn gas. You know what happens to me when you start talking that way.'

*

26

The small monogram on the back door of the limousine read SLM as did the Oklahoma license plates on the grey Rolls-Royce. The initials stood for Stella Lehson-Manchester. The steel grey paint had been specially mixed to match its owner's eyes. Stella's chauffeur wore a uniform of grey twill that complemented, rather than matched, the car. The metallic grey Silver Cloud moved easily along the wide avenues of Tulsa City's most exclusive residential section. Stella looked down at her watch—4.12. She would be a little late this afternoon, but knew her father had lost all sense of time two years ago. He measured his life as spans between their Sunday meetings. A few minutes either way wouldn't make too much difference. Stella settled back in the deep leather seat. It was odd, but she never could feel completely comfortable in this car. She tried to think why. A Rolls was, in many respects, like an opulent vicuna coat from Lehson's. It owned you, not you it. Lehson's even had their labels sewn in upside down so the wealthy women who did purchase a rare vicuna could casually place it over the seat of the chair in elegant restaurants and everyone around would know where it had come from. It wasn't her coat. It was Lehson's. The same held true of the Rolls-Royce. She accepted the analogy and felt better about it.

For the first time in months, Stellar thought about Brian Manchester. He was her husband as well as the last initial in her monogram. Of the two, the monogram was more important. She and Brian had been married for more than twenty years. She had loathed him the first three years, become bored with him the next seven, and dismissed him for the last ten. They slept in the same house, but in different wings and were seen together only at those large public functions that demanded husband and wife. Privately, they were total strangers whose paths never crossed. Brian was a big, roughly good-looking Oklahoma gentleman with an income from family interests. He had dabbled at land development, real estate, tried a restaurant and failed and finally settled down to being her husband, even if in name only. The only time that Brian had been a whole man, one alive, had been during the war. He was a captain and a good one. He loved the service and the war. He would have made it his life, but a stray piece of German flak had ended his career and his service. The entire experience had lasted less than a year, when he was repatriated back to Tulsa City on crutches. There was a minor hero's welcome and he settled down to being the mate of the heiress to a growing

27

department store and measuring exactly how much of Bourbon county's finest whiskey he could absorb before their stills or his liver broke down. Today, the contest was still a draw, but Brian Manchester wasn't giving up.

Stella never measured a man, Brian included, in terms of another man—not even her father. The yardstick was achievement of a tangible sort; the success and growth and importance of the store. That was her measure. No man could compete with steel and concrete, and Brian had the bad grace not to even try. Stella detested him for not trying, knowing full well no one could succeed. The reason she thought of him at all today was the delicate problem that would face her as ambassador. It was out of the question that she would take him along, not that he would go, but she didn't like the idea of not having a reasonable explanation for his absence. Divorce was never considered—though he had begged her for one often—since that might indicate some unseen weakness, or confession of error, on her part. There was nothing that even remotely suggested any urgency to keep him in Tulsa City. It was a problem. Bill Bethel might come up with some palatable explanation that would pass as a solution. 'Why is it,' she thought as she looked out and saw her father's house, 'that the wrong men always die?'

The Rolls braked silently before the two-storey oak doors of her father's massive Tudor mansion. She looked out over the manicured lawns, shrubs and flowers as her chauffeur opened the door. Even now her father's plans and projections were perfectly carried out, although he was a man more vegetable than human. The house looked exactly as it always had and always would as long as he was alive. As she allowed the driver to help her from the car, she thought of the problem of selling the huge residence when her father died. She checked herself for thinking such thoughts, but recovered in remembering that her father would be thinking exactly the same way were their positions reversed. Stella looked up at the stone edifice—the turrets on the corners, the leaded pane windows, the multiple chimneys, the gardens beyond the house, the circular front drive. It was impressive in a refined way that was out of place with the newness and architectural exotica of the other mansions in the neighborhood. When Mr. Abe had built the place, all those years ago, it had looked old from the beginning. A thing of substance, like the store he built. He created his own history and lived to see it fulfilled.

28

Abraham was the last of the great merchant princes and although the dynasty he founded was in the strong, safe hands of his daughter, he was still 'Mr. Abe' and Lehson's was still his store. Arthritis had crippled his body, emphysema defoliated his lungs and cataracts clouded his eyes. His breath oozed out in painful rasps and the vocal cords no longer responded to his will. He could stay awake only a few minutes at a time and those times he did awaken were getting farther and farther apart. The doctors told Stella that it was a miracle he stayed alive as long as he did. But she knew that these Sunday afternoon visits were the reason he lived. An almost umbilical link to his store. His life.

Stella strode up the wide stone steps as the tall doors opened to welcome her. Martin, perpetual Martin, the family's butler for better than fifty years, still in that elegant old-fashioned livery, his shining, black face wreathed in white wool. Martin had once again opened the doors of Lehson house to greet her.

'Afternoon, Miz Stella.'

'It is a good afternoon, Martin. I must say that you are keeping in splendid shape. Splendid indeed. And how, may I ask, is Mr. Abe?'

The black man's smile faded. He closed the doors behind them and indicated the way she knew so well.

'He's the same, Miz Stella, which is bad. His miseries don't seem to get no better, no matter what the doctors do. Ah despair sometimes, Miz Stella, ah'm 'fraid ah do despair.'

'Martin, you are the eternal pessimist. Mr. Abe isn't leaving us that quickly. He's a spiteful old man and wouldn't give you the satisfaction of not having anything to worry about.'

Martin broke into a smile again. 'How you carry on, Miz Stella, with your nonsense.'

They passed through the enormous living room with its priceless furniture that had been unused in over a decade, the masterpieces on the walls unseen by anyone other than the servants, physicians and herself. Through the room and to the solarium beyond.

The solarium was a large glassed-in rectangle. From the glass ceiling, down the glass walls, splitting on to the Portuguese tile floor and filling every foot of it were hundreds upon hundreds of lush, tropical plants that sweated in the ninety-five degree heat of the room. In the center of this controlled jungle was a smallish semicircle of clear space and it was here that a wizened old man sat strapped into a cripple's chair. The once large and imposing frame had been reduced to a flimsy limp sack of loose skin that held the bones like a string bag carrying some light groceries. He sat shivering and wheezing in the oppressive heat and humidity of the steamy solarium.

He sensed, rather than heard, the clickety-clack of Stella's heels as they crossed the perspiring tile towards his chair. He turned his rutted neck slightly and sought her out with sightless, filmy eyes.

'And how is Mr. Abe this lovely afternoon?'

She kissed him tenderly on the forehead and sat on the ottoman next to his wheelchair as Martin left them alone. One corner of his cracked lips twitched up, acknowledging her presence. Stella took a delicate embroidered lace handkerchief from her suede bag and gently wiped the spittle from the corner of his mouth.

For the next hour, Stella sat beside the dying man, rekindling in his brittle carcass the last vital area of his life—his imagination. Every detail of the preceding week's events at the store were capsulized and ingested. No happening was too minute for her narration. If all else failed him, at least—once more—he came alive and active in the mirror of his memory as Stella recaptured the day-to-day occurrences at Lehson's.

Lehson's! The family store of the Southwest that had grown in half a century to become the world's most prestigious and influential fashion emporium. Abraham Lehson had founded it on borrowed money. Nurtured it with his unique brand of style and innate good taste. Breathed life into it with understated flamboyance and seen it grow from a decidedly out-of-place shop in a dusty Oklahoma hamlet to the definitive and most-copied merchandising authority in all America. From the very beginning, before the century had turned and the world was still feigning innocence, Mr. Abe had brought a stamp, a mark, upon the great department stores of a rich and powerful continent; a land that had discovered its wealth and was now searching for a history and sense of place. Events gave America its history. Abraham Lehson and a few others like Field, Straus and Gimbel dictated its sense of taste. But those other merchants had huge, growing urban metropolitan areas to plot their paths. Only Mr. Abe had staked his claim in a West that was still territorial, let alone urbane.

And Mr. Abe was the last one to remain alive. What he had founded in 1899 had kept the shape he dictated and grown up to become America's most important store in those areas where good taste and style were concerned. He believed deeply in his motto, and at Lehson's, good taste was never, ever, compromised. Abe Lehson built a store that shaped a city that influenced a nation. The incidental fact that a huge underground sea of petroleum was discovered a few years after the store opened just a few miles from Tulsa City, was—to Mr. Abe—merely a happy coincidence.

His daughter Stella joined his store the week of the Wall Street crash; tried her wings in the early Depression years and by the mid-thirties walked beside him as heiress apparent. When World War II ended, Stella was able to tread in his bootprints and fill them well. He had watched as she enlarged the store's horizons and increased its prestige. Mr. Abe was filled with a sense of pride, of accomplishment and dynasty. Lehson's lived and Mr. Abe would never die.

Stella's recounting of the past week's activities faded as he let his imagination take over. It was all bright and beautiful once again. The crowds, the clothes, the glitter and pomp. A soft euphoria of content prevailed and lulled Mr. Abe back into a blissful sleep.

Gene Zeller, the buyer of Lehson's better dresses, sat nursing a Scotch on the rocks at the long bar of the Saddleback Country Club. His wife, known not too affectionately as 'Pushy Sylvia', was in the club's card room dominating a rubber of bridge with three of the wives of other Lehson buyers. Zeller stared into his glass and wished he was still single and had never heard about retailing, when the courtly Brian Manchester, Stella's husband, walked over to him, a Bourbon and branch water secured firmly in his large hand. Manchester was quite drunk, but in control. It was still only four-thirty on a Sunday afternoon.

'I say—don't want to appear rude—but I'm afraid I've forgotten your name. You're with the store though, aren't you?'

Zeller looked up at the big man and read concern on his face.

'Yes, of course. Gene Zeller. Buy the better dresses.'

Manchester leaned against the bar.

'Zeller. Of course, how stupid of me. 'Scuse. Stella has mentioned you quite often. Hope I'm not intruding?'

'Not at all, sir. May I get you a drink?'

'Champion suggestion. And I'll get you one. Sandy! Same around again, please.'

Manchester drained his glass and waited for the refill. He was noticeably anxious. Sandy, the barman, brought the drinks, wiped down the bar in front of them and left.

'Cheers, old man.'

Manchester downed half the amber liquid at one pull.

'Ahh. Bit of a problem, Zeller . . . don't know whether you can help or not, but I'm damned if I know what to do. This is something of a first—even for the fabulous Lehson's.'

'Anything I can possibly do to help, Mr. Manchester. Please . . . just ask.'

'Decent. Definitely decent attitude. Real Lehson spirit, I might add. Yes, Zeller, bit of a dilemma . . . yes. You see . . . it's this way. . . . I mean . . . well, I just can't go barging in, can I? I'm still only an in-law, if you get what I mean.'

'Sorry, Mr. Manchester, but I'm afraid I don't.'

'Dammit, boy . . . Lyla. My sister-in-law. Stella's little sister. Got herself into the men's locker room! Well? Can't you see it's a bit of a problem? Yes . . . a problem.'

'Miss Lyla? In the locker room? Is she ill?'

'Sick boy, Lyla's sick.'

'We've got to get her out.'

'Of course we must. That's the problem, Zeller. She is, even as we speak, blowing the golf pro.'

Gene Zeller's eyes bugged out from his head and he choked on his drink.

'But the real crunch is that there is a rather prominent foursome waiting their turn.'

Gene Zeller was as stunned as if Manchester had swung a bat across his stomach. His jaw slackened and his knees went weak. The drink in his hand trembled and his voice cracked as he spoke.

'God, Mr. Manchester. What are you going to do?'

'Yes . . . do. Well, I never really fancied Lyla, though she is an attractive woman, so I think I'll just have another Bourbon. Sandy! Same again, please.'

'You've got to get her out of there!'

'Don't think we can, Zeller. She's sworn to remain in that rather awkward position until she's unloaded the entire greens' committee.'

'But . . . Miss Stella will . . . oh my God!'

Manchester turned to him and smiled a big, grateful, evil Oklahoma smile.

'Exactly. And thank you, Zeller. Thank you very much. You've gotten right to the core of the matter. Speaking for the family—don't think we all don't appreciate it.'

Josh Frankel sat in a window seat in the first-class compartment of American Airlines Flight 10, nonstop from New York's Idlewild Airport to Tulsa City, Oklahoma. The giant jet was circling the field, waiting for clearance to land. Josh had just finished his copy of Friday's *Women's Wear Daily* and held a half-finished Bloody Mary as he looked out the cabin window. Below him the sparkle of Tulsa City's lights twinkled in the crystal-clear Oklahoma evening air.

'What a nice place to live in,' he thought. 'No smog. No crime to speak of. No corrupt politicians—at least no obvious ones. Best of all, down there somewhere is America's most prestigious fashion store. And they want me.'

What they didn't know was that he didn't want them. Josh was flattered and intrigued, but he had no interest in changing jobs at this stage in his career. Thirty-four years old and up for the job of divisional merchandise manager at Alleff's. Dammit. He'd earned it. Fusty old Alleff's, doyen of Fifth Avenue. That was five years ago when he started as assistant buyer for the medium-priced coats. Made buyer in nine months. They never saw such figures. Buyer of better dresses and a complete reversal of the matronly, dumb styles the store stood for. Today, after two years, Alleff's didn't have to take a back seat to L. & T, Bonwit's, no one. And Josh Frankel had done it. Yes, he had a great future at Alleff's. If only they paid better. Big deal. He was young, healthy and tomorrow was his. That's what Cindy had said. Wife, mother and nudge. They were all settled down in Long Island, and Westchester wasn't too far away. Kids in school. Friends. Perfect. 'Who needs the damn desert?'

Josh smiled to himself as he thought of her petulant surprise when he blithely announced he was flying down to Tulsa City as Lehson's guest for a few days. 'Honestly, Josh! Is it too much to ask that you spend a little time with your family?' He guessed that Cindy was a good kid, though he really didn't particularly like her. Guess that means he must love her. In any case, she sure as hell was a great screw and that was important to Josh. It would be fun getting away for a few days. See for himself what all this hoopla was about. This famous, above-the-crowd Lehson's. A store. Like any other store, only better. Personally, he felt it was just the superior image-building press campaign that Bill Bethel did for them. That guy could make anyone look good. Imagine. Working with Bethel. With Stella Lehson. That sensational-looking Lyla. And he'd case the store thoroughly. See for himself what made it so special—if it really was all that special, which he doubted. Wonder what they'd offer? He sure as hell wasn't saving any money on the lousy twenty grand Alleff's paid him.

Josh leaned back away from the window and finished his cocktail. Mediterranean gala! Imagine, a store so powerful that it could dream up a sales gimmick just to boost profits during the two worst weeks of the fall season and see it turn into the most copied merchandising event in the country. Josh boy, that's some store! Wonder what else they have? Dream on, Joshua Frankel, just dream on. You're not going anywhere and you know it. Cindy sure knows it. Still, let your imagination run around for a while. Lehson's. They are a power. The prestige. Goddamn it, they're merchants! Creative merchandising that no one anywhere did half as good as Stella Lehson and her crew. And Stella wants little Josh Frankel for her team. Thank you very much, Miss Stella—must remember to call her Miss Stella—but I can't really consider making such a decisive move for anything less than fifty thou and a tight contract. That would be something for her to think about . . . coming from a scrawny kid from South Philly. The skinny Jew in the ghetto neighborhood. His old man peddles junk and his old lady took in boarders. Long time ago, but you never really leave all the way. Do you? Joshua Frankel, vice-president and merchandise manager of fine apparel for Lehson's and Company, Jesus Christ!

'The field has cleared us for landing, ladies and gentlemen, so if you will please fasten your seat belts and extinguish your cigarettes we shall be on the ground in seven minutes. We hope you've enjoyed your flight and we hope to see you soon again on American.'

Cindy was probably right. What kind of life would it be in an overgrown cowtown? The schools? What about the schools? Probably have only one temple. Oil men never have been known to be too friendly to Jews and it is an oil man's town. Too many unknowns. Stop daydreaming, Josh. New York is just fine. Fine and safe in the jungle. That's where the action is. That's where your future lies. Yep, that's all there is to it. Still, this would be very interesting. Might even be a lot of fun. Careful, Joshua, curiosity killed the cat.

The plane nosed down toward the runway; the wheels moved mechanically from the belly of the plane and Joshua thought, 'But most of all, I wonder what kind of broad this Miss Stella Lehson really is. Finding that out could be worth the entire trip.'

Curiosity killed the cat. Satisfaction brought him back again.

'Turn this way, Miss Stella. Thanks.'

'Mr. Ambassador, suh, y'all hold the scissors a little higher? Fine.'

'Hey, Princess honey, smile now. Hey! Great.'

The outside of Lehson's had, over the weekend, been roughly plastered a stark white, and the coats of arms and flags of all the nations that bordered the Mediterranean studded the areas between the windows. The four-sided clock above the main entrance at Mesa and Grand chimed, the hands slid into the nine-thirty position, the Marine Corps Drum and Bugle Band struck up the 'Marseillaise', flashbulbs popped and His Excellency, Count Ramon Villanueva y Portolo, Spanish Ambassador to the United States, cut the red, white and blue ribbon that officially opened Lehson's Mediterranean gala. Her Pacific Highness, Princess Judith of Monteblanco and Boston, assisted him with a glacial smile. Mayor Herman Cupp of Tulsa City was unsuccessful in upstaging the visiting aristocrats. Mrs. Stella Lehson-Manchester stood a little to one side, smiling and enjoying the spectacle thoroughly. The more periodic press was somewhat overshadowed by the presence of television cameras. The phalanx of invited dignitaries witnessing the opening included Oklahoma's junior senator (up for reelection); Morgan Moore, dean of American couturiers; all the Lehson vice-presidents; a three-star general assigned to America's NATO forces in the Mediterranean; Perk Polk, star quarterback for the Oklahoma Sooners, with his wife; Alain Pierre Boufort, enfant terrible of the French cinema and Seth Stein, grand old man of American sculpture. His Excellency, never an avowed Francophile, winced at the blaring strains of the French anthem and handed the scissors to the mayor, who hadn't the remotest idea of what to do with them, and ushered the procession into the store.

Stella took the lead. Inside Lehson's was a set designer's dream come true; C.Z. had outdone himself.

Stella commentated as the visitors, with the press following, marveled at the wonders on the main floor. They were on a wide esplanade traveling down the Italian Riviera. The colors, flora, and scents of San Remo seemed to be everywhere. Whitewashed walls, cascading bougainvillea, brilliant land- and seascapes on the walls, a strolling trio of imported Italian musicians serenading the early morning visitors and the merchandise—cases of magnificent costume jewelry, hand-crocheted stoles and sweaters, elegant handbags of softest leathers and embroidery from cloistered nunneries; over to the gift department—which was now the intriguing and inviting Casbah —tented, awninged and incensed. The most unusual and compelling assortment of presents ever assembled were heaped together in the native quarter of downtown Tulsa City. Through a wide Roman arch and into the men's department, or rather, the Grand Casino at Monte Carlo with all the salesmen ready to greet the day's first potential customers. Rich silk ties, jeweled cufflinks and sheer voile handkerchiefs were displayed on the green baize of roulette tables. Fine Italian men's hose adorned the baccarat table. French velour sweatshirts were neatly stacked where one would usually play chemin de fer. The tiny coffee bar tucked beneath the escalator had been changed into a sidewalk stand where bright Italian ices were vended by middle-aged black women dressed in the authentic garb of Sicilian peasants—a nice touch, thought the Spanish ambassador, as they stepped on to the moving stairway and up to the second floor.

Here the wide and diverse assortment of all categories of women's moderately priced merchandise was shown against a backdrop of strong sunlit colors. The fabrics and textures of the Mediterranean were the unifying theme that united this, the most uninspired of the fashion floors. A cursory exploration, not too many photographs, a sense of briefness Stella felt. This was, after all, where the average customer shopped. Only Morgan Moore seemed more than casually interested at the racks of medium-priced apparel. He was intently examining one particular section of dresses as the main body of guests boarded the escalator and was carried up towards the third floor.

On three, the impressed assembly marveled at the transformation that had turned the sportswear and casual shoe sections into a stunning reproduction of the essence of Mykonos's stark grandeur. Again the clothing and accessories were, in the main, specially made and styled from the Mediterranean resorts. The displays framed the nonchalance and understated elegance of the world's most expensive watering spots. Sweaters of every fashion and occasion predominated the merchandise, but golf and tennis, swimming and sunning were all represented by appropriately stunning apparel. The area which only days before had housed the sports and casual shoe department had been miraculously transformed into an authentic duplicate of a Spanish cobbler's workroom, complete with a real Spanish cobbler. The young, darkly handsome shoemaker looked up from his half-finished sandal as His Excellency detached himself from the crowd and crossed to him. They conversed in Spanish and it was obvious to all that the young craftsman was delighted at the honor. The ambassador thanked the Spaniard for his artistry and patience. The out-of-place shoemaker could only beam in gratitude. His open smile was not lost on Lyla, who had been noticeably bored with the routine so far. She watched as the two men shook hands in parting and was impressed by the muscular strength of the young man's grip. Her eyes expertly wandered down to the crotch of the tight-fitting leather trousers he wore and her excitement at the prominence of that particular muscle triggered a mental note to investigate his Latin inventory at a later date. Her eyes lingered for a moment on the young man and, as he caught her gaze, Lyla turned away to spy Morgan Moore arriving on the escalator. He was obviously upset. She was about to go to him, find out what was making this talented and gentle man so apparently troubled, when the crowd, at Stella's insistence, moved her towards the escalator that led to the fourth floor.

The fourth floor was Lyla's area. Couture. Moore's anxiety was quickly forgotten as the 'oohhs' and 'ahhhs' of the delighted guests punctuated their impression of the jewel in Lehson's mercantile diadem. The entire area was a re-creation of the breathtaking splendor of ancient Persia. Even Lyla and Stella, who had spent so many hours working out the stunning fashions inspired by the gems and tapestry of this opulent empire, were caught by the majesty of the finished show. This was the first time they had seen it as a fait accompli and their awe matched that of the others. The glory of an older Persia was magnificently reflected in the incredible housing that had been erected in two short days to reflect the costly and unusual fashions that had been specially designed for this event. Lyla took over as guide and led the visitors through the wonders of the fourth floor.

Princess Judith, that austere actress-cum-Highness, turned to Stella.

'It's quite impressive, Stella, but I don't remember Persia being on the Mediterranean.'

'Oh, it's not. But it does make for a truly gorgeous effect, doesn't it.'

'Yes.'

'And if Lehson's can't juggle a little geography, well, who can?'

Sonia, who had slipped behind the scenes, scooted out five of Lehson's top models who mingled with the guests. Everyone was duly awed by the fantastic designs the quintet wore. An exact replica of the Shah's crown rested in a glass jewel case watched by two uniformed guards. In another, identical case an array of Majorcan pearls of rare color and size had been mounted into gold, platinum and jeweled settings of Renaissance splendor. At the entrance to Lehson's famous fur department, a six- by nine-foot Tabriz rug was framed in gilt. It was a genuine marvel as it had been painstakingly crafted from sheared mink pelts that had been dyed to match exactly the shading in the rare original rug used as a model. There was no price tag, naturally, but its outrageous extravagance was obvious. The accessories, the dressy evening slippers, the handmade lingerie, all that was costly and unique and decidedly beautiful had been gathered together on this one floor to astound, intrigue and be coveted by the very rich and the very fashionable. This, in essence, was what Lehson's was all about. The guests separated to explore individually the various items that had caught their interest. Lyla made her way to Morgan Moore.

'Morgan darling, something seems to be bothering you.'

The courtly, elegant designer set his jaw and turned away from her and the question. Lyla realized that this unusual mood from the kind old man was something that she would have to find out about as soon as the tour was completed. She frowned at his retreating back and returned to the group which had re-formed in front of the escalator where Stella was ready to lead them all up to the fifth and final floor.

The public area of the fifth floor was a delight, for here, in addition to the crystal, linen, silver and china of the home furnishings department, was where the children's apparel was found. The gaiety, color and exuberance of the Mediterranean Sea had been ideally focused into the small and exciting fashions displayed for children's wear. Young boys and girls, the offspring of Tulsa City's finest families, had been recruited to model for this first day and were earnestly diligent in performing this exacting function before their elders. The children's department was a singular success. It was with more than usual difficulty that Stella led them all away from the youngsters into the store's restaurant.

Lehson's restaurant, the Five Seasons, had always ranked as the premier dining facility of any department store in the world. But, for the Mediterranean gala it was stupendous. The Five Seasons had been transformed into the Blue Grotto of Capri. One of Rome's leading chef's had been flown in to supervise the menu and the kitchen. The entire physical aspect of the café had been miraculously changed so the diners seemed to be actually in Capri. A soundtrack of the sea, the gulls and the laughter of the bathers was piped discreetly throughout. Deeply niched windows had been erected, behind which three-dimensional images showed the clouded skies and azure waters of that fabled isle. The cloths and napkins, the dishes and cutlery were perfect in their duplication of Capri's best eateries. The waiters and busboys were authentically dressed. The selection of food and wines totally emulated the best of Italy. The Blue Grotto was Capri and Capri for two weeks belonged to Lehson's.

It was all so exciting and time passed so quickly that the guests were surprised to learn that it was well past noon. Name cards had been placed at each seating in the Blue Grotto and the dignitaries had little problem in finding where they were to enjoy lunch. Each Lehson executive hosted a different table. As the waiters poured the first glasses of the chilled Italian white wine, the models started their fashion parade of the newest resort clothes inspired by the Mediterranean spas. The strolling musicians ambled through the sea of tables and all was festive and gay.

Downstairs, the store was already packed with customers and lookers, and as the cash registers rang discreetly, the honored ones who relaxed in the Blue Grotto were unaware that they were but the vanguard of this highly organized and extremely profitable merchandising promotion. The opening had been perfect.

Laughter mingled with the music and appreciative comments. Glasses clinked and the zesty aroma of the delicate antipasto permeated the room. Even the rich and famous got hungry. At Lyla's table, the mood was somewhat down. Morgan Moore, taut and petulant, refused to either speak or eat. Lyla tried her best to bring him out of his funk.

'Morgan dear, at least tell me what's the matter. I hope it's not something I've done.'

The old man's eyes shifted to hers and stared down.

'If it is, I shall soon find out.'

He could no longer contain his inner fury. Moore rose, pushed his plate aside with a clatter, and addressed her in a loud, tight voice.

'Follow me . . . please!'

All heads turned toward them as Morgan Moore bulled his way out of the room, his rage obvious. Lyla, truly mystified, excused herself from the table and went after him.

Moore pushed through the customers fawning over the children's clothes and made his way to the down escalator. A now worried Lyla tried to keep up with him as he elbowed and sidled his way through the people on the moving staircase. Finally, he reached the second floor.

Moore's anger had risen as he descended down to the floor where the moderate-priced apparel was displayed. He hustled through the scores of clutching women and made directly for the section where the dresses were receiving the lion's share of attention. Lyla could hardly keep up with him.

He had reached a long rack of garments, grabbed one piece out and wheeled to face Lyla. He thrust the dress in front of her.

'This!'

The dress trembled in his hand.

'Oh my God!'

It was an exact, line-for-line duplicate of Moore's most successful, best dress of the preceding season. Even the fabric had been copied. The only thing that told this original from this wide selection of copies was the five hundred dollars difference in price. Walter Culbertson's buyer had marked them ninety dollars and, at that figure, they were selling like hot cakes. Moore, warming to his rage, threw the dress on the floor and dashed to another track. Again he grabbed a representative style. Again it was a duplicate of his original.

'This rag is only seventy-five dollars!'

And that dress followed its sister to the carpet.

Morgan Moore went through the department, flinging styles out and down. The customers retreated from his frenzy and Lyla stood aghast as the couturier pulled out an even dozen styles that had been duplicated exactly from his expensive originals.

'Was I invited to this charade merely to be mocked? How dare Lehson's do this to me! Is that all that forty years of doing business with the store means to you?'

The full realization of what Culbertson had done was not lost on Lyla. She tried to rationalize, but even in a business where piracy is common, this was a singular insult. Still, Lehson's and its policy must come first.

'Morgan, I swear to you that neither Stella nor I had any idea this had been done. You must believe me. It is the truth.'

'So what do you intend to do?'

'Apologize. Profusely if necessary.'

'That is insufficient.'

'What can I do?'

'For a start, every single piece of these shoddy imitations must be instantly removed from the store.'

Lyla's expert eye told her that there were several hundred dresses displayed on the floor, which meant that an equal amount must be in stock in the warehouse. To even consider his demand would mean not only a huge financial loss, but a depletion of the second floor dress inventory that would be disastrous.

'I'll talk to Stella the instant lunch is over.'

'That, my dear, is entirely up to you. If your ad and my schedule are correct, I am slated to preview my entire new fall collection tomorrow afternoon. Obviously, I refuse to add injury to insult by even considering such a showing.'

'Now Morgan. Let's go up to my office, have coffee and we'll find some way to work this out.'

'Your coffee, like this vile prairie called Oklahoma, would stick in my craw. I'm returning to my hotel. I shall expect Lehson's decision within an hour.'

Moore's reserve of dignity was called up as the proud, hurt designer left her and the store. That was all there was to it.

Lyla never lost her control. Back in the Blue Grotto, she sought out Stella, whispered in her ear that a meeting between them was imperative, and returned to her guests to continue the luncheon as if nothing had happened.

Lyla briefed Stella quickly and thoroughly. It took only a few minutes.

'Eleanor? Ask Mr. Culbertson to come in now, please.'

The door to her office opened and the man who accounted for the largest profit segment of Lehson's income casually entered. He nodded to Lyla, cracked his chewing gum and sat in a chair next to her. He slouched down, rumpled, and lit a cigarette.

Lyla eyed the merchandise manager carefully as Stella spoke. She was as calm as ever.

'Mr. Culbertson, I'm afraid the store has a serious problem on its hands.'

'Yeah?'

'Elena Rogers buys the dresses on your floor?'

'That's right.'

'Did she buy these?'

Stella's hand indicated the twelve Moore copies that now hung on a rack near her desk. Culbertson's glance was merely cursory.

'Naw, those are mine. Rogers just worked out the colors and sizes.'

'You know that these are identical duplicates of Morgan Moore's things?'

'Of course I know. That's why I went in so heavy on them.'

'Mr. Moore, our honored guest, is furious.'

'Big deal.'

'Mr. Culbertson, it is a big deal. No one in this store appreciates more than I do the successful operation you are running, but we have not built Lehson's into what it now is without ethics. These copies, especially at this time, are highly unethical.'

Culbertson stiffened.

'Careful, Miss Stella.'

Stella arched an eyebrow and with a voice of acid, said, 'I beg your pardon.'

'Facts! All these styles are from Zack Purlmutter. Purlmutter is one of my three top volume resources. Purlmutter does better'n ten million nationally. Rogers and I saw the line together and spotted these knock-offs right away. I knew if we didn't get them confined to Lehson's, our competition would get them. Nothing was going to stop those dresses getting into Tulsa City. Last fact, I knew that Moore's stuff had always been exclusive with the store. I felt it was only prudent they continued to be. There was no alternative.'

'Your logic is impeccable, but our problem still exists with Mr. Moore.'

'Not our problem, Miss Stella, your problem. Yours and Miss Lyla's.' He rose. 'Can I get back to the second floor. Your precious Morgan Moore has wreaked havoc in my dress department.'

'Thank you for the explanation.'

Culbertson's cigarette ash snowflaked down on to his jacket as he turned and left the room. Even after he had gone, his presence remained.

'What do we do now, Stell?'

'Tell Moore the truth.'

'In the mood he's in?'

'Can you think of an alternative?'

Lyla was silent as Stella dialed the hotel. She was connected to Moore's suite. The phone rang once. He answered.

'Morgan, it's Stella.'

'Yes.'

'I'm not going to apologize, dear, that would be insulting. I've found out what happened and why. May I tell you?'

'What happened is too painfully obvious. The why won't change anything. I'm interested only in how you intend solving this mess.'

'The only feasible solution is for you to charitably excuse the store; and you can rest assured that nothing of this nature will ever happen again.'

'I? I should excuse Lehson's? You can't be serious?'

'Quite serious. We're all adults and while I won't for a moment try to mitigate the seriousness of what's happened, I only know it has happened and there's nothing that can be realistically done.'

'I don't believe my ears! Well, Mrs. Manchester, I can certainly do something. I can return to New York on the next plane.'

'That would be foolish, Morgan. Your customers don't even know our second floor exists.'

'Not even when their maids come in wearing copies of my originals?'

'Lehson's moderate-priced department does not cater to servants.'

'Will you arrange that my samples, all my samples, are packed and returned to my showroom today?'

'Of course, if that's what you want.'

'That is what I demand!'

'Morgan, you have no idea how unhappy this all makes me.'

'But not unhappy enough to remove those copies?'

44

'You know I can't do that.'

'Miss Stella, you know exactly what you can do.'

And the line went dead.

Stella replaced the receiver and sighed. A major crisis this early in the promotion didn't augur well for the remaining days.

'We've lost Moore, Lyla.'

'Shit!'

'Exactly. Get a hold of Sonia and have her remove all his samples down to shipping. They are to be packed with great care and air-freighted back to New York immediately.'

'And tomorrow's showing?'

'Canceled. In fact, I assume we shall no longer carry Moore's things in the store. Sorry.'

'So am I. He's the one constant talent we've got.'

'Had.'

'Had. Goddamn that Culbertson!'

'What could he do?'

'He could do plenty as far as I'm concerned.'

'Forget it. Now then, how do we fill in tomorrow afternoon?'

'Better get Della up here for starters.'

'Right.'

How Lehson's handled a big problem was testimony to its reputation. Della Blye called the *Tulsa City News* and pulled the ad that was to announce the Morgan Moore showing. Bill Bethel used all his persuasion and got the closing time for advertising moved ahead two hours at the paper. Della, Lyla and Stella personally wrote the copy for the substitute ad—once the new idea had been agreed upon. Again, it was Bethel who filled the gap.

'We've got a fashion museum, haven't we? Examples of the most important styles since nineteen hundred. What's more interesting than a retrospect showing? It's fun, it's fascinating and it's news-worthy.'

Della's mind whirred and she blurted out, 'Lehson's presents a Golden Jubilee of Fashion. Fifty years of all that has been beautiful.'

'Dammit Della, that's good enough for an entire two-week promotion.'

'Thanks, Bill, but let's just salvage tomorrow.'

And together, they did save Tuesday afternoon. While Della worked on finalizing the copy for the ad, Lyla alerted Sonia to what was happening. Bethel contacted the Tulsa City Museum of Fine Art and they agreed to help in any way possible. Stella phoned Princess Judith and the iceberg of the Mediterranean thawed enough to agree to personally model a few of the antique styles, provided of course that they fit her perfectly. The wheels of talent spun and within seventy minutes it was all systems go. Della was on her way to the paper with the new copy. Bethel was off to notify the press of the exciting new event. Sonia was happily busy rummaging through the perfectly maintained relics of six decades of styling, selecting those obvious and startling choices to overwhelm tomorrow's ladies with Lehson's history. Lyla was about to leave the office when Stella stopped her.

'Have Sonia select the things with a mind to the Mediterranean, if at all possible. The only word of caution is to make absolutely sure that not one Morgan Moore costume is included.'

'That may be difficult. He's been among the best for over forty years.'

'Maybe, but Lehson's is the best and has been for over sixty years. The store, still, is more important than any individual.'

Walter Culbertson's office reflected its occupant. Messy, frenetic, blue hazed with cigarette smoke. He'd barked at his assistant that no calls were to be allowed and slammed the door to insure privacy. He used the private, outside line that didn't go through the store's switchboard.

'Operator. Person-to-person to Mr. Zachery Purlmutter . . . M-U-T-T-E-R . . . New York. Yeah, got it right here . . . area code is 212 . . . Longacre 4-6649. Yeah . . . 4-9. Make it a collect call. Culbertson . . . 448-2239. No . . . I'll hold.'

Culbertson extracted the wad of gum from his mouth and stuck it under his desk. He cradled the telephone as he lit another cigarette. The operator informed him that the call was accepted and his party was on the line.

'Zack? Walt.'

'Hey, how's it going, buddy boy?'

'Stuff that crap . . . listen. Listen real good. If you or anyone in that crummy joint so much as mumbles in his sleep that I gave you those Moores to copy, I'll see your fat ass stretched all the way across Seventh Avenue and you'll never get so much as a sleeve into Lehson's ever again. Is that clear?'

'Hey Walt, no sweat. Cool down.'

'Fuck you, Purlmutter. I'm not kidding. Your mouth better be tighter than a fly's asshole or I'll break you, so help me God.'

'Walt, I've just gone mute.'

'Good. Any reaction on the styles yet?'

'Only sensational, that's all. Tested 'em at Magnin's and the one-piece jerseys checked right out.'

'Figures. I'm having Rogers put through a reorder next week. Figure about a hundred pieces.'

'Good. We can deliver.'

'I want a price break, Zack.'

'Hell, Walt, I already shaved the cost for you.'

'So what, I gave you the dresses didn't I?'

'Yes, but . . .'

'No buts, we're a house account, aren't we?'

'Yes.'

'Then how about the salesman's commission?'

'Christ, Walter. You'll kill me.'

'We all gotta go. I'll tell Rogers to knock off eight percent.'

'Okay, I guess so, but . . .'

'Yeah, yeah . . . just remember what I said.'

'Well, Mr. Frankel, what do you think of Lehson's so far?'

'To say I'm impressed would be an understatement. I never would have believed it.'

Eugene Boardman sat back and allowed himself a rare smile.

'Then we do live up to our advance publicity?'

'With honors.'

'Of course, we are at our best during these annual fashion events. The Mediterranean theme is particularly good, I think. Allows the buyers ample latitude to create.'

'I think I see why Lehson's is such an emulated operation. Fifth Avenue didn't follow your lead until six years ago.'

'Uh, five. Five years to be exact. But, that is what this store is all about. I'm sorry that you haven't had a chance to meet Miss Stella yet, but it is opening day. You understand.'

'Of course. Besides, there's an awful lot to absorb. This is quite a plant.'

'As modern as tomorrow inside. Still the public sees tradition, history, a sense of definition and place. A most pleasant combination.'

'And I've only seen the first three floors.'

'You will need an entire day for the fourth floor alone. We want you to get used to it.'

'Well, now let's not rush things, Mr. Boardman.'

'Not rushing, merely being optimistically hopeful.'

'As I told you over the phone, sir, I am extremely happy at Alleff's.'

'Of course, but that doesn't mean you can't be happier somewhere else.'

'I don't want to appear rude, but may we hold off this area of conversation for a while?'

'Of course we can. I'm the one who seems to be rude, after all . . . you are our guest. Now, then, is there anything at all we can get you? A guide, perhaps?'

'No, not yet at least. I'm like a kid lost in a toy store. It's more fun finding out for myself.'

'Well good. You did bring your dinner jacket, didn't you?'

'Just like you suggested.'

'Fine. The cocktail party this evening at Miss Stella's is semi-formal. Hopefully, we'll all be able to chat freely there.'

'I'm looking forward to meeting her.'

'And she you. You just make yourself at home—roam about all you want. Anything you wish to see, call my secretary and she'll arrange it. I'll pick you up at your hotel at around six-thirty. Will that give you enough time to change?'

'More than enough. Thank you, Mr. Boardman.'

'Thank you, uh, Josh.'

'Well, Eugene, is he impressed?'

'Yes, it would be hard not to be.'

'Good. Is there any particular tack you feel I should take this evening in chatting with him?'

'Your usual charm will suffice, Miss Stella. If he's going to be won over it will have to be with more than money.'

'The Lehson mystique shall be supercharged, I assure you. Has Mr. Frankel any obvious Achilles' heel?'

'None that I can see. He's all we knew him to be. If there's anything that will help decide him, I'd suspect it would be the kind of life he would expect away from the store. Most New Yorkers still look upon this part of the world as the sticks, you know?'

'Yes, unfortunately. I'll do my best to convince him otherwise.'

'Then we can assuredly count on his joining Lehson's.'

'We know better than to count on anything. A party is a festive affair. I don't want Mr. Frankel to feel too out of place. I want his visit to be a perfect one. Perfect in all respects. Can you see to it that nothing is left to chance . . . about his getting the wrong impression of our hospitality?'

'No problem. Until this evening then.'

'Yes, it should be a lovely party.'

The Junior World, that department which specialized in those young ladies from midteen to twenties, occupied its own special place in the store. The concept and new sizing were the last radical departure that Lehson's had allowed in its structured merchandising. Juniors, as a size and as a concept, came into being just after the Second World War. Lehson's quickly grasped the significance of this potential and revamped their mezzanine to hold this latest innovation. Junior World was reached by its own staircase and was, besides this, isolated from the rest of the store. A soda fountain and Coke machine were as prominent as the clothing. Pop music was piped in and the sales-girls were only a bit older than the customers. It was *Young. With It. Alive.* It was a fun section for everyone and, therefore, highly successful.

Ann Carter, who bought the junior apparel, had started with the store right out of college, as a salesgirl. She had grown with the de-partment during the last four years and today was, at twenty-four, a seasoned veteran of the merchandising wars. Since the department was still relatively new, though growing, a merchandise manager had not as yet been appointed to oversee things. Ann pretty much functioned on her own, though she did report to Walter Culbertson four times a year. Culbertson seemed satisfied with her profits and left her alone. He didn't understand Junior World, Ann Carter or anything at all on the mezzanine but the Coke machine.

Ann Samantha Carter, Tulsa City born, cute, perky, bright. Some-thing of a swinger. Definite intellectual leanings. What was a super girl like Ann doing in a place like Tulsa City? Lehson's was the answer. She loved the store. Her job. And Ann adored her father, city editor of the *Tulsa City News*, and was just waiting to really fall in total love to complete her ideal existence. It was all still new and exciting, and since the store didn't seem to intrude too much on her Junior World, she functioned just splendidly. She was just a little surprised when the banker-clad Eugene Boardman made his way up the stairs to her department. Outside of Bill Bethel, no major store executive ever found their way to her little domain.

'Why Mr. Boardman, welcome to Junior World!'

'Yes . . . quite a climb.'

'Sorry about that. I keep forgetting all my customers are usually hyped up.'

Boardman, like everyone else, couldn't help but like the girl. He managed a smile.

'I foresee the day, and not too far off at that, when we'll have to find you larger and more accessible quarters, young lady.'

'Oh, I wouldn't like that.'

'A buyer who doesn't want a larger department? Will wonders never cease.'

'Junior World is quite happy in its own little island, thank you. Confidentially, no one bothers us up here. I think they don't know we're even around.'

'I shall guard your secret.'

'Something for your daughter, Mr. B.?'

'No, she's far too sophisticated to let her father do any shopping for her . . . other than a gift certificate.'

'Wise child.'

'Indeed. The reason I braved those steps was to invite you to a party.'

'Super! When and where?'

'Tonight and at Miss Stella's.'

'I'm impressed. Why?'

'Forgive the lateness of the invitation, Ann, but it actually is an official store function. Under ordinary circumstances, we wouldn't bore you with it.'

'I'm never bored. Curious, but never bored.'

'That's good to know, dear. There's a visiting fireman here, the store's guest for a few days, and since he's a very nice chap we figured he might enjoy some . . . uh . . . super company.'

'Sounds dreary.'

'Not at all. Mr. Frankel isn't all that much older than you are. From Alleff's in New York.'

'Married?'

'Yes, I think so.'

'Dreary.'

'I'm not suggesting a rendezvous, Ann, just an escort for a few hours. It is store policy to be polite to our guests, you know?'

'I'm sorry, Mr. B., of course I'll be delighted to be his date. What does one wear?'

'Well, it's semiformal and, as I said, at Miss Stella's. I leave the wardrobe up to you.'

'Can I filch something from stock?'

'Anything you want.'

'Super. Should be fun.'

'You'll see how the older half lives.'

'Why not? Have to get used to being a merchant princess, don't I?'

'Yes, you do.'

'Frankel? Hey, not Josh Frankel?'

'Why yes. Do you know him?'

'No way. Just saw him in the market last year. He's groovy-looking. Say, this might just turn out to be fun.'

'I knew we'd selected the right escort. I'll collect you at your place a little after six, if that's convenient, and we'll pick up Mr. Frankel at his hotel.'

'No. I'll want my own car. I'll meet you at Miss Stella's at seven, if that's all right?'

'Fine, Ann. Glad you can come.'

'So am I.'

Better than two hundred fashionably attired guests mingled easily throughout Stella's large Colonial home. Those that were there for the first time marveled at her brilliant collection of priceless Fabergé. Those that had been there before never ceased to be impressed at how easily she handled a large and diverse party. The decor and service was the finest. The food, drink and wine superlative. The guests were often witty; they were always rich and important. It was an impeccable affair. That such a function was taking place in Tulsa City was lost on no one. Even the waiters and bartenders were singular, chosen as they were from the handsomest and most knowledgeable of the entire Latin community. Alex, the Lehson caterer, was a past master at perfection.

Stella was the ideal hostess. Her guests felt perfectly at home. She sallied through the little groups of people—chatting, laughing lightly at their little jokes, seeing they were attended to, and always selling in the softest possible manner. Stella was thoroughly enjoying herself.

Stella greeted Boardman, his wife, Mary, and Frankel with genuine warmth. It was really a pleasure to see them. When Ann Carter arrived, just a few minutes after them, Stella personally sought Josh out to introduce his date. No sooner had they met when Stella excused herself and whisked Josh away to meet some of the others. All the while, she was selling softly. As long as the Spanish ambassador was here, why not take something back for his stunning wife? There was such a sameness in Washington, and, after all, her Iberian beauty could certainly carry off the more dramatic styles. The NATO general, getting along so famously with Bill Bethel's gorgeous wife, Tina, needed no prodding to remind him of the little woman back in Brussels. It was the same wherever she went. The suggestion, always in perfect taste and always right on target. Josh stayed with her, her escort of the moment, but never really a part of it. When Stella had a captive clientele, no one could stop her. Still, it was never offensive. Never obvious. Always perfect taste. Joshua was thoroughly charmed. The magic aura of Lehson's pervaded even the drawing room.

Stella released Josh back to Ann.

'She's sure something!'

'Indeed she is, Mr. Frankel. Our Miss Stella is a oner.'

'Hey lady, it's Josh. Mr. Frankel is my dad.'

'That's funny, mine is Adam Hadley Carter.'

He laughed. In those few moments, he knew he really liked this girl. Together, they sampled the caviar. Too fishy. Sipped the champagne. Too dry. Tried the smoked Scotch salmon. Better with cream cheese. And they laughed. Josh and Ann had performed that rarest of all miracles ... instant warmth and rapport. Ann seemed to become a little older, Josh grew younger. They met. And the party disappeared. The suggestion was Ann's.

'If Joshua doesn't think Miss Carter is too forward ...'

'Never.'

'. . . then Miss Carter would like to suggest cutting out from this posh, but slightly aging group.'

'Joshua agrees. Where?'

'A super groovy little place that I've discovered.'

'Lead on, Christopher Columbus. Is it really fun?'

'Not only that, it's fairly close.'

'The gentleman from Manhattan is intrigued. Where goeth us?'

'It's called my apartment.'

'Like the name.'

'Will you promise to be good?'

'I swear to it.'

'Then let's go.'

They made their apologies to Stella. Boardman and the few others who seemed to notice they were there. Stella saw them off and smiled as the butler closed the door behind them. She turned to Eleanor Long, who stood discreetly in the entrance hall.

'Now Eleanor, you're a guest this evening. I hope you're enjoying yourself.'

'Always, Miss Stella. It's a splendid party.'

'Yes, such attractive people. Have some champagne, dear. I must chat with Princess Judith. Been neglecting her all evening. Excuse me.'

The older guests started taking their leave a little after nine. Such a marvelous party. Stella's farewell to each guest was a final reminder of that one perfect something at the store they simply couldn't live without. As a sales effort, the evening was a smashing success. Slowly the party wound down and the end was, at last, in sight. The house would be empty by ten o'clock. Tomorrow was another big day. Eleanor, always the efficient secretary, supervised the caterers' dismantling of their tables and service and the eventual cleaning up. The lights were lowered as the men quickly packed up and the last guest was seen out. Stella knew that it had been another good evening.

'Eleanor dear, I'm afraid I have to leave you to close up. I'm exhausted. Do you mind?'

'Not at all. You hurry on up to bed. I'll see to everything down here.'

'Thank you, dear. See you tomorrow.'

'Yes, ma'am. Goodnight.'

'Goodnight, Eleanor dear.'

Eleanor crossed from the wide stairway and over to where Alex was instructing his waiters and barmen on getting everything together.

'Everything seemed to go well, Miss Long.'

'Yes, Alex, it did.'

There was a pause.

Eleanor Long finally asked, 'Which one?'

Alex, the immaculate caterer, smiled and pointed out a tall, muscular young bartender stacking cases of empty champagne bottles.

'That one.'

'I'm sure he'll do nicely, Alex.'

'I guarantee it.'

'He understands what's to be done?'

'Perfectly. We shall be finished here within twenty minutes. The young man will be in Miss Stella's bedroom exactly at ten-thirty.'

'Good. You'll see his gratuity is put on the store's bill.'

'As always, Miss Long.'

Ann Carter's apartment was a refreshing departure from the grandeur of the day's activities—small, warm, cozy and decorated in a bright style that speaks of a home. Ann and Josh slowly danced to the soft music that purred out of the stereo. Only the flicker of the small fire in the fireplace illuminated the room. It was normal—perfectly normal and unaffected.

'Not too much of a comedown from all that chic at Miss Stella's?'

'Ummmm. No, ma'am. Hate cocktail parties.'

'But you can meet the nicest people there.'

'Umm, you can that.'

'Hi!'

'Hi yourself.'

'How 'bout some wine?'

'Champagne?'

'Nope.'

'Cheap domestic stuff?'

'Yep.'

'Make it a big glass.'

Ann slid out of his encircling arms and to the bottle of California Chablis that stood in the ice bucket. She held it up and the water dripped on the thick shag carpet.

'Want me to open it?'

'Nope. You're my guest.'

She struggled for a few moments, as Josh stood and watched her efforts with a broad grin.

'Give up?'

''Fraid so, here.'

He took the bottle with the corkscrew and expertly opened it. He savored the bouquet with mock severity.

'Not an important wine . . . but quite heady.'

He poured it into two tall-stemmed goblets and they both sat down on the soft sofa. They clicked glasses and sipped the wine. Two healthy, attractive people thoroughly enjoying one another. The song on the tape ended and Lionel Hampton's version of 'Getting to Know You' quietly filled the room. Josh cocked his head and listened for a moment.

'Appropriate. You do this often?'

'No.'

'Good.'

It was easy to accept Ann's open candor. It was apparent that she was intelligent without pretension. She was also accessible. Josh Frankel discovered that the young buyer from Tulsa City turned him on in more ways than sexual. He scrunched down into the deep cushions as she snuggled warmly up next to him. Ann listened to the music, examining her glass.

'This isn't as innocent as you might imagine.'

'Oh?'

'I'm not certain, but I think I'm supposed to seduce you.'

'Be my guest.'

'Be serious.'

'Who's kidding?'

'When Mr. Boardman asked whether I'd be your date, well, I'm not too sure what he meant by that.'

'You're not suggesting the fabled Lehson's stoops to procuring?'

'Good God no. The store is too subtle for that. It's just that . . . well . . .'

'Come on, honey, tell me. Let's get it out of the way.'

'Why did he pick me for you?'

'What about the obvious? He figured we'd be compatible.'

'They're very anxious to have you join the store, you know?'

'Yes, but do you honestly believe that an evening with a girl—an

55

admittedly sensational one—would really influence any decision I might make?'

'I guess not.'

'It wouldn't, believe me.'

'You think I'm reading more into it than exists?'

'No, I don't. It's just that it wouldn't work, for either of us. Now, can we change the subject?'

'Done.'

'Good again.'

'Except that . . .'

'Oh God.'

'Okay, just let me finish, then you'll hear no more of it.'

'So finish.'

'Josh, I appreciate your honesty and being so polite. I just didn't want there to be any misunderstanding. That's all.'

'Fine.'

'The store has an almost mystical pull on those of us that really love it. If Lehson's want you than I should help them get you.'

'Help yourself.'

'No, Josh. That's what was lurking in the back of my mind. When I go to New York to buy . . . the same feeling's always there. I must do it better than anyone else. For the store. Now I'm mixed up.'

'Jeez Ann, can't we just enjoy ourselves and forget the damned store?'

'That's exactly the problem . . . I have forgotten it. I just wanted it clear from the start. Cards on the table sort of thing. Sorry.'

'You are a special lady, you know?'

'Oh Josh, I want you just for myself tonight.'

Her hand trembled, but she couldn't control it as it slid easily inside his shirt and caressed the thick hair on his chest. Her smooth white skin tingled at the sensation of feeling him. She licked her lips and gave a little pull on his nipple. The touch of her cool fingers against his body, the little tweak of his teat ignited a passion that had been growing in him all evening. Josh drew her firmly towards him. Their mouths opened and joined. Their tongues met and a wave of sinuous sexuality electrified them both. Josh's hands enveloped her and his searching tongue explored the warm, moistness of Ann's mouth, plunging in, teasing back. Her hands were now clasped around his neck, bringing him even closer to her. Josh moved his mouth away from hers and with both tongue and lips kissed the hollow of her neck in a passionate, exploring movement. His searching mouth kissed, caressed and moved upward on her taut neck until it discovered her small, delicate ear. His breath was hot, and he was sure as once again the tongue found the shell of her ear and kissed it both front and back with ever-increasing fervor until it entered her pulsating shell to drive her into a state of near frenzy. Ann's eyes were closed but the entire universe was exploding before her as her hand found the pulsing bulge that stretched the fabric of his crotch.

'Oh my God! Oh Josh—you're driving me crazy! Ohhh, ohhh Jesus . . .' Her grip on his straining sex drove him with a sensation he would later remember as unique. Josh's tongue glided in—out—around her ear. His heavy breath surged into her, igniting the flame of her ecstasy into a conflagration of sweet animality.

Her massaging pressure against his massive erection was more than he could stand. Josh quickly moved his strong hands down her writhing body, under her skirt, slipping them between her moist thighs. Deftly, expertly, with firm fingers, he fondled the quivering vagina to even more erotic heights.

'Oh, Josh . . . let's get undressed,' she moaned.

Without disengaging, they quickly stripped. As Josh removed his jockey shorts at last, Ann inhaled with anticipation as his huge hard-on slapped up against her taut stomach. He smothered her breasts, freed from the brassiere's confinement, with his anxious mouth. Josh kissed, caressed, fondled and sucked at the soft, firm bosoms as Ann writhed in the primitive experience of sensuality. Her hand was tight around his cock. His tongue found the hot valley it sought between her legs and slowly, hungrily entered that promised land. It moved, flicked, explored, licked, and moved on—farther in—no area unloved until her loins became a raging eruption of uninhibited desire.

'Oh my God. I love it so much . . . oh Josh! Oh God! Ohhhhhh my sweet God!'

Their simultaneous climax was a pulsating gush of molten lava spilling, pouring, rushing out to release the power of their intense, pent-up pressure. The first climax had not even ebbed when the second began in even greater intensity. Their moment became infinity and time and space were erased as they exploded again into immortality and oneness.

Much later, Ann lay cradled close to him, Josh's arm around her naked shoulder. She took a quiet pull on her cigarette and offered one to him.

'No thanks, honey, I don't need to relax.'

She snubbed out the cigarette and turned again towards Josh. She nibbled invitingly on the lobe of his ear and murmured . . .

'Forgive the vulgarity, darling, but fuck the store.'

'Maybe later, sweetheart, but tonight I'm going to fuck you. Into insensibility with a little luck.'

'Promises?'

'Facts, Miss Carter. Hard, hot facts. Now for Christ's sake, don't turn off that light!'

Carl Guest hosted his own party in the reconverted loft he had turned into a dazzling, eclectic apartment. Candles danced inside pierced brass globes; huge silk pillows were piled into seductive seating arrangements; ornate mirrors lined the tapestry-covered walls; reproductions of ancient statues stood sentinel; rattan peacock chairs, draped with elaborate fabrics, were stationed between the stone gods. A flaking sarcophagus was propped in one corner. It was open and filled with ferns and greenery. A Jacobean table at one end of the room was piled high with a staggering buffet and scores of crystal decanters, each filled with a different-colored liqueur. Bottles of wines and spirits dominated a large, low cocktail table. The wall art was a mixture of pop posters and old masters that somehow managed to get along harmoniously. From the eight speakers strategically placed about the place, *Carmina Burana* blared forth.

Carl, in an extravagant brocade caftan, was incredibly drunk. The black cigarette in his holder had been crushed in a fall and refused to be replaced. He was sprawled amidst a hill of pillows, a jeweled goblet of gin doing its best to leave his fingers. His head had dropped back to the support of the pillows and he was singing loudly along with the profane mass from the stereo.

Three husky construction workers from the display company building the Mediterranean theme were stripped to the waist, nearly as drunk as their host, and trying to manage some food while being somehow attentive to Carl. His pale head turkeyed up from its resting place and he surveyed the trio of muscular physiques that smiled dumbly back at him.

'My Gawd, I just thought of something!'

'Wha's that, Misser Guest?' answered one of the torsos.

'It's a goddamn good thing that Lehshon's issen in Texas.'

'Wha-y is thay-t, Misser Guest?'

'Because then everyone would call her Schtella Dallas.'

And he fell back agasint the silk, his frail body contorted with unrestrained laughter.

TUESDAY, OCTOBER 4

The morning meeting in Stella's office was a scant ten minutes old when the first of the parade of telephone calls that punctuated her life began. As always, Eleanor Long answered the phone.

'It's Princess Judith, Miss Stella.'

Stella automatically took the receiver from Eleanor, continued to check the computer-tabulated receipts of yesterday's business and spoke.

'Dear, I thought you were going to nap till noon?'

The store executives seated around the conference table relaxed a bit and chatted quietly among themselves as Stella held her conversation. They had been joined this morning by an almost exhausted Josh Frankel, who could no longer stifle the mounting yawn—just one of the several physical residuals from a six-hour session of discovering the incredible depths and passions of the pert buyer of Lehson's Junior World.

Eugene Boardman forced his thin smile and asked Josh, 'Don't tell me our sleepy little town is boring you?'

'Your sleepy little town,' Josh grinned back, 'could teach Manhattan one helluva lot. Sorry about my yawn, but yesterday was quite a Monday.'

'Then you really were impressed?'

'Deeply.'

C.Z. was having his usual morning tremors and after several futile attempts to encase a cigarette in his trembling holder, finally abandoned the prop and stuck the black tobacco tube in his dry lips. Lyla charitably lit it for him. His rheumy eyes blinked his thanks as he inhaled deeply, coughed contortedly and then sank back in his chair.

'Nothing like a good smoke to revive sluggish organs.'

Walter Culbertson took the momentary break to survey and estimate the competition for Stella's chair. Boardman and Bethel, the obvious choices other than himself, he knew well. He'd plotted ways to work one against the other and, hopefully, weaken their individual positions. If Lehson's were a public company, responsible to a group of profit-oriented directors, his chances for the presidency would have been even money. As it was, they were only one in three. Or were they? This Frankel. Culbertson didn't like him sitting at the antique table on this particular morning. Too good a reputation. Obvious hot shot. Sharp merchant. Young. The odds just might be more like one in four today and Walter favored a better chance. He had a few days to do whatever he could to encourage Josh Frankel to stay right where he was in New York. He didn't want to revise his strategy this late in the game.

'I wouldn't think of letting you take a taxi, dear. My car will pick you up promptly at eleven. You can do a little shopping before lunch and the retrospect show this afternoon.'

Stella smiled.

'Yes, it should be great fun. See you a little later.'

Walter Culbertson made his way back to his office. As he passed through his women's coat and suit department, he stopped before a rack of black wool coats collared with small mink pelts. His assistant's eyes saw him examine one of the collars and she hurried up.

'Anything the matter, Mr. C.?'

'This is a female skin.'

'And?'

'And female skins stink. No sheen, no gloss. Dull. Haven't you learned anything yet?'

'Sorry, furs are new to me.'

'Then learn. Go through all these coats and send those with female skins back to the manufacturer.'

'Yes, sir.'

'That California creep. Thinks he can pull a fast one on me. I paid for male skins.'

'Sir?'

'Yeah.'

'Aren't these from Justin?'

'That's right, what of it?'

'He gave us a five-dollar advertising allowance on each coat. Who'll pay for the ad if we return too many?'

'He will. Return the coats after the ads run. Learn something, will ya!'

In the privacy of his office, Culbertson slithered into his chair and called Zack Purlmutter in New York. Collect.

'Zack? Walt here.'

'Hi babe, what can I do you for? A reorder?'

'Shit no! Business sucks. Zack, how much business you do with Alleff's?'

' 'Bout a hundred thou a year. Why?'

'Be too bad if you lost it.'

'Whaddya mean, lose it? You gotta be kidding. Our record is sensational there.'

'It won't be if Hal Spink becomes merchandise manager.'

'Spink? You're crazy. Josh Frankel is the fair-haired boy of Fifth Avenue. He'd never leave.'

'Never is a long time. Even as you and I speak, Mr. Frankel is right here in Lehson's. He's being wined and dined and flattered by the top brass.'

'Frankel? In Tulsa City? Jeez.'

'Yeah, treading our marble floors and getting wooed and screwed right and left to join the store.'

'So what the hell can I do?'

'Not a damn thing, Zack. Except lose Alleff's if he leaves. Spink is the only man besides myself who could fill the job and I ain't leaving here.'

'So tell me what to do?'

'Who am I to tell a friend anything. If it was me though, I'd damned well see that old man Alleff knew his treasured wunderkind was negotiating behind his back. That can only mean he's unhappy there. Alleff will know how to make him happy. If it were me, a three-year new contract with a hefty raise would do the trick.'

'Is that all?'

'Does Alleff know that Tulsa City has one of the broadest foundations of anti-Semitism in the entire Jew-hating Southwest? Frankel's wife and kids would love moving here, if you get what I mean.'

'Ya don't say. I'll find a way to get it to Alleff tomorrow.'

'See that you do.'

'I will. I will. I got a lot at stake, y'know.'

'Protect yourself. That's all.'

'Thanks, Walt. I really mean it. Thanks a helluva lot.'

'Hey, whatter friends for?'

The well-to-do Oklahoma matrons were curious. A real, live American princess wasn't your everyday type of Lehson celebrity. The couture floor was more crowded than usual, but discretion ruled as their curiosity was satisfied at being able to occupy the same quarter-acre of fashion as the Pacific Highness from Boston. Her face, that famous cameo of alabaster beauty multiplied and enlarged by the motion picture screens of every nation on earth, showed nothing as the truly magnificent clothes were modeled before her. The Princess looked casually away from the delustered ivory satin ball gown that Lyla was explaining and saw Stella enter her line of vision. Princess Judith smiled and waved a subtle greeting. Stella waved back and started toward her.

Stella was interrupted in her short journey by Claudia Wright, senior saleswoman of better dresses.

'Good morning, Miss Stella.'

'Claudia. Good morning to you, dear.'

'How is Mr. Abe this morning?'

'The same. He's always the same these days, I'm afraid.'

'I do wish the doctors would allow me just one short visit.'

'It would depress you, Claudia. It's best we leave it as it is for now. He's a very ill old man.'

Claudia's eyes misted.

'You do remember me to him, don't you?'

'Of course, Claudia. It does him good to know he's remembered.'

'I do that, Miss Stella. I certainly do.'

Stella watched as the tall woman turned, dabbed her eyes and returned across the floor to her department. Even in her midsixties, Claudia Wright was a handsome, prepossessing woman. Not beautiful, but with strong, definite features that belied the years. For seven years Claudia had been Mr. Abe's mistress. Stella wondered what the relationship had been like. It must have made a deep impression on the woman, since it had been over for twenty years and the usually controlled Claudia still could not contain herself when she spoke of the eldest Lehson. As long as Claudia lives, Stella remembered her father's order, she has her position with the store. Stella had no idea how exceptional a mistress Claudia was, but as a saleswoman she had no peer. Her father's order had never been questioned.

Stella acknowledged the 'good mornings' of the salespeople and regular customers as she made her way to where Princess Judith sat. Lyla smiled a greeting, excused herself, and left the two women alone.

'See anything you particularly liked?'

'Stella, your collections seriously rival the Paris houses. I don't see how you do it.'

'Ah, Paris has only itself for inspiration. Lyla has the entire world for hers. It's geographic, really.'

'Like putting Persia on the Mediterranean?'

'Exactly.'

The two women smiled as warmly as they could. The Princess spoke first.

'All right, Stella, what is this season's little Lehson surprise?'

'How you see through me. Very well, follow me.'

They rose and the elegant Highness marched alongside the mercantile queen toward Lehson's sanctum sanctorum . . . the fur department.

'You're not going to show me that mink rug by any chance?'

'Heavens no. After all, it is a copy. Besides that piece is just a trifle theatrical for you, dear. No, what I have in mind is unique. Please, sit down and make yourself comfortable.'

Princess Judith sat on a delicate Sheraton settee while Stella went to a distinguished, elderly man who stood discreetly back from the two women.

'Max, may I have the keys?'

'Certainly, Miss Stella.'

And he handed her a set of two keys. These unlocked the doors to the fur vault where the world's costliest skins and coats were stored. Stella went through two paneled doors and into the vault. The Princess amused herself by affecting boredom, but inwardly she was quite excited over what little treasure the fabulous Lehson safe held for her eyes alone. Whatever it was, it would be outrageously expensive and, as always, she'd fall instantly in love with it. The good Lord knew her handsome Prince couldn't afford it. She even had to dip into her personal income to help maintain that mini-castle she reigned over. Still, it was a small price to pay to be genuinely Princess Judith of Monteblanco. And thank the Lord again she had borne two deliciously perfect little heirs to insure the postage stamp principality would continue to be a prime tourist target for at least fifty more years. If only that Greek would return the casino concession back to to them. Still, time was on her side. Time and the title. Stella returned with a large box. To hell with it, she thought, I don't care what it costs if I really do like it. After all, they did sell six of my old films to television last month. My share will pay for it with enough left over to see to the castle's plumbing.

'Dear Princess. I hope you're going to be as pleased as we are.'

'Darling, if it's as smart as the presentation, I know I shall.'

Max gently removed the lid from the box. Small waves of white tissue billowed up. He laid the lid to one side and stood back, for this was where Miss Stella's star shone the brightest.

'Your face has always been perfection and that golden hair the most lovely crown any titled head could wear . . .'

'Yes, and thank you.'

'I don't know when I've ever seen such soft, silky, elegant hair. In fact, until last summer, I hadn't.'

Stella moved alongside the open box and caressed the crest of tissue paper.

'And what was last summer?'

'The sable auction in St. Petersburg . . . I mean, Leningrad.'

'This is a better beginning than my last film.'

'And all true. Highness, do you remember a year ago when you had your hair done in our salon?'

'Did I? If you say so.'

'Yes, you did. Had it cut as well. Max.'

He handed her a small simple brown leather ring box.

'I took the liberty of keeping one curl. I return it to you now.'

Intrigued, Princess Judith accepted the box, opened it and smiled down at the golden ringlet that reposed on the satin.

'It is mine. How nice.'

'That incomparable color could belong to no one else. Until last summer. At the auction.'

Stella gently removed the tissue. Several sheets floated gracefully to the carpet. With genuine love. Stella removed a cluster of sable pelts . . . each a color-perfect duplication of the Princess's hair. The match was flawless. In spite of her reserve, the mini-monarch gave a tiny yelp of delight.

'One full-length coat. That's all there is and, I doubt, ever will be. We will have it crafted by Beverly Hills' leading furrier, Elias Cohen.

A pale blond sable coat fit for a Tzarina.' And Stella tenderly draped the precious pelts across the delighted shoulders of the monarch from Massachusetts.

Max handed a large looking-glass to Stella who moved it in front of the royal customer. She looked in the mirror and the reflection that came back confirmed the color duplication. The match was perfect.

'Is it going to be frightfully expensive?'

'Not really. Not for a singular treasure. You'll wear it a lifetime. Fifty thousand, but since we'll be sending it to you abroad, there's no tax.'

The Princess thought, 'Damn, now I'll never be able to grow gray gracefully.'

Aloud, she told Stella, 'I'll take it.'

While Stella and the Princess enjoyed a light lunch in her office, the organized well-oiled machinery of preparing the extensive fashion retrospect show moved swiftly along on the fourth floor. A runway was laid, three hundred and fifty gilt chairs were arranged for maximum viewing, the public address system was hooked up and the models were assisted in donning the antique apparel that would soon delight Lehson's honored guests. Sonia helped the eighteen high-fashion models as Bill Bethel went over the historical notes that documented the fifty years of fashion that would parade once again down a Lehson runway. Guests from the Tulsa City Museum and other cultural organizations would be in attendance as well as the press, who, being alerted, had welcomed this unusual presentation for a fashion gala. Bill would personally handle the commentary, though Stella would be on hand to greet the three hundred and fifty guests. The star attraction, of course, would be Princess Judith modeling several selections. The Princess had been reluctant to model, but after the exhilaration of her new sable creation, she was genuinely delighted and would indeed be the day's shining star.

But, it was the guests—those haute couture customers with engraved invitations—who were a special show in themselves. They felt no fashion competition from the aged apparel that came down the runway; only the inevitable sizing up and gauging of each other—a singular peer group on gilt chairs. Many of the ladies could and did remember the clothes dating back half a century. The majority responded to at least three decades. The younger guests and the newly rich wrapped themselves in the semisecurity of either youth or estate. They all, these pampered, polished, posh socialites, had a common denominator—they had defied nature. In the world of animals only they stood erect and in that superior position they were the only drab females of the species who had managed to camouflage themselves with a gay and gaudy finery that passed for fashion. There were a few, a mere handful, who were truly secure. Their unerring good sense of taste and propriety made them aloof to the vagueries and conceits of couturiers and designers who each year frenetically tried to establish something 'new' that would, for at least a season, secure their toehold on the peak of haute couture. They were above any crowd. Olympian in their security, though—alas—still forced to belong to the erect anthropoids.

And Stella Lehson-Manchester greeted them all.

Michelle De Soto, her personal maid and physician in tow, had flown in from New York to buy a few things. When this wrinkled, wealthy harridan had been a lovely Georgia belle (before the turn of the century) she had made the annual required grand tour of Europe with her governess. She was sixteen, the year was 1890 and the ship was the *Kaiser Wilhelm De Grosse*. The crossing took two and a half weeks. Michelle had eluded her nanny long enough to flutter the sixty-year-old heart of one Barney Demerrit. The romance was whirlwind and when the mighty liner was halfway across a turbulent Atlantic, the ship's captain had married them. Her latent passions unlocked by the elderly Demerrit had proved his ruin. He never left his stateroom, but her complexion blossomed even richer. By the time the boat docked at Southampton, Demerrit was dead and his grieving teen-age widow found herself back with the governess plus a legacy of seven city blocks on Manhattan's Fifth Avenue. Michelle never looked back and in the ensuing sixty-odd years had married and loved to death a succession of five more gentlemen of property. True to her first, she refused to wed a man whose last name didn't begin with a 'D.'

'Hell, y'all think I'm goin' to change mah monogram for something as temporary as a husband?'

The small minority of men who would view the retrospect fell mainly into two separate categories: elegant under-forties in the arts or in tow, and the leisure-rich over-fifties who escorted their wives. One dramatic exception became theatrically apparent with the entrance of Belle O'Hara and her constant companion, Salvatore A'Patico. Belle was the lead singer of America's most popular sister singing group—the O'Hara sisters (Belle, Brooke and Kendell)—and a dear and close friend of Lyla's. Brassy, outgoing and possessed of a warm candor that evoked instant likability, Belle adored the fashions she could never successfully wear. No matter what the label, no matter how hard Lyla tried, the most elegant designs ended up a costume on Belle O'Hara's back. In direct contrast to her red-haired, fair-skinned, blue-eyed prettiness and large-framed voluptuous body, was the oily squatness of A'Patico. He managed to combine heavy-lidded pop eyes with a ferret's face, and his dress was strictly more tout than smart. He was an unashamed villain, a senior Mafioso, a reputed assassin and absolutely mesmerized by his adoration and worship of Belle. Together they made the most startling entrance the couture floor had ever seen.

Belle acknowledged Stella's welcome, introduced her friend and swept over to a smiling Lyla for the open hug that was so happily offered. A'Patico's swarthy lids louvered up a fraction and he actually permitted his coarse visage a brief smile. He too was fond of Miss Lyla. 'We just flew in for the day. Belle's gotta sing in Vegas tonight, okay?'

C.Z., standing to one side watching the mismatched pair, remarked to no one in particular, 'I wish she'd kiss him so he can turn into a prince before the gowns appear.'

Film directors' wives, Eastern socialites, career women and the very rich of the great Southwest swooshed and sidled into the area. The faithful of fashion had begun their annual pilgrimage to the Mauve Mecca.

The babel of voices waned as the always splendid Bill Bethel walked toward the small dais and adjusted the microphone. He smiled down at the assembled crowd who returned his smile.

'Ladies and gentlemen. Friends of Lehson's. Welcome to a special premiere that, we all hope, will become an annual event. Welcome to the Lehson's Fashion Hall of Fame Retrospect.'

From hidden speakers around the floor, the very soft strains of music began. Della had added a special dimension to the event by rummaging through the local radio stations' vast library of music and piecing together a tape of music that echoed the bygone years which the gowns that were to be paraded represented. As subtly as the styles

68

changed from decade to decade, so did the tempo and rhythms that backgrounded them. This was just another little Lehson touch that evoked the proper mood for the aged moths that were being displayed in the cosseted coccoon of the fourth floor.

'And let us begin when Lehson's and the century were both very young.'

From behind a series of lovely screens, the first model appeared. The dress and the music were fin de siècle and several audible sighs of nostalgia were heard from the older women in the packed make-shift theater. The retrospect had begun and Morgan Moore, for the moment, had been forgotten.

Josh Frankel and Stella stood at the back of the crowd as the models moved the years away.

'I do hope this isn't boring you, Mr. Frankel.'

Josh suppressed a yawn and reddened just a bit.

'Bored? This is the most interesting showing I've ever seen. Mr. Boardman explained to me what happened with Moore and knowing the short time you had, I still don't believe it.'

'Why thank you. Lehson's has a singular team.'

'I don't mind telling you that I shall copy this for Alleff's as soon as possible.'

'The sincerest form of flattery. New York should be even better. Your Metropolitan Museum has a stunning collection that goes back to Colonial times. You must invite me.'

'Guest of honor.'

'How very nice.'

'One question?'

'As many as you like.'

'How do you manage to keep topping yourselves?'

'The blood of any successful store is its people. Lehson's has combed the world for the very best. There is no better group of merchants anywhere on earth . . . including Manhattan. We also keep the team at their peak by carefully selecting new executives to inspire us and keep us on our mettle. The formula, my father's, works.'

'It's really amazing, here in Tulsa City, I mean.'

'To get and keep the best, we give the most in every way. Tulsa City can be a very exciting place. Any city can. It just depends on what you as a person put into it, that's how much you can take out.'

'I never thought that any place could hold a candle to New York.''

'I hope you won't think me rude, but I find New York's constant preoccupation with tension an unhealthy reason for progress. If that's what you call it. You work so hard to enjoy yourself that it's all a little like New Year's Eve. Holidays are only special when they're not too frequent.'

'Agreed.'

'I hope you'll forgive the late invitation, but I'm having a few interesting people in for dinner tonight and would love to include you. If you haven't made other plans, of course.'

'Thank you, but I have plans as it happens. May I take a rain-check?'

'With pleasure. Yes, Mr. Frankel, I'm genuinely pleased that you've already found our city somewhat to your tastes.'

Josh, his tie and shoes off, lazed on the sofa in Ann's living room and read the little handwritten menu she had handed him, a glass of the iced white wine already half-sipped.

'Chinese? Hey, do I get one from column "A" and one from column "B"?'

'I'm trying to impress you with my cooking genius and you make jokes.'

'Are you serious? I mean, you didn't really cook this, did you?'

'Of course I did.'

'No sneaking out to the corner restaurant?'

'You sure know how to hurt a gal, Mr. Frankel.'

'Really, honey, working all day at the store and then this . . . wow. Rumaki and fried shrimp to start. Oriental pork chops with Chinese vegetables . . . wait a minute. Shrimp and pork. Fine thing, you must not know I'm Jewish.'

'Know? Darling, I saw!'

'Hussy.' Josh laughed deeply. 'Get your arse into that kitchen, chop chop. Your master is starved.'

'Ah so, to hear is to obey.'

Josh laid the little menu on the side table and sipped at his wine as she left. There was a small, cozy fire in the grate and the lights were low. Henry Mancini was on the record player and Josh Frankel was as content as he had ever been. Ann had not left his thoughts during the entire day and he marveled that a girl, any girl, could so impose her personality on his entire being after such a short period of time.

He thought again of her incredible sexuality and was rewarded with a stiffening in the muscle overworked the previous night. He thought with a smile, 'Thank God I can still reorder.' Then his thoughts shifted to the non-bed Ann. It was equally pleasant. She was a girl he was totally unprepared for. Whatever she did, whenever she did it, was with a special grace—a seemingly virgin expectation and excitement. She was calm, unruffled and yet everything about her and being with her was exciting. If this kept up he would . . . he broke the thought off before it could completely form. That was the kind of serious thinking that didn't belong in his life plan. A good dinner, a sensational screw and good-bye Tulsa City. It was great. But, and this time the question was finished, he was already missing her and she was just a few feet away in the tiny kitchen. Damn her. He stopped thinking. Then it came. No . . . bless her.

The dinner was perfection.

They made love on the thick shag rug in front of the fireplace and it was even more beautiful than the night before. It was even more wonderful, because it still seemed to be all new and shining and original. Josh had never been happier, more complete in his entire existence. It was like being reborn into some poetic paradise. If this continued he knew he would sell his soul to keep this idyllic woman and their fantastic relationship.

'If I ever feel, even for a second, that you're doing all this to get me to join Lehson's, I'll kill you.'

'You, sir, are an insulting moo.'

'I mean it, Ann.'

'Tell me, Josh. Please tell me.'

The words stuck for only an instant.

'Oh Annie, I love you so. So very, very much. I love you and worship you and am jealous of being away from you. If you want me I'll call Boardman tonight and tell him he's got himself a new V.P.'

'You silly big city slicker, I love you more than that. I spoke with our resident buying office in New York this afternoon. I've got a super good friend there. She's already looking around for something sensational in one of the better Manhattan stores.'

'You'd do that for me?'

'Try and get rid of me.'

'It's indescribable how I love you.'

'Try.'

71

'You ever loved another man before?'

'Just one.'

Josh's back stiffened just a little.

'Who?'

'My father. Still do.'

He relaxed.

'Him I gotta meet.'

'Oh, you will. Maybe tomorrow if you're good.'

'Good, Annie? I intend to be superb!'

And he rolled over on top of her, her entire body ready to accept the challenge of his unquenchable desire.

WEDNESDAY, OCTOBER 5

All the executives were clustered around the table in Stella's office for the morning meeting. Josh was there, too, eyes bagged and darkened from lack of sleep.

Stella noticed his condition and appreciated how well Boardman had selected Frankel's escort for this visit. The cold merchandise manager had an uncanny knack for creating human chemistry.

'I think we can begin.'

The chattering stopped and everyone turned towards Stella.

'Before we go through this morning's agenda,' she returned to Josh at her left, 'let us find out how our guest is faring. Well, Mr. Frankel, we assume that you've had sufficient time to explore our workings. What have you decided?'

'Miss Stella, you and everyone else here have not only presented an enlightening perspective on the store's operations, and the range of Tulsa City, but you've all shown me a marvelous time—as my tired state indicates. However, I'm going to need more time to make up my mind. There are many variables involved, and I can't make a definite decision right now. I wouldn't want you to build up strong expectations that I will join the company. I'm not sure that this is the right time for a move and I do have my family to consider. I thank you again, all of you, for your courtesy and hospitality. And, Miss Stella and Mr. Boardman, I'll let you know my final decision within the week.'

'All right, Mr. Frankel. Frankly we had hoped for a more positive response but we do appreciate your candor.'

'You'll excuse me then, I have some gifts I'd like to purchase before my flight this afternoon.'

'Surely, Joshua, good day.'

Downstairs, as he leisurely made his way through the heavy crowd of shoppers, Josh was again impressed at how well the Lehson machine rolled over the inhabitants of this overly rich community. Here it was, the beginning of October, a traditionally slow time in retailing, and this old store in the middle of nowhere was packed with people spending ridiculous amounts of money on things they couldn't possibly need. That was the guts of great merchandising. He stopped before the gleaming glass display counters of the fine jewelry department. A sleek but charming woman clerk smiled a plastic smile.

'Is there anything special I can show you, sir?'

'Perhaps.'

'Is it for a gift?'

'Yes. Something rather special.'

'Of course. For a lady?'

'A young lady. Nothing extravagant please and in excellent taste.'

'Lehson's motto is "Taste Can Never Be Compromised". I shall try to live up to it. Ahhh, this is charming.'

She removed a golden object from a tray of brooches and laid it on a black velvet cushion. It was a filigreed pin set with five small diamonds.

'Nice, but much too ornate for what I had in mind. I want something simple. Simple and casual. Nothing too dressy.'

'I think this just may answer the bill.'

It was a heart. A plump little golden heart. Polished to a high gloss, but definitely understated beauty. The saleslady opened a drawer beneath the counter and extracted a tray of thin gold chains. Deftly she selected an appropriate chain and attached the heart. She put it around her neck and the shining metal shone rich and young against the somber grey of her flannel dress.

'Any young lady would treasure something like this. With the chain it has the added advantage of being worn beneath one's dress as well as out. It's like monogramming one's intimate apparel. Only the wearer knows it's there. Do you like it?'

'Very much. It's exactly what I had in mind.'

'I'm so glad.'

'How much is it, with the chain of course.'

'With the chain . . . let's see. One hundred and twenty dollars. An excellent value, actually.'

'Fine. Can you gift wrap it, please.'

'Of course. Cash or charge?'

'Cash.'

'It will only take a minute. Perhaps you'd like to look around while it's being wrapped?'

'No, I'll wait.'

Alone in the bustling crowd, Josh thought of Ann. But the ease with which the expert saleslady made the quick sale had impressed him, and his mind shifted back to the great class of this store. No attempt to get him to spend more than he could afford. No intimidation. Perfect taste in selecting exactly the correct item. He thought of the same experience as it might occur in Manhattan. At Alleff's. He was forced to laugh and admit this was indeed a far cry from downtown New York. The saleslady reappeared with a delightfully wrapped little box.

'I hope it didn't take too long.'

'Not at all. I think this is correct,' he said as he handed her several bills and accepted the box.

She didn't even bother to count the money. Only a smile and, 'I'm certain it's all here, Mr. Frankel. If we can be of any more service, please let us know. My name is Mrs. Gunther.'

Josh smiled, genuinely pleased at both the gift and the professionalism of the saleslady. She'd known all along who he was. Didn't even count the money. That's the way to run a business.

Wading through the mass of postpubescents that seeemed to fill Ann's junior department, Josh once again had to admire the skill with which every section of the store captured the spirit and excitement of the store's theme. He marveled at how a bikini bathing suit could be both sexy and demure at the same time, but there they were. Three Oklahoma teen-agers were modeling the skimpy creations for each other with accompanying giggles and squeaks of delight. College girls were selecting sweater and skirt sets in vibrant Mediterranean colors by the armful. In New York, for fall, all the stores were featuring dull heather shades. It took this store and this staff to beat the whole country to the punch by injecting high colors for drab seasons. Everywhere he had gone in Lehson's he was astounded to see new ideas being promoted and sold. This is what his business life was all about and it wasn't happening with him at Alleff's. Ann spied Josh and excused herself from the tennis-tanned mother and her leggy deb daughter who were trying to decide on the right fun fur for fall.

'Hello there.'

'Hello yourself. God, you look beat, Josh. But super beat.'

'I was, but suddenly I'm revived.'

'What's the good word on the fifth floor?'

'I gave them a definite "maybe".'

'Good, keep them guessing.'

'Ann, I'm taking the afternoon plane.'

'Oh.'

'Can you make lunch?'

'I don't think I should. I'd make a mess out of this good-bye.'

'Who said anything about good-bye? Dammit Ann, don't make this any tougher than it is.'

'Don't be cross with me, darling, but I'm so very much in love with you. Please?'

'Sorry honey. You're the last person I want to be brusque with. The thought of leaving you, even for a while . . .'

'If you start in, I'll break out crying right here. We'll have lunch.'

'That's better. Besides, I brought you a present.'

'You've already given me the dearest gift in the entire world.'

'I'll meet you in the restaurant, with your present, at noon. Don't keep me waiting.'

'Make it twelve-thirty. I'm still a working girl, remember?

'Twelve-thirty then.'

Ann gave his hand a discreet squeeze, but even that slight contact stimulated the electricity she generated through him. A girl trying on a camel's hair coat near them bumped against Josh and pushed him into Ann.

'Whoops, sorry mister. Isn't this a dreamy coat?'

'Super,' he said to the girl.

His stiffness as his body moved close to Ann's showed his love for her. Ann blushed, pushed him gently away and, as she walked back to the customers and their fun fur, told him, 'I won't be late.'

The Oak Room Bar at the Plaza in New York was a male-only retreat until five when ladies and well-dressed homosexuals mingled with the resentful regulars. The dark paneled walls with their quaint murals of an earlier and more elegant Manhattan, the old waiters and prompt service, the perfectly mixed drinks and clubby atmosphere combined to make this last refuge the ideal place for a serious business lunch. Since Frank Preston's office was a short walk from the Plaza, he enjoyed being a 'regular' regular. He had just ordered his second

Chivas on the rocks when Amos Barron arrived at the table. Frank attracted his waiter's eye at the bar and held up two fingers. The waiter caught his order and Amos elegantly sat down across from Frank.

'The whole goddamned morning at the U.N. was wasted—a lot of bullshit.'

'Why Amos, how undiplomatic of you. What would they say at the State Department? Here's your drink. Relax.'

The white-haired waiter set the two glasses down, slipped menus discreetly to one side of the table and left. Barron managed to drain his drink at one slow, practiced swallow.

'Ahh, that's better. It's been a rough morning.'

Frank signaled the waiter who nodded and went to the bar for Amos Barron's refill.

'What I meant to say,' Amos continued, 'was that nothing ever gets done.'

'Let's turn to pleasanter matters then.' Frank picked up the menu and studied it. 'Now then, what could be more soothing than a plate of subtle soft-shell crabs flown in fresh from Maryland this morning?'

'Perfect.'

The waiter arrived with Barron's drink and Frank gave him their order. Alone again, he quietly resumed the conversation.

'Any indication yet which country my Miss Stella might be vacationing in?'

'Nothing definite, but the climate in Italy or any of the Scandinavian countries seems best this time of year.'

'She is anxious to go anywhere, as you know, but there is no question that her personal preference would be Rome. She has strong attachments to Italy, both personal and economic. You know, Amos, that the store almost single-handedly helped revive Italy's fashion industry after the war. Stella's been decorated twice by their government. The mutuality of rapport indicates, to me at least, the logic of an Italian vacation.'

'Look Fran, again, I can't speak with any real certainty right now, but I assure you everything is being done to see that Stella's trip works out to everyone's satisfaction. I can tell you this, though, the Italians are especially keen for her to vacation in Rome. That's half the battle.'

'That's very nice to hear.'

'Yes, I'm sure it is. One appreciates being wanted.'

'Another Scotch before the food comes, Amos?'

'If you'll join me?'

'I will indeed.' He caught the waiter's eye once again and the signal for another round was received.

'Frank, let me get back to you on Friday with, hopefully, a clearer picture of the situation.'

'Thanks, Amos, I'm sure you'll do what you can. It would be a marvelous public relations coup if we could announce the trip at the end of the store's annual fashion gala.'

'Oh, when is that?'

'Unfortunately, a week from Saturday. Too soon?'

'Possibly not. We'll talk again on Friday.'

The waiter brought the drinks and the two men silently toasted each other with pragmatic smiles.

The Tulsa City International Airport, an enormous architectural complex far too vast for the occasional traffic it supported but a structural testament to the mineral and animal wealth of the area, lazed in the brilliant midmorning sun. Bill Bethel sat in the back seat of the Lehson VIP limousine reading *Women's Wear Daily* while waiting for the plane carrying Ceil Bordon to arrive. The long black sedan had been parked in the LOADING ZONE–THREE MINUTE PARKING ONLY area for fifteen minutes. It would be there for another half hour until Madame Bordon and her numerous pieces of luggage were packed into the car. In Tulsa City, a Lehson automobile merited more respect than that of the mayor.

Bill turned to the page that featured cosmetics and, as expected, the first thing that caught his eye was the quarter page ad for Ceil Bordon's 'Ultra-Svelte', an expensive lotion that promised to remove the oily fats from m'lady's skin and reap an unusually high profit for the better merchants who vended her wares. In a relatively few years, Ceil Bordon had emerged as the high priestess of cosmetics, eclipsing even Helena Rubinstein and Elizabeth Arden for the scented throne of number one in the makeup world. Her laboratory was near her chateau on the French Riviera, her headquarters were in New York, her packaging was from Italy and the whole business was carried in her head.

When Ceil had first emerged from the relative obscurity of her small Manhattan salon to stab her way into the lucrative wholesale field she had approached Lehson's, in the person of Stella. Stella had used the initial products herself and did not find them lacking in either performance or potential. Lehson's launched the line in their magnificent Christmas catalogue of 1956 and Ceil Bordon was made. Ceil ruled her powder puff principality with the absoluteness of a Catherine the Great. Her flair in developing new products was inspired and her innate sense of merchandising a marketing wonder. Many times a millionairess, Ceil clung to the precarious heights of ruling the rouged roost with a tenacity her competitors found alarming. None of this showed in the elegant, understated advertisement that beckoned out from the pages of *Women's Wear*, wooing those few reluctant retailers to join the prestigious roster of fine stores who were growing fiscally fat with 'Ultra-Svelte.'

'American Flight number one from New York arriving at gate twenty-seven,' boomed the loudspeakers. Ceil Bordon was arriving on time. Bill folded the paper neatly and opened the door. He made a fast mental calculation as he walked toward the gate.

'Eleven in the morning in Tulsa City. Nine hours difference between here and Paris with an hour layover in New York to change planes. Ceil must be exhausted.'

He stood back from the crowd that pressed against the glass of the waiting room and watched as they slid the landing stairway up to the huge aircraft. It was secured and opened. The flight attendant accepted the clipboard from the stewardess and stepped aside to allow the first-class passengers to disembark. The first one to the door was Ceil Bordon. Her luxurious mink coat was thrown casually over her smartly dressed shoulders and, even at this distance, her jewels sparkled in the sunlight. He could see Cecil gesturing dramatically to the stewardess who was following every word of the makeup messiah with mesmerized fascination. Ceil took a small bottle from the alligator travel bag she carried and pressed it into the grateful girl's hands. The stewardess beamed her gratitude and Ceil Bordon at last left the interior of the plane. The flight attendant saluted smartly and Ceil descended the stairs with a speed and precision that belied the long trip's expected fatigue. Bill made his way to the railing and when Ceil emerged into the waiting area, he broke into a wide smile and a schoolboy's wave.

'Hey! Welcome to Tulsa City.'

Ceil responded with a bright grin and, as they met, handed him her coat, baggage checks and the alligator carryall.

'Lehsonland would be more like it, Bill. What the hell time is it here, anyway?'

'Eleven straight up.'

'The sun's out so it must be A.M. I stink at all these time changes. Car in front?'

'Yep. Come on with me. You must be beat.'

'Never felt better.'

The woman was indefatigable. Bill held the door of the car open for her, gave the baggage checks to the driver and slipped in beside her.

'We'll stop by the hotel and give you a chance to freshen up. You probably want to take a nap.'

'Why? I told you I feel great. Raring to go, in fact.' She thrust her dynamic face up at him. 'Do I look tired?'

'I've got to admit you don't. Honestly, Ceil, how do you do it?'

'Priority, honey. Today's priority is to show Stella the new line we're introducing this week at your shindig. It's sensational!'

He looked at her as she glanced out the window at the enormous terminal. Bright as a penny, this small vivacious woman from the Bronx with her Parisian clothes and fabulous jewels could do without rest or pause when it came to evangelizing her cosmetics before an audience of the faithful. Since she had started at Lehson's it was back to the store each year at fortnight time to introduce the miracles and wonders that the French chemists had wrought from the chemicals and oils to restore and rejuvenate the rich ladies of America.

'This is some airport you got here.'

'The most modern in the country.'

'You think the town will ever grow big enough to warrant the size?'

'No. Then they'd just have to build a larger one. That's part of the ego of this part of the country. In every other major city the airports are too small; in Tulsa City, it's got to be too big.'

'My kind of town. Where's that driver?'

'You do have quite a bit of luggage, Ceil.'

'Yeah, but I'm itching to get to the store. Ah, here he comes.'

The chauffeur was leading a trio of skycaps who wheeled three dollies loaded with more than twenty pieces of luggage and tightly sealed packing boxes. He supervised the storage of the cases into the trunk, the front seat and the available space in the rear. It was a tight squeeze.

When it was completed, the driver handed each skycap two dollars, returned to his place and started the engine for the drive back to Tulsa City. He half-turned his head and inquired, 'Tulsa City Royal, Mr. Bethel?'

Bill looked at Ceil. She answered for him.

'The store, and step on it!'

Lehson's—the store—was a magnetic temple that attracted both customers and suppliers from all over the United States, all over the world in fact. An aging nondescript downtown department store whose stolid façade hid its treasures for those with the pocketbooks and taste to appreciate its eclectic trove. It was a palace of pleasure and a delight for all ages and sexes, provided they could afford the prices and have the good sense to accept what Lehson's dictated was the fashionable change for each season. Fashion was change and change was profit. After all, what woman really needs another winter coat?

The door to Stella's palatial office was held open by a happy Eleanor Long as Ceil Bordon, exuding confidence, prosperity and surprise, swept into the room. Stella embraced her with a warmth reserved for those few women friends and associates who were truly her peer.

'My Gawd, Stell, you look fantastic!'

'And you, Ceil, how do you manage to do it? And don't tell me it's just Bordon cosmetics.'

They both laughed as Ceil sat herself down in a large leather chair and fanned out the mink coat like some regal slipcover.

'The damned stuff really does work, y'know? But just between us girls . . .' Bill entered the office with a large packed case, put it on Stella's desk and play fully cupped his hands over his ears. Ceil continued, delighted, 'Say, Stell, does the hear-no monkey also speak-no?'

'Only when it's good press.'

'Well, this isn't. My secret is the most fabulous Swiss plastic surgeon. The good doctor makes a teeny slice behind the ear, a stretch and smooth up the cheeks and—*violà*—ten years younger.'

'His name?'

'Ah ha, that would be telling. Later, hon. Bill! Uncrate those goodies and get the rest of the crew in here. I'm as excited as a bride.'

'They're on their way.' He expertly sliced away the protective wrappings and carefully opened the box. Ceil got up and moved her hands into the excelsior shreds, extracting scores of tiny plain boxes of various sizes and shapes. Bill put the wrappings into the box and placed it out of sight, as Della Blye and Carl Guest made their way into the office. Both were delighted to see the Bronx warhorse again and showed it.

'Madame Mascara, you're to swoon over!' chortled C.Z. as he pecked a kiss on her taut cheek.

'Ceil Bordon! You've got to have found the youth fountain. I'll take a double scoop.'

'How are my two favorite people? C.Z.? My displays had better be sensational this year, 'cause we're going to set them on their well-upholstered keesters before this fortnight is through.'

'Madame will be enchanted. A Barcelona bordello, if I say so myself.'

'And the ads, Della?'

'Nothing, 'til we see what you've got.'

'I've got a double-page spread worth of miracles this time, plus a little zinger that will set the whole damned world spinning. My little surprise!'

C.Z. unfolded into a chair, lighted a black cigarette and asked, 'Instant martinis with chlorophyll?'

'Better!'

Stella resumed her seat behind the desk table and eagerly awaited the always exciting performance when Ceil dramatically presented a new collection. Everyone was caught up in the excitement that oozed from Ceil as she lovingly and theatrically undid package after package to reveal the latest line of oils, lotions, scents, conditioners, rouges and creams that constituted a complete array of necessities for the aging rich. Everyone knew that the basic preparations were the same as in years past—what Ceil was selling was the new scents, new packaging and the blanket advertising campaign her agency in New York had formulated to herald this year's bag of toilette tricks for a hungrily awaiting horde of women.

Her audience reacted with the pleasure of children at Christmas. It was a fine line, eminently salable and exquisitely wrapped. A natural. Another winner. Another first for Lehson's. The final unopened box was cradled in her bejeweled hand as she stopped for a tense full minute—waiting. Even Eleanor Long, sentinel at the closed door, stood in semibreathless anticipation. Finally, Cecil was ready.

'Okay, you divine friends and buyers. Here it is. The zinger for 1964 . . . and 1965 and forever!' She slowly lifted the lid, laid it on Stella's table. She unwrapped the pale pink tissue that guarded her secret, and finally removed the object.

'Ceil Bordon's *Epidermal Rhythmizer!*'

They would have applauded, but no one in the room knew what it was she held up so proudly.

The Epidermal Rhythmizer was a pink plastic cylinder about seven inches in length, with a softly smoothed pointed end and a diallike flange at the bottom. Ceil beamed at their stupefied faces.

'Of course you don't know what it is! That's because it's a genuine first. An original! My technicians have been working on this in secret for eighteen months. It is now perfected. It's the wonder of the century! Watch . . .' Ceil turned the tooled flange at the bottom to its first position, 'Turn it once . . . and a small essence of dermatic balm is emitted from the tiny holes at the base. Turn it twice,' which she did, 'and the interior battery starts to run the miniaturized engine inside the Rhythmizer. Now, the application!' As the pale pink plastic tube began to quietly hum, everyone could see it vibrating steadily in her hand. She put the device up to her face and softly, gently, carefully, expertly massaged the crevice where the nostril met the face. Then to the eyelids. Behind the ears. Every area on her face that was vulnerable to lines and aging was massaged effortlessly by the whirring Rhythmizer. Then they knew what she had wrought. A battery-operated face vibrator that contained her special blend of face creams. It was a first, and certainly a zinger. Stella was the first to react verbally.

'Ceil! It's really marvelous!'

'You've got your double-page ad!' chirped Della.

'My God, we'll go to town on this one!' from Bill.

'I love it,' yelped C.Z., 'it reminds me of my first husband!'

The room filled with laughter as Carl reddened at the effect of his blurted reaction, but the truth of his observation was not lost on Della Blye. Instantly, she recognized the phallic qualities of Ceil's invention. Everyone else in the room did as well, but their awareness was mercantile. Hers was personal.

'Is it a one-speed engine?' asked Della.

'Nope, three.' As they crowded around her, she demonstrated the three speeds. The last one, where the pulsing became quite heavy, most impressed Della.

'Can I have the Rhythmizer for the week? The art work must be done to perfection. Miss Stella? Can we have a double-page ad?'

'You're only budgeted for one page, you know.'

But this is everything Ceil says it is. The splash is worth it.'

Bill Bethel sided with the boss. 'Della, we're over budget as it is.'

Della turned to Ceil Bordon and gave a hopeless shrug.

'How much is a page . . . the store rate now?'

'Twenty-six hundred.'

Ceil turned to Della. 'Take it and give us a great two-page spread. I'll pick up half the tab.'

The little charade was over. Ceil hoped she wouldn't have to split the ad, but knew all along it was expected of her. She didn't really mind. That ad alone would result in a million dollars' worth of orders before the month was over. It had been a profitable meeting. As they all stood about congratulating a jubilant Ceil Bordon, the first wave of tiredness started to sweep over her. The debut was over and the deb's exhaustion became manifest. Bill recognized it at once.

'Okay kids, back to work. I'm taking Ceil to her hotel and she's going to rest whether she likes it or not. Madame, you happen to be tonight's honored guest at a rather important party; and since our Swiss doctors are on vacation, this physician insists you follow his sleep prescription.'

Twelve-twenty. Josh sat at the small table in the corner of the store's restaurant sipping iced tea and waiting for Ann, when Walter Culbertson passed by on his way to lunch.

'All packed, Frankel?'

'Yes, but since the plane doesn't leave until four, I figured I'd take my last meal here.'

'Not a condemned man, I hope.'

'Hardly. It's been an impressive few days.'

'Yeah, they fattened me up with sweet talk and broads, too, before I said "yes".'

84

Josh stiffened slightly. He didn't like the man, but then nobody did, so what difference did it make.

'Are you glad you did?'

'Yeah, I guess so. One job's as good as another, but the wife and kids hate this lousy town.'

'Oh?'

'Goddamned bunch of Jew-haters, when you scratch the surface.'

'I hadn't noticed.'

'Yeah, but you don't live here. Whatever you decide, good luck to ya' kid,' he said, and shuffled away.

Josh's eyes followed the sloppy Culbertson as he wended his way to a table where his assistant was nervously waiting for him. He thought to himself, 'That guy could turn Ben-Gurion into an anti-Semite.'

The delicious stabbing pang of sensual reawakening coursed through Josh as he saw Ann enter the dining room and look around to find him. He stood and waved to her. She saw him and made her way through the luncheon crowd toward him—stopping at two tables to say hello to various friends.

He held her chair and as she sat, her eyes turned up towards his. They loved each other and the power of their feelings was silently communicated. They finished with the business of ordering quickly and sat gazing fondly and a little sadly at each other, trying their best to appear casual about the meal for the benefit of those in the dining room who had seen them. Josh was the first to speak.

'I'm not going to lose you, you know.'

'You're terribly young to be so old-fashioned. It's been the most important three days of my entire life, and you're leaving me a fulfilled woman for the very first time.'

'This isn't just another Lehson first, Ann. This is something that we both have to grab. With both hands. Grab and hold on to forever.'

'Please don't. I cherish you so. Love . . . love you so. Let's not even think, let alone plan anything beyond this lunch. This time together. Please, Josh, don't add pain to my heart.'

'I'm going to love you. Protect you. I don't know how yet, but we're not going to lose something so perfect.'

The waitress brought their chef salads and left. They toyed with the greens, but neither could eat. Ann spoke softly, her eyes cast down to the table.

'You're making it very difficult for me, darling. Your plane leaves in just a few hours.'

'Take the afternoon off.'

'You know I can't do that. I'm certain too many people are already gossiping.'

'To hell with them.'

'No, you don't mean that. I have to work here. These are my friends as well as associates. Besides, I like them.'

'Then come to New York. A job . . . a good one . . . that's no problem.'

'This is my home. Besides, I'm in New York for buying trips at least six times a year.'

'Do you honestly think I'm going to wait two months to see you?' His voice grew louder—more insistent. 'Two months' vacuum between loving you?'

'Shhh, Josh. Please.'

'It's damned unfair!'

'Say, where's that fabulous present you promised me?'

'Oh, that.'

Josh took the small package from his pocket and moved it across the table to her. She took it and put it in her purse.

'I'll open it tonight. When I'm alone.'

'When you're alone. Ann, I don't want you to ever be alone again.'

'We'll work something out. Really we will. But we both need time to figure out how. I know I'll adore the present; please, be as generous and give me the time. Please?'

'What a lousy way to end our first experience. Catching a plane to the East while you unwrap a stupid gift by yourself here. It's just not fair.'

'Love isn't always just. But no amount of distance can erase it if it's real.'

Ann reached over and took his hand in hers. 'I'm going back to my department now. It's been a lovely lunch and the happiest three days of my life. Thank you, Josh.'

She stood, serious yet smiling. Josh didn't rise. He sat glumly, staring at his uneaten salad. As she turned and left the restaurant, he muttered to himself. 'Dammit! It's just not right. Why can't it ever be fair?'

*

The Bethel's Georgian home in Tulsa City's nicest residential section was ablaze with lights prior to their party for Ceil Bordon. More than sixty of the city's most prominent citizens, store executives and visiting dignitaries were invited for cocktails, buffet supper and entertainment from Madrid's premier flamenco troupe, the Golendrinas. The store, of course, was paying for the entire event. C.Z. and staff had seen to the decor, Alex handled the catering (which featured rare Iberian delicacies) and the portable stage in the rear garden had been covered with a gaily striped marquee under whose candlelit roof the guests would enjoy the music and dance of the Golendrinas.

Upstairs in the double dressing room that adjoined their bedroom suite, Bill and Tina Bethel were putting the last finishing touches on themselves prior to going downstairs to receive their guests. Bill finished arranging his perfect black bow tie, but Tina was far from ready. A Baccarat balloon glass of Napoleon brandy and Dr. Pepper on the rocks sat, half-finished, next to her as she worked on her makeup.

Bill couldn't help stealing glances at her, marveling at the exquisite perfection of her form and face. He smiled to himself, remembering the force of her almost pagan demands on his manhood just a short forty-five minutes ago. The hot shower and after-shave lotion could not conceal the animal quality of their mating as it continued to glow in his mind and his loins. Not only was she the most gorgeous woman in the entire state, but her lust for him and him only was a never-ending source of joy and amazement. If only she would make some attempt to improve her mind. Her mind . . . a great, grey wasteland inhabited only by insecurity and jealousy. The two years' tutoring by the head of the Speech Department from the University had managed to glaze a veneer of vocal culture on to her; but in moments of stress —and she tensed easily—the guttural, shrill drawl of her poverty-stricken, red-neck origins broke through. In those awful moments when jealousy surged through her body, her high whine could grate horseradish. Bill prayed for calm sailing tonight.

Bill loved her, almost blindly, and tried to understand the torment this magnificent creature constantly endured. Her first job had been as a wrapping clerk at Lehson's. She was fifteen and had been out of school for three years. Her dirt-poor family had wandered around the Southwest and had finally lit in a shanty suburb of Tulsa City. All nine children were put to work. It was Mr. Abe who had first recognized the possibilities of this striking teen-ager. He had mentioned the scruffy child with the incredible bone structure to Claudia, who, after looking, had agreed about her potential. She was taught to walk, to use makeup properly, to do her hair, the way to stand to show off clothes to their best advantage. Tina took to the excitement of being noticed with a hunger that made her expert in all the model's arts. On her sixteenth birthday she was presented with a full-time modeling job with the store. She tried to forget everything about her family and past, but could never completely conquer the gnawing fear and loathing which were so deeply ingrained. Tina was total surface and her personality never attempted to compete with her looks. After she had met Bill and fallen desperately in love with him, she tried to correct this, but by then it was too late. The elocution lessons worked a little, but that was all. It wasn't too bad when they were alone, but her pervasive insecurity magnified itself at any social function where she was limelighted and forced to react and respond intelligently to people far more cosmopolitan than she could ever hope to be. Bill understood and kept their social encounters to a minimum. He handled the inevitable suicide threats that followed her rare excursions into society with love. In fact, he was so smitten that only one habit of hers made him angry: Tina's practice of regurgitating her evening meals.

'Hones'ly, Bill hon, how else's a gal to keep her figure?'

Bill glanced at his watch. The guests would be arriving any minute and Tina was far from ready. He noticed her high-strung agitation as she sat in front of the mirror, sipping the cognac concoction while hassling with her makeup.

'Dammit! Ah can't hold my hand steady.'

'Relax, lover. Slow down,' purred Bill as he walked over and put his arm around her. 'That dress is stunning; it looks tremendous on you, baby. Don't worry, there won't be a woman within miles who can hold a candle to you. Relax, just take it easier.'

'These do's ain't like modelin', Bill. As soon as ah open my ignoramus mouth, my looks stop workin' for me. You know ah jus' don't have a thing smart to say to these slick folk.'

'C'mon, doll, this isn't the first party you've ever been to—or hosted. Everything will be just fine. Try to remember what Dr. Austin taught you. Speak slowly.'

Her face froze into an elegant mask, the eyelids half-closed. Her facial poise became extraordinary. She answered with pearl-shaped words.

'My de-ah Willyum . . . these people do not know me. The real me.' He smiled a broad grin and winked.

'They're all going to love you, baby, just like I do.'

The chime of the front doorbell floated up the stairs.

'I'd better go and see to our first guests. Hurry now.'

Alone Tina squinted into the mirror, took a long pull on the drink and reverted to her normal whine.

'Goddamned cultured jet setters an' their goddamned in'ernational carryings on. Sheeet!'

Bill entered the spacious entry hall. Hilda, their Swedish house-keeper, had opened the door for Dorothea, Lady Vidal, who strode in with a sable floor-length coat covering her athletic shoulders. Bill watched as Hilda started to remove the fur. Lady Vidal preferred to remove it herself. Jealous of her household sovereignty, Hilda re-fused to abdicate her duty. There followed a slight tug-of-skin, when the sixty-year-old peeress caught sight of Bill, smiling at their little dance of extrication.

'Hi, Billy boy!' enthused m'lady. 'First one here, huh?' Her Okla-homa twang didn't fit the title, but there she was—little Dorothy Mason from Enid, Oklahoma, swathed in sable and dripping dia-monds. She allowed Hilda to take the coat.

'And a good evening to you, Lady V.'

Lady Vidal, built like a female physical education instructor, had been the most energetic and popular registered nurse in the county. Her open good humor and no-nonsense capabilities had endeared her to every patient she treated. It was in this humanitarian capacity that she had first met Vincent, Lord Vidal. It was many years back and he had been in Oklahoma to purchase thoroughbred jumping horses to add to his already world-famous stables in Ireland. Lord Vidal en-countered a particularly virulent influenza germ and, rather than jeopardize his sizable buying power, his hosts had engaged Nurse Mason to tend the aging baron. Her ministrations, blond hair, sturdy build (Lord Vidal would later remark to a fellow breeder, 'The lass has hindquarters like a champion!') and genuine candor so refreshed his lordship that her employment became permanent. They stayed together for eleven years when the nobleman suffered a mild stroke on his seventieth birthday and had the marriage banns posted the next day. That was over a decade ago, but Dotty still upheld her end of the bargain well. Lord Vidal remained alive, and though her flaxen hair now shimmered with a bleach, Lady Vidal remained earthy and regular. She was a loyal friend, and no friendship was greater than that of her income and Lehson's marvelous wares. Every year, she and her lord sailed across the sea and trained into Tulsa City for the annual fashion fortnights.

'Where's Lord Vincent, Dotty?'

'Popped him into the oxygen tent tonight. Seems spending all our winnings from the Grand National was too much for the old dear. Where's Tina?'

'Be down in a minute.'

'Good!' she lilted, then turned and surveyed the rooms. 'Hey Bill, mind if I snoop? Never been in your house before.'

'Of course not,' he replied, only seconds after she had set off on a frenetic course which encompassed a round of hors d'oeuvre-tasting, a scan of art, books, furniture, and records, and somewhere along the line, a visit to the bar.

'Ummm,' she cooed, 'food's good, and so's your taste, just like I expected from a suave dog like you.' Affecting an exaggerated, mock Groucho Marx stance, Lady Vidal chortled, 'My God!' and held up a record album. 'Who in the hell listens to Kate Smith?'

'I do, your ladyship.' Tina entered the room. 'She's so terribly American. Oh my God, but are you ever stunning!' Lady Vidal rolled her eyes. 'Honey, you are really something else. Come on over here and let an old horse trainer look at your teeth.' They all laughed and Tina embraced the delighted lady. Tina could relax with Dotty, and she reverted to a softer Southern accent, 'Ah do thank you, Lady Vidal, you're looking real well yourself.'

Bill left the two women and their mutual admiration to attend to the first wave of guests. Eugene and Mary Boardman escorted Ceil Bordon, the guest of honor, into the Bethel house. There was much handshaking and kisses. Sonia Angelini and her husband, Roger Gregory, who was Tulsa City's foremost society photographer, followed. Sonia's sultry beauty contrasted strongly with Gregory's bland, blond, cultured demeanor. The party quickly filled out and the tinkle of glasses mingled with the chatter of a successful evening on its way.

The cocktail portion of the party was in full swing when the doorbell chimed for the last time. Hilda opened the door and, in spite of her Scandinavian reserve, emitted a little gasp and attempted a clumsy curtsy. Framed in the door of the charming house stood a regal Princess Judith, her escort, C.Z. Guest, two paces to her rear. All eyes turned to the stunning blond beauty who had been type cast in the role of monarch. Tina shuddered beneath her gown and slipped to the bar for a large refill of straight brandy. Bill, his eyes glowing, escorted Ceil as guest of honor to meet the royal visitor.

'Princess Judith, how very nice of you to come. May I present our guest, Madame Ceil Bordon.'

Ceil dropped in a practiced curtsy as the Princess smiled and lifted her up. 'Madame Bordon and I are very close . . . as close as the marvelous preparations she allows ex-film actresses to use.'

'Thank you, Princess. Any time you'd like to pose for a testimonial ad just say the word.'

'Unfortunately,' Bill interjected, 'the Princess has a long-term contract with Monteblanco's postage stamps.'

'Then I shall,' continued Ceil, 'use them for our next mailing.'

The audience gently applauded the exchange of light pleasantries, as Bill and Ceil led the Princess in to meet the others. C.Z., basking in the wake of so much chic, followed them until he passed a bar and detoured towards a double martini. His damask brocade dinner jacket with its sequined lapels didn't, for some strange reason, look all that out of place among the richly dressed assemblage.

Bill tried to find Tina, and when at last he did, he was oblivious to how much she had already drunk. He led Princess Judith towards his wife.

'Princess, I'm afraid Mrs. Bethel is terribly nervous about meeting you. She's really just a simple girl.'

'Don't worry, dear, she'll be fine.'

Tina was terrorized as they approached. However, the model's training came through and she managed to stand erect and smiling as Bill presented her. She couldn't navigate the curtsy and had the good sense not to try.

'Oh, Mrs. Bethel,' the Princess said as she held out her hands to clasp Tina's, 'what a ravishing creature you are. Bill, you lucky fox. She's the most beautiful thing I've ever seen.' She turned toward Tina and smiled a dazzling smile. Tina's lids slid down to half cover her onyx eyes, and in the same modulated voice that had greeted Lady Vidal, answered, 'Just terribly native American, your Grace.'

'No dear . . . that's the other one,' piped in C.Z. and Bill knew Tina had passed the first hurdle of the evening.

The party proceeded to the buffet and compliments abounded at the charm of the evening. Bill was too busy to stop Tina from drinking far more than she should. Like society, she could not hold her liquor. But everything was progressing smoothly and Tina seemed to be doing fairly well.

Much gay laughter could be heard from a circle in the corner, which included Mary Boardman, Sonia, Tina, and Princess Judith. They were running on about the charms of Tulsa City.

'I'm sure the climate here has a lot to do with creating this marvelously relaxed atmosphere,' offered the Princess.

'Yes,' agreed Mary, 'and the smaller population helps avoid a lot of tension, too.'

'Are you happy here?' the Princess asked Tina, who hadn't contributed a whole lot to the conversation up to this point.

'Happy? Why ah'm happy as a sow in shit!' burst out Tina in a drunken version to the vernacular of her youth.

The wince was heard round the room. Tina finally realized she had erred terribly, but before she could react, Bill made an announcement.

'Ladies and gentlemen, your attention please. We have more of the Mediterranean with us tonight than just her Serene Highness. If you will all follow Madame Bordon into the garden, the entertainment will soon begin!'

From C.Z.: 'It's going to be pretty hard to top Tina's act.'

Bill, ever smiling, turned the host duties over to Ceil, who picked up immediately.

'Come on now . . . out to the fresh air. I'm so excited . . . all this for little me!'

As the guests filed out, Bill crossed the large room to Tina, standing erect, her face galvanized into her stage mask. As he reached her, he realized she was trembling from head to toe.

'Hey there, it's going just fine.'

'Ah ruined your party. *Ah ruined . . .*'

'Tina! Please, our guests.'

'*Your* guests, y'mean.'

'Ours, darling.'

92

'How dare you embarrass *me*?'

'Tina, what did I do?'

'*Ah's the hostess!*'

'Tina, lower your voice . . . please.'

'Ah was the one supposed to lead them into the garden. You let that cow do, *do what ah was supposed to do!*'

All the guests were outside, sitting on folding chairs as Pablocito, star of the Golendrinas, flung his hat to the stage and started stomping a welcome staccato from the cries inside the house. The guitars strummed and the dancers cavorted. While all eyes focused on the entertainment outside, all thoughts remained with what had just gone on inside the house.

C.Z. casually cradled his drink and shifted his weight in his chair so he could pretend to be watching the dancers while actually watching Tina and Bill as they argued behind the panel arch of the bay window. He mumbled a ringside commentary to Ceil Bordon, who passed it along to Princess Judith.

'She's dropped her composure. Oops, she's waving her arms. Poor child, her hair's fallen out of coif. Pity. Oh, my dear, Bethel's getting physical. He's shaking her by the shoulders . . . but ever so gently. My, he always is the gentleman. Aha! Tina's broken away from him . . . oh, oh, he shouldn't do that . . . grabbed for her . . . she's turning, she's pushing him away . . . Good God . . . Bill! Watch out! *The window* . . .'

The instant was frozen by a loud smash and the crashing shattering of glass. The music stopped and all heads turned to see Bill Bethel come flying backward through a sea of splintered window panes, falling hard on to the flagstoned path beneath the house. His loud cry at impact indicated his pain. The guests were stunned. Only Lady Vidal, her nursing instincts aroused, rose. The others stared up at the now drafty ruin of the window to see a shocked Tina, her hands up to her mouth. She screamed sharply, turned and dashed out of their line of sight.

Lady Vidal reached him first.

'Don't move, Bill, you might have broken something.'

'How stupidly clumsy of me, Dotty, slipping like that. *Ouch!*'

'Just as I thought, that arm's busted. You've got to get to the hospital, and right away.'

Ceil, Eugene, and Mary Boardman were now circled around him.

'Gene, do you mind?' whispered Bill.

'Of course not, old fellow. Just relax, I'll drive you.'

'The party. The party must continue. Ceil . . . it's for Ceil. Oh, my God, what a thing to do to the store . . .' and he passed, thankfully, from consciousness.

Eugene and two other male guests carried Bill to the Boardman car as Lady Vidal issued practical instructions. Ceil took command over the astounded guests and insisted the entertainment continue. C.Z. quietly allowed his martini glass to be refilled as the people nervously resumed their places and tried to pretend that nothing had happened. Carl glanced up to the second floor and saw the lights in the master suite go out.

'Tina, Tina . . . such a cunning stunt. And vice versa.'

'Oh my God! Oh God! I can't wait . . . harder! Ohhh . . . oh sweet God! Now. *Now*! Ohhhhhhh . . . oh my God. Don't move, Josh . . . please don't move.'

The all-enveloping power of Ann's last climax pulsated through every fiber of her body and brain as Josh, ebbing with the exhilaration of release, smothered her trembling body with his athletic frame. His mouth again found hers and he tenderly, gently kissed her. Twice, in that last few hours, he had satisfied her. He was still in her, as erect as ever, but it was gentler now. Less demanding proof of their oneness. Ann's legs, which had wrapped around him in such a frenzy of passion, relaxed and moved down his back to the bed; but her arms still held him in a grip of warmth that did not want to yield to the reality of the waning orgasm. Tenderly, Josh moved out off her, his kisses leaving her mouth and moving down her moist neck until they found the soft abundance of her firm young breasts. Ann shuddered at the surprise of instant reawakening and permitted herself a silly giggle.

'My heart tickles.'

Josh unlocked his lips from her firm, brown nipple and looked up at her face. Ann tried to stifle a schoolgirl laugh.

'Your heart tickles? I'm not that big.'

That did it. She broke out in a peal of laughter.

'Animal! My golden heart . . . your present. It's gotten cold and it tickles me.'

'I'll rip it off.'

'You'll do no such thing.'

She unfolded her arms, removed the chain from around her neck, and placed the little trinket on the nightstand next to the bed.

'Cigarette time,' she said, as she took two from the pack and lit them.

Josh rolled off her and lay back against the headboard. He accepted the cigarette and inhaled deeply.

'Thanks.'

'And after this one, you're getting dressed and catching that last plane. You're expected in New York, you know.'

'Big deal.'

'You are going to be on that plane. I couldn't live through another surprise.'

He smiled, impishly.

'Didn't expect me here when you got home, did you?'

'I certainly didn't.'

'Fooled you?'

'You did. I hope you're proud of yourself, Mr. Frankel.'

'Before I catch that plane you'll see how proud I am.'

'Josh! I couldn't.'

'Oh yes you will. I've got over an hour and a half to make the flight.' He turned over on her and buried his mouth over her ear.

'Oh, my darling. I'll drive you to the plane.'

'Yeah, but until then I'll do the driving. Okay?'

His tongue caressed the inside of her ear and his hot breath once more fanned the flame of passion inside her aching body.

'Oh my sweet Josh, if you only knew how much I love you. How very, very much.'

'I know, baby, I know because I feel the same way. That's why you and I are never going to be apart. I've found you and I'm never letting go.'

'Promise?'

'Promise. Ann, it's settled.'

He moved easily inside her, amazing himself at the recuperative sexual powers of a man who has, at last, found what he's always searched for.

THURSDAY, OCTOBER 6

Manny Berns was that rare and exotic animal in the silken jungle of almost couture: paranoid, megalomaniacal, devoid of any human sentiments (except, perhaps, the sodomite's lust), capable and expert at every devious, obscene vice in that broad roster of depravity. He was generous in business—bribery—to the point of bankruptcy, a consummate liar, carrion feeding on the loneliness and fear of middle-aged women buyers, compulsive and awesome. He was also a master salesman with a modicum of good taste. This vile, reprehensible sub-human connived and cheated his way into the sinew of better dress departments through exploiting the talents of others mingled with the insecurity of those unfortunate ladies who, under his influence, filled their stores with whatever wares he was currently promoting. Manny was tall, weakly bloated, wore an obvious toupee and flaunted his homosexuality in a theatrical manner. He was evil, able and totally obnoxious. In the past decade, he had managed to build up and eventually put out of business three once-prominent manufacturers. For the past two years he had been partner and sales force for Juan Felipe, the now-famous designer. Their business was in Los Angeles and exceeded two million a year. Due to Manny's extravagance, they had yet to show any respectable profit. As he did with any vulnerable person he used, Manny had managed to keep Juan Felipe's mind else-where. A string of occasional boys accommodated and pacified the warm-blooded Latin. Pimping was Manny's strongest selling tool—second only to the well-placed lie that could destroy a career.

With the single exception of Juan's inclination towards deviate sex, he was a talented and thoroughly charming man. Tall, movie-star handsome, perfectly groomed, intelligent and nice, he was a delight to workers, buyers, textile salesmen and the fashion press. Juan Felipe was the instrument to exploit to the fullest that Manny had searched for all his life. Being a gentleman from a fine, old Dominican Republic family, Juan refused to listen to the ugly stories that filtered back about his partner. He had watched the sales volume multiply since Berns joined the firm and, since Berns had managed, so far, to expertly explain the lack of profits, he was letting things ride. Now, at last, Juan was the recipient of a major fashion honor—a coveted Lehson's trophy. His star had emerged and he was taking full advantage of this singular award to consolidate his thoughts towards the future. Juan had a plan. He was almost ready to tell it to Manny.

The plane that had carried them from Los Angeles to Tulsa City was circling the airport. The stewardess had removed the champagne from their first-class seats. Manny and his star were landing.

Lyla had asked Sonia to be with her as she met the plane. Sonia, ever cryptic, stood with the youngest Lehson and observed to herself that Lyla seemed slightly on edge.

'Cigarette, Lyla?'

'Hmm? Oh, yes. Thanks. Why are they taking so long to get the passengers off? That's all we need today is a delay.'

'I could have met Juan by myself.'

'Oh, no dear. I adore him and while he'd never say a word, I know he'd be a little hurt if we both weren't here.'

'I have never met his associate, this Berns chap.'

'You can thank your God for that small favor.'

'Is he so difficult?'

'No, I guess not. It's just that . . . well, Manny, can have a profound effect on one. Be careful, is all I can say.'

Sonia allowed herself a rare, tight smile, 'Do not worry about this Mr. Berns and me.'

'Lucky girl. Oh! Here they come now.'

Lyla and Sonia extinguished their cigarettes and made their way to the foot of the departure ramp to greet Lehson's latest guests. Juan led the way from the plane, spied the women, broke into a radiant smile and waved. Manny fussed with his fur-collared raincoat and tried to catch up with the striding designer.

'Hello, Juan!'

He reached them and warmly embraced them both. Lyla asked, 'How was the flight, darling?'

'*Magnifico*, Lyla. Sonia, *como está?*'

'*Muy bien, gracias. Y usted?*'

'Like the trip—*magnifico*.'

'Well, I feel like *merde!*'

'Ah, Manny, what is the matter now?'

'Would you believe they served domestic champagne? I mean, really, carbonated Lysol.'

'It was a domestic flight, Manny.'

'Double *merde*. The service was foul.'

'Until Señor Berns informed them how important we are, yes?'

'How thoughtful.'

'And those stewardesses uniforms. It was gag time! They looked like trolls in polyester gaberdine. I mean it was a *gag!*'

Lyla turned from Berns, locked her hand in Juan Felipe's arm and said, 'Juan darling, I must have you meet the wife of the president of Consolidated Airlines. Working through the store, you just might be able to do something to spice up their drab costumes.'

Manny spat. 'And Lehson's would keep the lion's share of those enormous profits.'

Juan saw only Lyla. 'It would be my pleasure, Lyla, anytime.'

'Thank you, darling. Who has the luggage checks?'

'I do, here . . . I'm getting a headache from that tacky *vino*.'

'Allow me,' said Sonia and took the checks from Manny and gave them to the chauffeur. 'Williams will collect the luggage.'

They were just about to enter the main terminal when Sonia noticed an emerald green luxurious private jet whiz down the runway and land with a whoosh. She pointed to the striking aircraft and said, 'Mrs. Hightower is arriving.'

Juan was curious, 'Mrs. Hightower?'

'Yes, unbelievably rich. Mr. Hightower owns Four Leaf Clover Oil, hence everything they own is green.'

'Money's green . . . cute idea,' said Berns.

As a crew dashed towards the plane to prepare the landing steps Sonia continued, 'She flies in from her ranch just to shop at Lehson's and have lunch with a few friends.'

'That is a good customer, *si*?'

Lyla added, 'Good is the wrong word. Great is better. Juan darling, last year she bought over six-thousand dollars' worth of your clothes alone.'

Sonia mused, 'And looked terrible in all of them.'

Juan smiled his winning smile again. 'Then I shall personally assist her this trip, to make certain she does not make the same mistakes.'

'That, as my sister Stella would say, is one of the reasons you're here.'

The cabin door of the emerald jet opened and a handsome, tanned pilot stood to one side to assist Mrs. Hightower down the steps. She was sixtyish, flaming red hair, two-way mirror goggle glasses and wore a brilliant green suede cowboy outfit with a huge four-leaf clover design in rhinestones studded to the back of her jacket. She dragged a white ermine cape behind her as she gingerly descended. Lyla was sizing up the good-looking pilot.

'Say,' she half whispered, 'that captain is groovy-looking.'

Juan patted her hand and replied, '*Si*, so I noticed.' The two laughed and led the rest into the terminal.

Lyla and Sonia ushered the Californians into the lavish suite readied specially for them at the Tulsa City Royal. Every detail had been attended to from the fully stocked bar, to well-placed bouquets of beautiful flowers, to the luscious assortment of fruits arranged about the room on silver trays. Even Juan's well-known penchant for coleus plants had been taken into account: the red and green leaves hung abundantly from the ceiling and nearly filled the spacious patio.

'Now listen, Juan,' said Lyla, 'you're our guest of honor here, and darling, we're going to cater to your every desire. No matter what you want, no matter how miniscule or outrageous, please just call down to the desk. Everything you desire is yours. Promise me that you won't be shy.'

Juan smiled warmly. 'You Lehsons never cease to amaze me. Thank you so much.'

'How about a *TV Guide* for starters?' said Manny as he stomped about the sitting room, throwing his clothes into drawers and closet.

'Juan, your new designs arrived last week and I must say they are simply smashing,' enthused Lyla.

'Oh, yes!' agreed Sonia.

'We've set them up for your show this afternoon and everyone at the store is terribly excited. This's got to be your best year yet!' said Lyla. 'Rest up now, Juan, your showing is at two o'clock and we're looking forward to a prime performance.'

'I can't wait either, Miss Lyla,' smiled Juan. 'I'm ready to shine.'

'Good. We'll send a car for you at one-thirty. See you later!'

Juan showed Lyla and Sonia to the door, then walked over to

Manny who was comfortably plunked into a plush divan, drinking a gin on the rocks and watching Rocky and Bullwinkle flit across a glowing screen.

'Manny, I've been thinking . . .'

'Could be dangerous,' chortled Berns.

'No, Manny, seriously. I desire the ultimate in retailing and this is the time for us to make such a move. A "Juan Felipe Boutique" in every important store across the country. My clothes, my name, my own space in the finest merchandising houses of the Western world.'

Manny, engrossed in the cartoons, replied in an offhand manner, 'Yeah, fantastic Juan . . . that's a tremendous idea.'

'It'll guarantee us hundreds upon hundreds of thousands of dollars a year, Manny, you know that. And when we're dealing with a fickle public and the uncertainties of creativity, that kind of old age insurance is very appealing.'

'Look, fella—we haven't done too badly with my selling, so let's leave it at that, huh sweetie?'

'No, Manny, I do not think I shall leave it. I have made up my mind that from this day forward there shall be profits to divide. My boutique will give me those profits. I trust you follow my thinking.'

'Hey, if you feel that strongly, I'll do something. Don't worry, kid.'

'I am not in the least worried. Either you settle it—and I have decided that Lehson's shall be my pilot store—or I shall find a sales manager to give me exactly what I want.'

Juan smiled, turned, and entered his bedroom, closing the door behind him. Manny's eyes followed him and focused on the shut door. This was the first time in two years that Juan had ever challenged his authority. Now it had come, and with a direct command. He knew his Latin and realized that his mind was set. Manny Berns was shaken. He tried to cap his rage, but knew that if he didn't obey, he'd lose Felipe and the leverage he had so carefully built up. His oily mind slipped into high gear as he started the necessary mental machinations to effect what he now realized was a superb merchandising concept. This slimy slug oozing across the leaf of Juan Felipe's talent knew he needed at least two more years before he was ready to dump the designer and branch out alone. 'Hell,' he fumed, 'I haven't stolen enough yet for even the first season!'

★

Perhaps no segment of the seemingly Alice in Wonderland world of a department store is as profitable and mercurial as the cosmetics department. Boiled down to essentials it is nothing more than packaging, presentation and a big promise. Cosmetics are always on the main floor of a store—the highest trafficked, heaviest selling area. It is here that the store's accountants calculate the real estate is the most expensive. Here must be the fastest selling, money-making items. If you make it on the main floor, you've made it big. If you don't make it and make it quickly, you are politely shoved out by the next aggressive manufacturer waiting in the wings to wear the star's crown.

Each year for Lehson's fashion extravaganza, one of the leading cosmetic firms was singled out for stellar treatment. The competition was represented, of course, but only one firm got the lion's share of space, promotion and prestige. Ceil Bordon had astounded the entire industry by dominating these annual affairs for three years running. Rubinstein was too old, Arden too rich from her shops around the world, and Revson too big for any one store. By making herself available in person and never stopping her aggressive pitching, plus the fact that her products were as good (or as bad) as any others, Ceil Bordon had risen quickly up the ladder of lanolin fame. This year, with the Mediterranean for its theme, Lehson's had erected colorful intimate beach cabanas around the central display of Ceil Bordon's main floor area. Each was outfitted with an illuminated mirror (of a special pastel pink-tinted glass) over a clear glass work table and with a slightly uncomfortable beach chair for the customer. Each cabana was staffed by a personal representative from Bordon's who was paid by and accountable to Ceil. They were there to advise and sell. Consult and sell. Make up and sell. Beautify and sell. No area of the cosmetologist's stage magic was unavailable to them. A hundred thousand dollars in retail sales could be rung up during one successful two-week promotion. Cosmetics was big business.

Today, Ceil's first day personally on the selling floor, saw the richest and most important women reserved for the queen's individual attention. With two male assistants, Ceil devoted as much as fifteen minutes each to this herd of rich and aging women who stampeded Lehson's, excitedly awaiting their chance for an analysis of their unique cosmetic needs from the high priestess of sham.

One-by-one the delighted dowagers entered a cabana to be received by an expert cosmetician who studiously examined their faces and recommended that one special cream to subdue this flaw and a little highlight to accent that asset. Invariably, Ceil slid into the cabana to seal the close, her positive assurance guaranteeing that that extra touch around the eyes or mouth would mask away decades.

After the exit of a particularly satisfied customer, the technician remarked to Ceil, 'They always leave aglow.'

'Yes,' replied Ceil, 'intoxicated with their drink from a temporal fountain of youth—and we know damn well they'll be back to guzzle more.'

Another attendant peeked his head into the cabana and announced, 'Mrs. Michelle De Soto is ready for her consultation.'

'Well, show her in,' Ceil said, then turning to the assistant present she whispered, 'Watch now, honey, and learn what you can.'

Mrs. De Soto and her personal maid entered the tent. Michelle De Soto had kept only a small remnant of a once-smashing figure. The fading ruin of her once-glamorous body had been stuffed, mulched, coaxed and forced into the special corsets that hid the flab and sagging flesh and allowed the smart tweed suit to look its handsomest. She wore too much jewelry, but since it was ostentatiously expensive, that seemed all right. The milliner had craftily fashioned a hat with a suggestion of veil that complimented and disguised the wreck of her forehead. Her enormous fortune enabled her to resist the only two things she had ever feared—age and its camp follower, death. She fought death with the only charity she allowed—huge contributions to every church. Age she left to the purring ministry of the Ceil Bordons and Swiss plastic surgeons of the world. Considering that she was nearing eighty and still insisted on the sexual servicing of her fifth exhausted husband, she was at least neck and neck in the battle. Where most women were content to have a pussy, Michelle boasted a panther. She prided herself on her good legs and wore expensive, handmade shoes that showed the calf and ankles to best advantage. She also knew exactly what she wanted . . . Ceil Bordon's personal attention in creating an illusion to make certain age was knocking at the wrong door.

Madame De Soto sat in the beach chair and Ceil went to work. Michelle's face was washed and cold-creamed gently into its natural state, which more closely resembled a relief map of Greece than human flesh.

Pulling out mortar and pestle, Ceil cooed, 'Mrs. De Soto, we shall create something very special and uniquely designed for you. This is not for common people.'

A soft warm towel was placed over Mrs. De Soto's face to prepare it for the application to come while Ceil added softening cold cream and scent to what was essentially a plaster of paris base. The pasty concoction was mixed, enriched, remixed and then delicately applied to De Soto's face with what could only be described as an elegant golden miniature trowel.

'This marvelous mixture makes you look like a card-carrying member of a younger generation . . .'

Michelle De Soto's face split into a broad grin.

'Careful, precious! The cover cracks with exaggerated facial movements. We'll give you this exquisite gold carrying case so you can always have enough handy for touch-ups during the day.'

'Jackson!' called out Ceil.

'Yes, Madame Bordon,' he replied, peeking into the tent.

'Please bring the wig we've picked out for Mrs. De Soto.'

'Yes, ma'am.'

'Now, Michelle, the styling of this hairpiece is not only perfectly you, but it's also perfect for you. The soft undersweeping below the ears, the delicate wisps cascading down the sides of the forehead. It's marvelous, really.'

Jackson carried the costly wig in and Ceil discreetly stepped between Michelle and her reflected image in the mirror for those brief moments between wigs when her piebald pate was exposed. Ceil stepped aside once more when the new wig was fitted.

'It does look beautiful!' uttered Mrs. De Soto through carefully pursed lips, trying not to crack her mask.

'Yes,' agreed Ceil, noting that the wig hid all the worst betrayers of age of Michelle's face.

'Bill me, Ceil, and thanks, honey—thanks so much for everything! Ah'm so pleased,' lilted De Soto, exiting with over eighteen hundred dollars' worth of dreams on order.

The couture floor was crowded to overflowing as Sonia began her commentary, starting the Juan Felipe showing. His styling had never been better and his creativity had been honed by the successful history of the past years. His customers, 'My darling ladies', were for the most part tall, well-constructed, strongly boned women—wise enough to don Juan's dresses and wealthy enough to afford the considerable prices retailers charge. What was his secret? Firstly, he respected and admired a statuesque woman from a sincere aesthetic sense. He also believed that women want to accentuate their femininity without being coy. Woman to him was that proud Dominican grande dame who had been his mother. Tall, vibrant, the coal black eyes smoldering their promises of sensuality reserved for the head of the ranchero. The aristocratic señora. His madonna of the early years when Juan wanted nothing more than pleasing her rather than following his father on his daily excursions around the vast coffee plantation. As he stood next to Sonia, accepting the admiring stares and open invitations of the several hundred handsome women—but safe from any incestuous overtones that might occur in private—Juan felt pride in the fashion show. He knew how to expertly accentuate a woman's figure—show it off to maximum advantage. Draping the silk jersey in subtle folds around the upper bodice, the little bias cut flounces bordering the hem of the evening dress, the careful selection of those primitive prints that suggested untold adventures to come. A Juan Felipe creation rumored the hint of sexuality, but offered nothing overt. It was his father's oft-remembered advice, 'Always treat a lady a little like a whore, and a whore a lot like a lady.' His parents had earned more than a little share in his Lehson award.

One by one they paraded—those gorgeous, lean mannequins swerved to reveal the angular hip, turned to silhouette the delightful curve of the buttocks, reached to stretch the clinging cloth across unbrassiered breasts, moved to show that even those starkly thin creatures could look inviting and, yes, sexy. The audience reacted in unison to the exquisiteness of Felipe's designs and no one attempted to hide the little gasps of delight as each new creation came forth, more strikingly beautiful than its predecessor.

Manny Berns stood at the back of the crowd with the tough, professional buyer of Juan's collection for the store, Penny Black.

'It's too much, Penny, really too much. These bitches are positively in heat over Juan's clothes.'

'Shush, will you. I can't hear Sonia.'

'Hear? Look sweetie . . . look at 'em and get ready to listen to the ring of the cash register.'

'The line is great this season, no one can take that away from him.'

'*Him!* Us, you mean. I sweated piss getting him to put this collection together and he gets all the credit. Juan and I are an unbeatable combo and you know it.'

'Sorry, Manny, I lost my head for a minute.'

'Excused, sweetie. What I'm leading up to . . .'

'Here it comes.'

'What I am leading up to is a little idea that's been lurking in the back of my mind for months now. I want you to be the first to hear it.'

'I can't listen to Sonia?'

'That half-breed? Where'd they ever find *her?*'

'Claubert's.'

'I'd heard he'd slipped. Anyways, the idea. I've decided to allow Lehson's to be the first store in America to open a Juan Felipe boutique.'

'A what?'

'That's right . . . an entire little area of his own where all his clothes will be displayed under one roof. Sensational? Tell the truth.'

'Are you on the pipe? Lehson's sells Lehson's. You want a boutique? Then open your own. Don't ask us to do it for you.'

'You're missing the bigger picture, *sweetie.* Listen to me for a minute . . .'

'Now just stop it! Stop pushing while the show is going on, and I mean it. Up to now, we've only promoted Juan's things because of Miss Lyla. I don't know what her reasons were, but they seem justified now. He's reached creative maturity with this line. As he ripens, I'll buy them without any prodding from the fifth floor. Your charming of Miss Lyla has paid off, so stop pressing your luck, stop pushing, shut up and enjoy the show. Enough said?'

Manny was nonplussed. 'Penny, aren't we the little cunt this afternoon. I knew a girl named Penny once, named after her father's yacht.'

'I was named after my father's fortune.'

'Clev-ver. Clev-ver.'

She looked back at the showing and mocked him. 'Dear Manny, your toupee is slipping.'

'You think you can screw around with Manny Berns, Miss Thing? We'll see what Lyla thinks about turning down a once-in-a-lifetime opportunity.'

He wheeled around and headed for the elevator, his every fiber concentrating on the destruction of this impudent, self-assured buyer.

Lyla's secretary was adamant.

'I'm sorry, Mr. Berns, but Miss Lyla is not to be disturbed. I have my orders. She's working with a very important manufacturer from New York.'

'More important than The House of Felipe? I think not!'

He brushed past the protesting girl, who, startled, rose and tried to stop him from opening Lyla's door. Manny was too strong for her; he pushed her aside and threw open the door to the inner office, only to find Lyla fluidly unzipping the fly of a smooth-looking stud in a Brooks Brothers suit. Lyla was aghast at his presumption.

'Christ, Manny! Don't you know how to knock?'

His eyes widened, his mouth curled a mean smile, he shrugged, said 'Whoops, sorry,' pirouetted around and left, shutting the door behind him. As he passed the secretary, close to tears, he shouted, 'Tell Miss Lyla I'll be back when she's finished editing his line.'

The five-thirty bell rang and the last straggling customers were allowed to finish their purchases and were then let out. Lehson's was closing after another profitable day. Even though the public had left, many of the store executives still worked on. The big entertainment of the evening was to be the premiere of Quentin Kimball's long-awaited adaptation of Aristophanes' *Lysistrata* at the new Theatre Centre. The facile author had, it was rumored, reversed the sexes; and critics from Hollywood and New York had flown in for what promised to be an auspicious evening. Upstairs on Lehson's fifth floor, activity was starting to ebb as the merchandise managers and key personnel wrapped up their schedules. Stella, on her way home to change before the charity performance, looked in on Edna.

'Going to the Centre tonight, Edna?'

'No, Stell, Boardman is bringing Weinstein in for a meeting.'

'Don't tell me it's insurance time again?'

'Reassessment of our coverage. I don't think we're as protected as I'd like, which means Eugene will fight the increased premiums.'

'Weinstein will make a compromise and everyone will be happy. Good night, Edna, see you tomorrow.'

'Night, Stell.'

The intercom buzzed and Edna flicked the switch, 'Yes, Peggy?'

'Mr. Boardman wants to know if you're free to see Mr. Weinstein.'

'I am. Send them in.'

Jeremiah Weinstein was aptly named. The dour man had grown rich and prominent in insurance circles by predicting every conceivable form of doom and destruction imaginable. He insured ranchers against insect plagues, oil fields against earthquakes, and county fairs against storms as well as the more conventional areas of traditional insurance. The Lehson account was one of his most profitable since Edna and Stella ran a tight, safe ship. The incidence of customers slipping and suing the store was minimal, and theft was a minor irritation rather than a problem. Security at Lehson's was the best in the nation.

'Jeremiah, how nice to see you again.'

'Thanks, Miss Edna, but I'm coming down with a gout attack, unless I'm mistaken.'

Boardman helped the afflicted man into a comfortable chair. 'Would you like an ottoman for your feet?'

'No, Eugene, this will be just fine. God meant I should suffer. Who am I to argue?'

'How is your family, Jeremiah?' asked Edna, more polite than concerned.

'Living, which is something I should be grateful for. My son . . . no, don't ask!'

'Robin, what about him?'

'What an insurance man that boy would've made. But, who am I to have *mazel*?'

Boardman was unfamiliar with the Yiddish word.

'*Mazel* means luck,' volunteered Edna.

'It means *good* luck, Eugene. My luck is all bad.'

'He's not ill, is he?'

'Robin is sick in the head, Miss Edna. He informed his mother and me last week he has decided to become a rabbi. A rabbi, yet!'

'Why that's wonderful, Jeremiah, you must be so proud.'

'Orthodox! My son an orthodox rabbi. What did I do wrong?'

'I consider that an honor, if you don't mind my saying.'

'In Israel! He's going to live in Israel. Across the world. My wife is under constant sedation.'

'It isn't as bad as all that. He'll make a fine, wonderful rabbi. He always had a thoughtful, scholarly mind. The store will be privileged to make a substantial contribution to his synagogue when he's ordained.'

'Oh, he'll be ordained, don't worry about that. Anything that boy does he does better than anyone else. Frustrating? All he's ever done is give his poor mother and me ulcers. Do you know that he started earning his own money when he was eight? Eight! Imagine the *chutzpah*—that's gall, Eugene—of that child. I didn't even have the satisfaction of giving him an allowance to hold over his head. Ah well, enough of my misery. Why are we here tonight?'

Boardman, relieved that the biblical drama was over, began.

'Jeremiah, Miss Edna has been studying the computer output on our inventory and feels we should discuss additional coverage.'

'Actually, Jeremiah, we hadn't planned on the amount of business that the Southfield branch has done. Inventories are now above our line of protection.'

'Ah hah, one good Oklahoma electrical storm and a whole store could go. You're wise, Edna, too much isn't ever enough.'

The meeting continued. Edna wanted more insurance. Boardman felt the policies they had were sufficient and Weinstein mediated between the two. Stella was proven right. Jeremiah Weinstein came up with a satisfactory compromise that kept everyone happy, and the store and its two branches overinsured. He limped from the office at 7.50, richer by an extra two thousand dollars in commissions. He refused Boardman's help in leaving and parted with only one comment—'Rabbi Robin. It's a ridiculous name.'

Edna remained alone in her office for a few minutes. She had welcomed the meeting and always felt better after listening to Weinstein's never-ending accounts of the misfortune that was his lot. She locked her desk from force of habit and, as she rose to leave, glanced at the framed photographs of her dead mother and dying father that were prominent on the table top. Edna looked hard and her eyes misted slightly as she thought, 'Everything was always for you, Poppa. No one but you.'

She sighed, turned off the lights and left. In the parking lot, she got in her car and headed out towards the highway leading to her Circle 'O' Ranch. She reached the cloverleaf intersection when something came over her and her thoughts about the condition of

Mr. Abe. She made a full circle around the bypass and headed back toward the residential section of Tulsa City.

Night had fallen outside Abraham Lehson's Tudor mansion where the fleet of physicians' vehicles were silently waiting.

Edna pulled up in front of the residence. She paused, breathed a full sigh and got out of the car. Edna approached the oaken door, hesitated before the bell, then turned and walked around to the side of the massive structure. She surveyed the darkened outlines of rolling estate. Her eyes clouded.

She remembered all those afternoons, years back, when Mr. Abe never seemed to have time for her. 'Daddy, can you teach me to ride my bicycle today?' 'Can't you see I'm busy Edna! ... Now don't cry, I didn't mean to shout, but I'm leaving for New York in an hour. Why don't you play with your dolls or help your mother in the kitchen? I'll teach you another day.'

'Whatever I did,' she thought, 'it was never good enough, never the right thing ... The winter I nearly killed myself swimming across the river, my horses ... no matter what it was, it wasn't ever right with him. He never noticed me. I could never reach him, his affection was always for the store ... I know he didn't really mean to hurt me, but why wasn't he ever warm, ever loving?'

Edna scrambled over a knoll to the deserted play area originally built for her sisters and herself. The playhouse, swing, croquet court and play equipment unused for over a generation were perfectly maintained. He had always hoped to see grandchildren romping on them. Another disappointment. She walked slowly, touching the roof of the playhouse lightly, almost reverently. Her hand ran across a rung on the slide's ladder.

Edna eased into the swing's support and slowly, methodically, she started rocking back and forth. Only tears, dropping and coagulating into opals of wet sand, punctuated Edna's rocking on into the night.

FRIDAY, OCTOBER 7

Stella had forgone her breakfast at home today to enjoy a working-social session with the avant-garde American designer, Gari Reichman. Gari, last year's recipient of Lehson's 'Most Influential Creator of the Year' award, and his model and constant companion, Nicky Von Verde, shared a large table with Stella in the otherwise deserted Blue Grotto.

Stella's respect for this withdrawn trend setter was the highest. She knew that here was one man with a true vision of fashion's future; and a working breakfast to pick his sizable brain would influence the direction of merchandising plans that Lehson's would take in the year to come. Gari was too far ahead to be commercially practical, but his unerring gift of prophecy had been too right for too long to be ignored by anyone whose life and income were wrapped up in the intricacies of fickle fashion. Surprisingly, Stella was the only important merchant who sought his counsel.

Gari and the statuesque Nicky each ate a spartan meal of tea and one thin slice of whole grain toast as Stella set the mood for this encounter.

'I really think, Gari, that fashion is walking a treadmill. There's very little to get really excited about in women's clothes today, don't you agree?'

'Fashion, as you're defining it, ended with the stock market crash of '29. It was replaced by the snob appeal of opulence that continues today.'

'I certainly wouldn't go that far, it's just a little dull.'

'Miss Stella, I'm weary of being evangelical over something so basically unimportant as women's apparel. All I can do is state my beliefs. What anyone wants to do with them is their concern.'

'Gari,' murmured Nicky almost to herself, 'sees the world of to-morrow. Most people can't look beyond yesterday.'

'I agree completely, which is why I value his opinion and the guts it takes to do something about it.'

'Miss Stella, let us be perfectly honest. My clothes don't belong in Lehson's.'

'That's ridiculous and you know it.'

'I'm never frivolous—a large store is wrong for me and my things. You don't really sell them the way you should, you know that.'

'It takes a little getting used to, that's all.'

'No, my philosophy of clothing is merely an extension of my beliefs about where the world is heading. It's not heading to large fashion emporiums. Small individual shops, yes. Big chains, yes. But the thing that will eventually change Lehson's is two-fold. Your rich customers are dying off, and the caliber of salespeople you must have to properly project what you're doing will become extinct. No, Lehson's will change in the future. It's many years away, but it's there.'

'I agree that the store will change. Change, Gari, is the basis of the business.'

'I don't agree at all. Nonchange is where it's heading to. The caprices of this stylist or that, that's not change, that's whimsy. The young people are almost ready to storm the Bastille of Seventh Avenue, Miss Stella. I can see it as clear as the sun outside. It's already started in London—the so-called Mod look. British kids are finally throwing off the shackles of their establishment. The final destruction of Victorian values is beginning, first at the London School of Economics, and second on King's Road.'

'We feature some young British styles and are doing quite well with them.'

'But your thinking is all wrong. To you it's just a small trend. To youth, it's their answer to the disenchantment of today. The traditional fashion industry is rigid. The large manufacturers are stuck with inventories of worn-out concepts. The young are moving away from all of that.'

'You really think so?'

'I know it. I feel it will develop one day to a uniform that both men and women will wear. A uniform of freedom and common sense. I don't know exactly what it will be, but the shape and utility will certainly have something to do with work clothes. The coverall, perhaps; a variation of pants absolutely. Levi Strauss is the closest manufacturer to it, right now, but they don't know it as yet.'

'Are you seriously telling me that denim and twill will be fashion?'

'Why not? They're natural fabrics and we're going to return to the naturals. Leathers, for sure. Why not denims and that genre?'

'I hope I'm not around when it happens.'

'You'll not only be around, but once you've sniffed the trend you'll be the first to promote it.'

'Poor Aaron Seton and his sort. What will become of them?'

'Like the mastodon, they shall vanish. It's a long way off, though. There are still enough old witches who've killed off their husbands to keep the so-called couturiers alive for many more seasons.'

'Gari, you certainly paint a depressing picture for a fashion retailer.'

'Sorry about that, but it's what I see. Uniforms. Protective wear, armor, if you will, for outside; and nudity or something close to it for private times. It's basic, natural . . . it's where it's going.'

'Oh, look at the time! I'm afraid that I must be going as well. It's always such an interesting time when I can talk to you seriously, Gari. Disturbing, but illuminating. Will I see you and Nicky before the rodeo on Sunday?'

'I doubt it. I'm booked into the sports floor for showings today and tomorrow.'

'Then Sunday it will be. Good-bye for now.'

As Stella signed the check and left Gari and Nicky alone, her thoughts turned to the immediate problems of the day. Nicky quietly asked Gari, 'Do you think she heard you?'

'She heard me, and she'll do something about it.'

'What?'

'Haven't a clue, but she's not the queen of merchants for nothing. Stella Lehson knows I tell the truth.'

Much has been made of the Lehson Christmas catalogue—that full-color compilation of rare and tasteful merchandise gathered from the four corners of the earth. Nothing went into the book that had not been personally vetted by Stella. The catalogue was her child and no mother ever pampered and protected an offspring like she did. Manufacturers vied for an eighth of a page. Careers were launched by inclusion. Fortunes were amassed by the man who had the one unique, special item that Stella Lehson demanded. For the singular privilege of having your product photographed for the catalogue you gladly paid the thousands of dollars that the store said was to cover the cost of printing and mailing. Its publication was as eagerly awaited by more than a hundred thousand customers all over the world as the most heralded of best sellers.

A Lehson Christmas catalogue was displayed on the cocktail table of the super-rich as a status symbol par excellence. The majority of the glittering gifts displayed inside its vellum pages were of prices that most people could afford. The little salt and pepper shakers at ten dollars were the epitome of chic and, usually, exclusive with the store. However, it was the minority of 'unusual, costly items' that garnered the attention and notoriety. Syndicated columnists quoted the opulence of the most exotic. There was never a selling catalogue produced to rival Lehson's. It was as far away from Sears & Roebuck's robust, practical effort as a hand-machined Lamborghini was from a Ford Model A. Over a month ago, Clay Pepper had telephoned from his ranch, just ten miles smaller than Rhode Island, and asked if Miss Stella could give him and his mother a little time to help them select their Christmas presents from the Lehson catalogue. Today was the day for that rendezvous.

The Cadillac division of General Motors had been commissioned to create a special camper for the Pepper clan. Measuring thirty feet long, it was entirely plated with pure chrome. It was air conditioned, of course, and furnished like a comfortable living room. It also contained, and this was the reason it was custom-built, a large bathroom with a special, small-scale toilet. This was for Clay's Momma, a seventy-nine-year-old, Bible-quoting stooped runt four feet nine inches high whose liver-spotted skin hung loosely on brittle bones. Momma Pepper had lost partial control of her kidneys during the drought of 1936 and her bladder had grown increasingly independent as the years passed. The bathroom was kept at a constant seventy-eight degrees and was perfumed to fight the acrid smoke that billowed out from the oily black cheroots Momma smoked. Momma spent most her time on the toilet as her exhausted organ evacuated the almost constant dribble of liquid waste. Since arthritis had made Momma a virtual cripple, a huge black nurse was in attendance at all times. Her name was Blossom. Her function was to lift Momma up when nature called, place her on the commode and put her back on a chair when it was over. It was an easy, undemanding job.

Clay was the only issue of Momma's union with Big Ed Pepper. Her small frame could barely accommodate Big Ed's bulk—he had been aptly named—and she had gained forty-seven pounds carrying the baby. When Clay finally emerged, apologetically premature, he still tipped the scales at eight pounds and measured nearly twenty-five inches. Had he been born on time, Momma was sure she would have died. Big Ed had to seek satisfaction with fancy ladies in Tulsa City, after the dynasty had been insured with an heir, and blissfully passed away one evening in the saddle of a voluptuous nymph who raised her prices the next afternoon. Clay was two when his Daddy was called to that big roundup in the sky and Momma clutched the hefty lad to her milkless breast and promised the heavens she would conserve his estate with all her might. True to her promise, when Clay reached his maturity the spread had expanded to its now-gigantic size and Clay tipped the scales at 280, which was evenly distributed over the six-foot seven-inch frame. Docile and dumb, Clay remained a Momma's boy to this day. His only trace of personality was his love affair with custom-made cowboy attire and his warm, open generosity. Clay Pepper, at fifty, was a nice boy.

The Cadillac camper made its way into the Lehson parking lot. Blossom mechanically removed the dripping Momma from the toilet, and Clay held the door open for their entry into the store and up to Stella's office. He was inwardly excited as these annual sorties into the big town to select presents from that legendary catalogue was the high point of his year.

Stella greeted the unusual trio with a warmth and genuineness reserved for the wildly rich. As Blossom tucked the chinchilla fur lap robe around Momma's shriveled legs (which didn't even reach the floor in a sitting position), Stella helped the massive Clay into a large comfortable chair. Stella returned to her desk and smoothed the cover of this year's edition of Christmas creations.

'Well now, Mother Pepper, would you like a cup of tea before we begin?'

'Goes through me like a dose of salts. Got any Bourbon?'

'Of course.'

'Two fingers—straight.'

Stella went to the hidden bar and poured the order.

'Thankee, Miss Stella. Dang if that don't taste warm. A little wine to comfort the soul, as the good book says.'

'It's a special whiskey I have made for us by a very small distillery. Let me send a bottle home with you, my compliments.'

Clay quickly broke in. 'Oh no, Miss Stella. It wouldn't be right, us acceptin' gifts from you. But thank you muchly, ma'am.'

'Clay's right. Put down ten cases for our order. My, oh my, that's smooth drinkin' likker. Oops. Blossom! The good Lord calls.'

No one but Clay, her accountant and her physician knew Momma's Christian name. But, as always, whenever Blossom lifted the flowing parent and rushed her toward Stella's private bathroom, the one label Blossom thought of for the old lady came to mind—'They shoulda called her Toilet Pepper.'

Stella smiled understandingly. The sound of the flush signaled Momma's return. As Blossom carefully placed her down on the chair and retucked the lap robe, Stella asked Clay, 'I trust you've brought your list, Mr. Pepper?'

He beamed. 'Sure did. Right here on the back of this envelope. Momma an' I have gone through the book at least twenty times, but we want your okay on what we picked.'

'Of course, that's why I'm here.'

Stella fondled a slim silver pencil next to the pad of order blanks and waited for Clay to start.

'Well now, on page thirty-two, them elephant tusks . . .'

'Aren't they marvelous? An impressive objet d'art for anyone. The fittings are sterling silver, you know?'

'Yep, I sure do. Says so right here. They'll do real fine for Uncle Kincaid in Tylerville. He's partial to anything African, y'know.'

Blossom thought to herself, 'He sure is. Made seven passes at me the last time he was at the ranch.'

Stella, ever efficient, said, 'We have his address from last year. A matched pair of male elephant tusks in sterling mountings . . . three thousand dollars. The store will take care of the shipping costs.'

'Why thanks again. You'll gift wrap 'em, won't you?'

'Naturally, that is part of Lehson's service.'

'An' on page forty, them cute little china horses. My, they sure are pretty. Aunt Daisy'll go plum crazy over 'em. That's Mrs. Daisy Crabs, she's Daddy's sister y'know, number Two Sutton Place in New York, New York.'

Stella jotted down the address and repeated as she wrote, 'Two Ming porcelain horses on teak stands . . . sixty-five hundred dollars. Next?'

'Don' forget Cousin Deirdre in Kansas now.'

'Ah won't, Momma. That's Deirdre Hawkins . . .'

'Of course, I remember her. Such a sweet person. I think, Clay, that we have all the addresses, as I said. Mother Pepper, how is Miss Hawkins?'

'Poorly. Real poorly. Suffered a fallen womb on July fourth. She needs perkin' up.'

'Momma felt this . . . this . . .' he blushed terribly, ' . . . garment on page twelve . . .'

It was a section devoted to intimate apparel. Clay pointed to a silk peignoir set pictured in the center of the page. 'There! That one.'

'It's perfectly lovely. Ideal for a convalescent. Do you know her size?'

Momma knew. Cousin Deirdre was a sixteen.

'And in what color, Mother Pepper?'

'Why jus' send her one in every color. 'Bout all she gets any pleasure from nowadays is unwrappin' packages.'

'Lovely thought. It's available in twelve colors, including black, but if I may suggest. . . ?'

'Do. Please do.'

'No black. In her condition . . . if you know what I mean?'

'Dammee! That's why we like shoppin' here. You ain't no big town slicker tryin' just to sell us something. If it ain't right, then Lehson's won' have no truck with it an' that's for danged sure!'

'You and your family are our friends . . . not merely customers.'

'An you're like kin to us, Miss Stella.'

'Again, thank you, Mother Pepper.'

'Shucks, call me Momma. Everyone else does.'

'Very well, then Momma it shall be. Eleven peignoir sets at two hundred each to Miss Hawkins in Kansas.'

And so it went. For almost an hour the Peppers bought and bought as Stella wrote and wrote. When the final name on the list had been taken care of, the bill was a staggering thirty-six thousand dollars. Stella disliked herself for thinking, 'and no salesgirl's commission,' but there it was.

*

Frank Preston's office befitted the man who headed up Lehson's New York and International operations. Even though there were sizable apparel markets in Los Angeles, Chicago and Dallas—ninety per cent of all the store's goods were purchased in New York and Europe. Eight per cent came from Beverly Hills and Los Angeles and the remaining two per cent was scattered throughout the rest of the world. In this, Lehson's was no different from any other of the country's bigger fashion stores. Frank was the dean of that select academy— New York resident offices for stores away from Manhattan. His job transcended its initial purpose and he was, today, a high-powered voice in the affairs of magazines, society and diplomatic government, as well as the arbiter of several monthly problems that manufacturers had in dealing with the store. He was aware of his power and used it to the fullest. His devotion was to Stella and the store, and in this he slaved over luncheons at the Colony, cocktails at 21, and dinners at the Pavillon to ensure that all that was new, newsy, fresh and fashionable saw the light of day at the Tulsa City store.

It was to Frank Preston that Stella had secretly entrusted her unknown ambition for government service. Though Frank was secure, he realized that getting Stella an ambassadorship would culminate and guarantee his career. To this end, he used his long-standing friendship with Amos Barron. Barron, scion of a wealthy tobacco family, had selected diplomacy as his contribution to his nation and was now Director of Protocol for the State Department. When Amos had been between wives, it was Frank who introduced those correct models and editors who were only too delighted to be seen with the rich diplomat; and sharing his freshly laundered bed was an accepted pleasure for all concerned. Yes, being friends, Amos Barron owed Frank Preston (and therefore Lehson's) a favor. Stella being named ambassador would wipe the slate clean.

It was an unusual October afternoon as Frank sat looking out his window on the twenty-second floor. Manhattan shimmered in dry, clear sunlight. The spires of those architectural triumphs gleamed and shone, and far, far below, the ants and autos plied their way against the crush of traffic. Frank waited as the long distance operator tried to complete his Washington call. Her voice came back on the line.

'Mr. Preston?'

'Waiting.'

'Ready on your call to Mr. Barron in Washington. Go ahead, Washington.'

'Frank?'

'Right. Hope I'm not interrupting anything, Amos.'

'Not at all. In fact you've saved the United States government the cost of this call. I was just about to ring you.'

'We must all do our bit. What's the word?'

'Stella Lehson-Manchester can stop worrying about the cold. The Scandinavian countries are out.'

'Down to the short list?'

'We are. It's going to be a Mediterranean nation, if it's going to be at all.'

'The first part is just splendid. I'm not happy about the "at all," though.'

'Diplomatic hedging, Frank, that's all.'

'How come the field's opened up? We thought Italy was the only one possible in that part of the world.'

'Change is breezy, Frank. That's all I know right now.'

'Thanks, Amos—a lot. You will keep me posted, won't you?'

'Naturally.'

'My best to Norma.'

'Will do. 'Bye, Frank.'

'Good-bye, Amos.'

He replaced the receiver and tapped idly on his desk. He pushed the buzzer to his secretary. 'Get me Miss Stella, please,' he said, and swiveled around again to enjoy the startling autumn view outside his window. Within minutes, his phone rang. Stella was on the line.

'Good morning, Stella, any new crises?'

'No, but's still early here.'

'Spoke with Morgan Moore this morning and it's no go. He won't budge.'

'That's unfortunate. Do you think a little time will change his mind?'

'I don't. I understand he's already been in contact with Mallot's and offered them the entire collection on an exclusive basis.'

'Edith Mallot runs an extremely fine shop. She'll do well with Moore. It's been a long time since Lehson's has lost a line it wanted.'

'Stella, I don't care what Culbertson says, it just doesn't wash. Something's fishy.'

'Have you spoken with Purlmutter?'

'He's been ducking me. That's what doesn't gel.'

'Keep after him. Any word from Amos Barron?'

'Good words. I just hung up after a nice chat.'

'And?'

'You won't be chilly. The northern nations are definitely out. It's the Mediterranean for sure.'

'Oh Frank, I am delighted. Oh dear!'

'What is it?'

'It will be the European side, won't it?'

Frank laughed. 'I can almost guarantee that. You wouldn't be particularly welcome in an Arab nation and it would be a trifle chauvinistic sending you to Israel.'

'Yes, I imagine you're right. Israel. Oh my, that would be dreadful. It's so . . . pioneering. You know what I mean?'

'I do indeed. If I were to venture a guess, I'd take book on Italy.'

'Oh Frank, I do hope you're right. I would so love Rome. This is most unlike me . . . I'm so excited I'm almost quivering.'

'Now hold on, Stella. Nothing is certain until it's all settled. I don't want you becoming too confident.'

'I won't, Frank. Thank God everything's so busy with the gala and all. . . . It helps to keep the hopes and fantasies from taking over completely. I have never wanted anything in my whole life like I want this.'

'And you'll probably get it, Stella. Just be patient for a few more days. Anything else?'

'No, not really. I doubt you'll learn much from Purlmutter, but try. Thanks so for calling. Talk with you soon.'

There is a basic truism in the fine art of superior salesmanship. . . . You must sell yourself before you sell the product. This can be done in many ways, and the method that Juan Felipe successfully used was to first put his woman a little off balance. Once she had become unsure of herself, he showed her how to restore the shaky confidence. He became the undisputed authority. She trusted him totally. Then he was able to sell her anything.

Lyla led Juan into the large dressing room where Mrs. Hightower waited. As he entered, Mrs. Hightower broke into a wide grin.

'My God, you are a handsome one, aren't you?'

'The señora is too kind.'

'Now Helen,' Lyla smilingly interjected, 'you're a happily married lady. Dare I trust you two in here alone?'

'Absolutely not!' Helen Hightower chuckled. 'Get that skinny fanny out of here and leave us to our own devices.'

'Fair enough, but you can only have Juan for a few minutes. There are hundreds of anxious ladies all waiting to meet him.'

'Honey, when he's received the Hightower seal of approval, he'll be made.'

Lyla turned to leave, then laughed and said to Juan, 'Watch her in the clinches.'

Alone, Helen turned to Juan and became serious. 'She's a damn nice kid. Wish to hell she'd find one decent fellow, get married and settle down. Lyla flits too much.'

'An occupational hazard. The world of fashion is not well suited to conventional family life, I'm afraid.'

'Guess you're right. Well now, young man, what exactly have you whipped up that's perfect for me . . . in green, of course.'

Juan's expertise and sophistication came immediately to the fore. It was time to create the lack of balance.

'Mrs. Hightower, you wear entirely too much green.'

'Whaaa?' She was disarmed. 'I wear *only* green, young man!'

'No variety. No, excuse me, señora . . . no chic.'

'Just an ever-loving minute . . .'

'If the señora will allow me to continue?'

'Well . . . go ahead.'

'Green does become you unquestionably and is, perhaps, a lucky shade as well.'

'You bet your sweet . . . oh, go on.'

Juan had her on edge—good. He sized the now-tense woman up with expert eyes. Older than the majority of the women who wear his clothes. Still, a striking (albeit brassy) female whose main assets were the flaming red hair, strong eyes the color of a philodendrum leaf flecked with copper, and first-rate legs.

'If you'll excuse me for just a moment, I shall return with some things I feel will suit you,' he said, and left the dressing room before she could protest.

When Juan returned five minutes later, he was followed by a salesgirl who pushed a rolling rack filled with his clothes. In his hands, he carried a tray of jewelry, accessories and scarves.

'This better be good, Mister Felipe. I'm not used to waiting around.'

'My apologies, señora. I feel certain you will benefit from the next few minutes.'

Juan studied the rack of dresses carefully and then extracted a long shirt style in pale blue silk. 'Please try this on.'

'I've never worn a washed-out color like that in . . .'

'Señora, please indulge me.'

'It'll look like hell, but okay. Give it here.'

While she was changing, Juan selected a strand of milky green opaline beads and a long, flowing chiffon scarf printed in emerald and copper on a pale blue background. Before she had a chance to object, he placed the soft beads around her neck and draped the elegant scarf over her shoulders. The effect was a revelation. Mrs. Hightower had never looked so lovely in her whole life.

'Ah ha,' he beamed, 'that is more like it. You are wearing the gown, it doesn't wear you.'

The salesgirl marveled at the transformation, 'Oh, Mrs. Hightower, you're so . . . pretty!'

'Hmmmm, you know . . . it doesn't look all that bad when you get it fixed up. Not bad at all.' She turned and looked at her side and back views in the mirror.

'One more thing. . . . Miss, I want the dress slit fifteen inches on each side. The señora has magnificent legs and it would be criminal to hide them.'

'Say now, that's all right.' The overgrown cowgirl had been transformed into a creature of sophisticated beauty. Juan Felipe was home. From here on in, Mrs. Hightower was his tool.

Fifteen minutes later, Lyla stuck her head in the dressing room. The salesgirl was writing up still another order as a fitter kneeled on the floor pinning a dove green jersey evening gown to Juan's exacting dictates.

'Juan, Mrs. Mulein is getting impatient. She's been waiting all morning for you.'

'Lyla, just let her wait. Mary Mulein has more money than sense and a little patience is what she needs. This kid stays right here. Honey, Juan's sensational!'

Yes, the change was remarkable. So was the bill. Before the day was over, Juan Felipe would be responsible for more sales of his clothes than Lehson's had ever sold in any given month.

The store had been closed for fifteen minutes and most of the sales employees had already left. It had been a grueling day, with enormous sales figures, and everyone was exhausted. Upstairs on five, Manny Berns sat across from Lyla in her office.

'I'm sorry, Lyla, but your Miss Penny is a counterfeit. God knows I bend over backward to be fair and accommodating, but just between us girls, that bitch doesn't cut it.'

'Penny Black's as good a buyer as they come.'

'Then I'm going into a different business. Did you see today's sales? Well, did you?'

'I'll get the figures in the morning.'

'I've done a little totaling myself . . . the store sold over eighteen thou of Juan's clothes. *In one day!*'

'That's fine. You'll get a reorder tomorrow.'

'I'm not interested in her tacky reorders! That bitch hasn't the taste to buy correctly. You are the only one to select our things and you know it.'

'What's this sudden mad-on you've got for Penny?'

'I loathe lesbians, that's all.'

'Lesbian? Manny, you're insane. Penny's happily married with two adorable children.'

'Still waters run deep. She's a dike if I ever saw one. What real woman could hate Juan's magnificent clothes? Well?'

'Who said she doesn't like the clothes?'

'I said! Juan feels it, too. I refuse to sell her. Disgusting bull . . .'

'Manny, stop it. Do you hear me? Stop this raving about Penny! It makes no sense whatsoever.'

'Mark my words, Lyla dear, before this fortnight is over you'll realize I'm right.'

'Manny, can we change the subject, please?'

'When you change the buyer.'

'I asked nicely.'

'Oh, very well.' Then a sudden thought. 'Oh, my God, I almost forgot! When are you coming to L.A.?'

'I don't know. In a month or so. Why?'

'I've found the most incredible young man! Darling, this one is positively Olympic material! He walked in one day, blond and bronzed, and asked for a job in the shipping department. My dear, this number isn't something one hides in the back of a factory. Gorrr-jus! I've given him a job and told him all about you.'

'Manny! You're outrageous.'

'Why? Because my affection for you goes beyond business? You hurt me, dear. Anyhow, Rick—his name's Rick, isn't that sexy?— Rick is to faint over.'

'I take it you've sampled the young man yourself?'

'Lyla! I couldn't let you get a pig in a poke, if you'll excuse the simile.'

'You're a corrupting villain, you know that.'

'And don't you just adore it?' He rose and said, 'Must dash now, taken up far too much of your time as it is.'

'Good night, Manny. See you tomorrow.'

'You will that. Oh darling, do something about that Black les, will you? She really has to go. Ta ta.'

Lyla was alone. She sat at her desk for a moment, then opened a drawer and took out a bottle of scotch. She poured a stiff drink into her water glass and sipped the liquor thoughtfully.

She took out her purse and checked her makeup. 'Not a bad-looking broad for a gal pushing forty.'

She left the office and walked down the stairs to the third floor. She was heading for the escalator when she noticed the Spanish cobbler cleaning up his little area. He stared at her, almost as if he had been waiting. Still thinking about Manny's lewd invitation, Lyla felt her sex come to life, and she looked back into his dark, piercing eyes. The young man spoke no English.

He rose as she approached and Lyla saw something else had already risen. Staring transfixed at the huge bulge stretching his leather breeches, she thought, 'My God, that can't be true.' He was not smiling. He stood like a statue, his face angry.

Lyla looked around. They were alone in the department. She grabbed his hand and led him back into the shoe stockroom, checking to see that everyone had left. Without a word, his black eyes blazing, the cobbler took off his shirt and then his leather breeches.

Lyla, knowing he couldn't understand, said, as she started to strip off her dress, 'Baby, you've got a body like a god and that schvantz

123

of yours looks like a baby's arm with an apple in its hand. This is going to be heaven.'

He kicked off his shoes and the sweat that covered his body shone in the half-light of the stockroom. The danger of using a total stranger right here in the store had so excited Lyla that she couldn't control herself. She had no idea that, to him, she was the symbol of everything he detested. The smart, assured, American woman. Using him like a clown in that stupid cobbler's costume. He, a master craftsman, forced by his bosses to come to this rude land and lose his dignity by being put on display. He hated Lyla with an all-consuming fire.

He grabbed her with strong hands and shoved her down on the concrete floor. Before she could resist, he straddled her heaving chest and shoved his enormous tool deep into her mouth and down her throat. That was just for openers . . . to humiliate and debase her before he raped her unmercifully. Lyla reached a plane of ecstasy that wiped out time, unaware of his true motives. He felt her fingernails dig into his muscular back and he withdrew from her hungry mouth. In an instant, he was upon her and into her. She flailed with unbridled passion as he sledgehammered into her writhing body. Shoe boxes and small chairs were knocked over in their frenzy as they thrashed and thrust, oblivious to all else. Lyla was moaning and crying in guttural English, and he cursed her vehemently in passionate Spanish. His pride returned with each powerful lunge into her. This exquisite rape would repay in part the abject humiliation he had suffered. Lyla, reveling in the only fact apparent to her, had never been so deliriously and breathlessly happy.

SATURDAY, OCTOBER 8

Heymano, Europe's current premier couturier, was this year's recipient of the coveted Lehson award for 'The Most Influential Creator of the Year'—the esteemed 'AL' trophy. Above all the Lehson prizes, the small golden dressmaker dummy bearing Mr. Abe's initials had become the fashion world's most sought-after accolade. The person who received it each year zoomed light-years ahead of all his competitors and rested secure and rich (for a year at least) on the\pinnacle of the *peau de soie* mountain.

As testament to the importance of the 'AL' and those who received it, Heymano and his business manager-partner, Pepe de Santos, were personally met at the Tulsa City airport by Stella Lehson-Manchester, Lyla Lehson-Reid, William Warren Bethel (his usually impeccable tailoring distorted by the cumbersome plaster cast that encased his broken arm) and two reporters, each with a cameraman. One of the press team was from *Women's Wear Daily*—out of deference to the singular magnitude of the occasion. The other was from the *Tulsa City News*—out of respect to Lehson's huge advertising budget. In Heymano's case, there was some merit to all the attention, for not since Dior had a major authority emerged to dictate what is or isn't de rigueur for the wealthy super-chics.

Heymano and de Santos were natives of Madrid who, after a smashing initial success in the Spanish capital, moved their couture home to the hub of a decaying fashion world—Paris. Both men were in their early thirties—handsome and well turned out. Heymano truly looked the part of an internationally famous designer—thin, elegant and ethereal. As he stepped from the plane, he was wearing a fawn-colored cashmere jump suit, cut like workman's overalls, with a matching silk sports shirt underneath. The shoulder bag he carried was suede, dyed to match the rest of the ensemble, and marked with the bronze H that served as both his initial and trademark. 'Mano' was thoroughly charming and decidedly continental.

Pepe was also charming, though in a more parochial manner; studied and automatic rather than natural. He was businesslike, cold and his black eyes shielded an inner ruthlessness. Pepe chilled one a bit, while Heymano was gregarious and enthusiastic. They made an excellent, successful team.

They were the last passengers to leave the airplane. As they stepped to the top of the disembarking stairs, the Lehson trio, reporters and cameramen clustered at the foot of the ramp. As flashbulbs popped, the delighted Heymano waved his greetings to those below.

'Mano! Mano darling! Welcome to America,' cried an excited Lyla.

'Lyla, my love! *Salud!* Miss Stella! Even you? Heymano is overwhelmed!'

'Welcome to Tulsa City, Mano!' shouted the usually reserved Stella.

Bill started to wave with his fractured arm, winced in pain, but managed a wide grin.

'Our star is really shining. Welcome to Lehson's, Mano . . . and Pepe.'

The arriving pair scrambled down the steps. Mano embraced his dear friend Lyla with warmth and sincerity. Then a clasp for Stella, who offered her cheek for the kiss. Bill shook hands with Pepe as the cameras continued to record this minor moment of fashion history.

'Lyla, my precious, how must you be? And you, Miss Stella? Bill? It is so wonderful you all come to meet this plane! And cameras as well? *Mon Dieu!*' Mano stood alongside the plane, ran expert fingers through his well-styled hair, clutched the Lehson sisters on either side of him and posed happily for the photographers as Bill took the luggage tickets from Pepe.

'I'll have the chauffeur attend to all this, Pepe. How was the flight?'

'From Orly to New York it was pleasant; but from New York to here, that was an adventure. Such service and attention we have never seen. Your hand was in that, eh, Señor Bill?'

'For a Lehson celebrity, all the stops are pulled. Glad you enjoyed it.' They walked toward the terminal.

'Speaking of your hand, what has happened? The plaster?'

'Little accident. Be okay in a few weeks. You two look awfully fit.'

'Mano is fabulous. Really. He is thrilled with this award, you know.'

'As well he should be. Ahh, there's the driver. . . . Gus, will you attend to the luggage?'

A Lehson station wagon was parked behind the limousine for the numerous pieces of luggage the two had brought with them.

'Hey there, let's get in the car and get moving,' Bill instructed. 'Gus will bring your things to the hotel in the wagon. Come on, Miss Stella, in we go.'

Seated in the climate-controlled sedan, whizzing smoothly through the flat, dull countryside of un-oiled Oklahoma, Lyla snuggled up against the ecstatic Heymano and remembered her kinetic encounter with the cobbler last evening. She looked up at Mano, and meant it when she said, 'Oh darling, this really is the year for the Spanish!'

Edna Lehson's Circle 'O' Ranch was a large, prosperous property about twenty-four miles due north of the city. It was a working spread whose primary concern was the breeding and care of the superb thoroughbred horses that Edna raised for pleasure and profit. The barns, stables and work buildings were modern and immaculate. The riding areas were as manicured as a fine golf course and the pasture land a lush and verdant field of deep green. Aged oak trees shaded and gave form to the usual environmental monotony of this part of the state. The main house was a large, sprawling, modern version of a Spanish hacienda meshing the best qualities of those diverse architectures. An Olympic swimming pool with well-equipped cabanas stood toward the back, set in a wide plot of cropped turf. Trees circled the residential perimeter of the estate into a quiet, cool island, set off, but still part of the businesslike activity of the ranch.

Edna lived here alone, except for the forty hands and servants who maintained the place; and the considerable size of the house was justified by those rare occasions when the store used it for entertaining. Sunday would be such a day. Today, the entire ranch was busy with many preparations for the big barbecue and rodeo that Edna was going to host for the store's guests, employees and customers the next day. This major event culminated the first week of the Mediterranean gala.

C.Z. had been commandeered from the store to use his chameleon talents in transforming the main house into a festive and inviting Iberian country club. A crew from the display department worked with a score of ranch hands erecting the bleachers to accommodate hundreds of guests for the traditional Western rodeo, so much a part of the folklore of the Southwest. Pits were being dug just beyond the grassy area around the pool for the barbecue itself, while other workers and caterers arranged long buffet sideboards and umbrellaed table settings for the diners. The kitchen was packed with cooks and helpers preparing in advance the huge caldrons of spicy chili con carne, pinto beans, Spanish rice and various cold salads for tomorrow's hungry horde. Only the regal stallions in the pasture were unperturbed by the activity of the men—they looked on in aristocratic amusement, snorted and romped off to nibble God's transplanted grass and ruminate on the folly of animals who learned to stand erect. They knew such animals usually fell.

C.Z., as usual, had singled out the weakest and most vulnerable of the display workers as the object of his acid derision. Today his victim was a wispy black lad, and C.Z. periodically reduced the young man to tears by teasing him. C.Z. armed himself with a brandy snifter abrim with English gin and a touch of Italian vermouth. Thus he was able to cope with the major problem of staying out of the glaring sun and inside the air-conditioned house. Edna sauntered into the main living room, her jeans and checkered man's shirt starting to wilt from the day's pressure and the heat.

'How're you doing, Carl?'

'You may tune your castanets, Miss Edna. Mañana will be as Spanish-looking as the Prado in drag.'

As they were talking they heard a car approaching. Edna stepped from the veranda that ran around three sides of the house, and shaded her eyes to see who was driving up the long gravel road that led from the highway to the ranch. When the dirty white station wagon screeched to a halt in front of the house and the dust settled, Edna saw it was Della. Edna nodded a greeting to the store's advertising director, her lover of these past six years.

'You're up early, Della. Come to help?'

'You need it?'

'No, Carl's got everything well in hand—including a new-found whipping boy. Want to watch?'

'A drink would be better. Man, it's hot for this late in the year.'

'Come on in. The cooling's on.'

They entered the main house, went through the large entry area and into the living room. C.Z., sitting on a Grandee's chair, directed the workers to string a row of colored bulbs among the rough beams below the ceiling.

'Say, it is cool in here. Forget the drink,' said Della.

They walked towards the library.

'Not that I'm anything less than delighted to see you, Dell, but why are you here so early?'

Della tried to conceal her seductive secret, but the Cheshire cat in her smiled it away. 'I've got to talk to you, privately.'

'Is the library private enough?'

'No way.'

'Oh,' said Edna, the hidden implications of Della's purpose dawning on her, 'then I guess it's our room.'

'Absolutely.'

'Okay, Dell, let's go. Will this take long?'

'That, sweetheart, is up to you.'

Edna smiled and yelled across to C.Z., 'Take care of everything for a while, will you? I've got some store business to go over with Della. No interruptions . . . not for anything.'

Edna took Della through the large house, down a hall, and they stopped before a magnificent American Indian rug that hung as a tapestry. Edna took a key and, pushing the rug aside, inserted it in the lock of a door secreted behind the hanging.

They entered a windowless room and Edna snapped on the lights, locking the door behind her. The room was a rectangle measuring thirty-five feet by twenty-five feet. The floor was gleaming white tile. The ceiling and two opposing walls were lined in mirror. Whips and articles of bondage and subjugation hung neatly on pegs in the walls. Huge jars filled with petroleum jelly were everywhere. There was a metal chair with arm and leg stirrups to one side, and in the center of the room was a king-size bed. The headboard was a full-color blowup of Andy Warhol's 'Marilyn Monroe' poster, framed by studded steel rivets. The bed was covered with a black leather spread. Coming up from the tile floor next to the bed was a small contraption that looked like a miniature gasoline pump. It even had a canvas tube with a nozzle on it. It was for wet steam.

'Well, now what's this little surprise you have for me?'

'For us, Edna, for us.'

She reached into the pocket of her loose slacks and took out Ceil Bordon's battery operated 'Epidermal Rhythmizer.'

'Okay, so you got a new dildo. I've got at least a dozen that are bigger than that.'

'Maybe bigger, sweetheart, but not better. Just watch this.'

Della switched on the flange switch to full speed and the massager began to vibrate and whir seductively. Edna's mouth dropped at the wonder of the instrument.

'Jesus Christ, will you look at that damned thing go!'

'Like I told you, Ed, this is really something.'

Edna reached over and clasped the Rhythmizer. 'Holy cow, I can really feel it work. Where the hell did you ever get this?'

'This, my dear Edna, is Ceil Bordon's zinger for fall of 1964.'

'Does she have any idea of what she's made?'

'Not a clue.'

'Then we're the first?'

'The very first.'

'Blye baby, get out of those clothes. . . . You and I are going to have ourselves one helluva matinee this afternoon!'

As Edna and Della prepared to explore the mysteries of Ceil Bordon's latest, a solicitous Stella personally escorted Princess Judith through the swarms of happy, buying customers who jostled and politely shoved to get a good look at the Princess while scooping up the delectable trinkets and styles unique to this grand store.

Where else but in Lehson's of Tulsa City could one purchase an Israeli knit bathing suit, an exact copy of Cellini's salt cellar (manufactured in Italy with real Majorca pearls) while rubbing elbows with a real, living, breathing movie star who was also a genuine princess? New York? Where was that?

Stella steered her Pacific Highness to the less-crowded designer's sportswear section where the very latest and most costly fashions were available.

'We've just received some hand-crocheted three-piece suits that you'll simply adore. The most practical things I've ever seen for traveling. Do make yourself comfortable while I get someone to help you. Oh Claudia, are you busy?'

Claudia was a trifle preoccupied, but not busy. As she crossed over to the now-seated Princess and the standing Stella, she asked for a moment alone with her employer.

'What is it, Claudia? The Princess has a plane to catch.'

'It's Lady Vidal . . .'

'Well?'

'She's in dressing room 'C' and . . . well, perhaps you'd better look in for yourself.'

'Of course. Princess, I'll only be a moment. Claudia will be delighted to show you those new French knits I was telling you about.'

Stella excused herself with the promise of a prompt return and walked over to the area where the dressing and fitting rooms were located. Down the aisle to 'C' and a quick look through the small glass window told her why Claudia was ruffled.

Inside, on the floor, a prostrate Lady Vidal clad only in a bra and panties was performing energetic push-ups with the gusto of an athlete in training. Stella, composing herself, opened the dressing room door and greeted the strenuously calisthenic patron.

'Good afternoon, your ladyship.'

'Hi, Stell. . . . Fifteen . . . sixteen . . . seventeen . . .'

'Uh, Lady Vidal . . . excuse my interruption, but is this really the correct place for this sort of . . . of activity?'

'Nineteen . . . twenty . . . sure as hell is. It's the sports floor, ain't it?'

Stella quietly closed the door behind her and returned to the Princess and Miriam.

The salesgirl asked, 'Is everything all right, Miss Stella?'

'Of course. Lady Vidal merely reminded me what department we're in.'

The Derrick Club ranked as the state's number one private social organization for the oil-depletion millionaires and their friends. It was an imposing granite bastion for the genteel gentiles who formed the Tulsa City Establishment. As further proof of the sway Lehson's held over the city, this Jewish-owned mercantile complex was allowed to use the restricted chambers for their private party. The only condition was that the members and their wives, all excellent Lehson customers, were invited. The pull of foreign titles and world-famous celebrities was too much for the Baptist bigots of the Derrick Club. And it was in this setting that tonight's ball, hosted by Lyla, was to be held.

No outside embellishments were necessary to alter the impression Lehson's wanted to make. The Southern Confederacy Courthouse edifice was grandly imposing. Inside, it was ideal for a large semi-formal party. Lanny Lester and his orchestra had been flown in from New York for the dancing. Giselle Gamin, the Parisian song stylist, had been imported to croon her plaintive street songs for the guests. Since the dining room (which accommodated five hundred guests) boasted a ceiling forty feet high, the sensational Italian aerialists, 'The Flying Ughatzs', were brought in from the circus's winter head-quarters in Sarasota to perform their trapeze artistry while the diners enjoyed their meal.

Lyla received the guests in a stunning Heymano gown and con-fided to each couple that she had arranged for a perfectly marvelous surprise to cap the evening. Thus titillated, these men and women who had spent thousands all week at Lehson's entered the majestic dining room to be wined, fed and amused as the store repaid them with this star-studded evening.

They were all there . . . Michelle De Soto, her new wig and facial mask radiating a plastic calm she did not feel, attended by her New York physician, her lawyer, her accountant and his wife, plus young Christopher Flake, her nephew. This awesome group was followed by Lady Vidal and two porters who gingerly carried his palsied lordship in his wheelchair. Clay Pepper, Momma, and a metallic silver-sheathed Blossom followed the Vidals. Gari and Nicky, in matching knit body suits with frosted goggles, came in, murmured and slipped off to a quiet corner to observe. Heymano and Pepe arrived, blinking fashionably for the cameras. Quentin Kimball, fresh from his triumph of *Lysistrata*, was escorting the powerful Chicago newspaper publisher, Mae Ritz. Juan Felipe's date for the evening was the perennially beautiful and fascinating Gloria Titania, still as radiant and magnetic as she was when she graced the silver screens of the world as a superstar. Stella, a guest at the store party tonight, came with that infrequent squire, her husband. C.Z., splendid in an Edwardian costume of Danube brown velvet, arrived alone. Since wine was being served, he had his martinis in a champagne glass. And more, so many more. These were the customers who spent at least fifty thousand dollars each year at the store, and the executives and designers who earned at least that much from the store's success. An elite five hundred for this, the second biggest party of the fortnight extravaganza.

As everyone chatted, laughed and drank their way through this initial phase of a stellar evening, Lyla slipped out to the main doors and inquired of the head porter, 'Have they arrived yet?'

'They left the airport a good fifteen minutes ago. Their car should be coming any moment now.'

'Then I'll wait outside.'

'Certainly, Miss Lyla, may I?' and he held the door aside, allowing her to exit. Lyla spotted the headlights of the store's limousine as it cut off from the highway and up the wide circular drive to the club. The surprise of the evening was here—the O'Hara Sisters, Belle, Brooke and Kendell. All it had taken was a call to Las Vegas where the girls were appearing in the Valhalla Room of the Xanadu Hotel, a watering spot and casino owned by Belle's devoted Salvatore A'Patico and several of his syndicated associates. Sal, the evil genius from Palermo, ordered men to their death without the batting of an eye, but was no more than damp clay in the hands of his dazzling paramour.

Sal controlled the Xanadu. Belle O'Hara controlled Sal. It was only natural that when Lyla phoned and asked if the girls would be the store's guests, she accepted and Sal agreed. Of course the girls would sing a few numbers for the party—what were friends for?

'Lyla!'

'Belle!'

'We're all here.'

'Brooke! Kendell! And Sal! It's good to see you all.'

They scrambled out of the car and into Lyla's warm embrace. They were delighted to see each other and Sal felt good at having been able to effect the visit.

'Let me look at you. Oh, Lyla, that dress is fantastic!'

'A Heymano no less,' she said as she modeled the gown for them.

'Got 'em at the store?'

'Scads of yummy things. Come on inside, Sal, you're looking great. Still loading the dice?'

He laughed at her friendly impertinence. 'No need when ya own the house.'

'Tell me! Dropped a small bundle myself, last year, didn't I?'

'You can afford it.'

They followed Lyla into the entry hall. 'Reserved a special dining room just for you. You're the big surprise, you know. This way.'

'Have you really got Gamin here?'

'Of course.'

'Oh, she's really sensational. Tough act to follow.'

As they went into the 'Spindletop Room', Lyla, arm around her adored Belle, answered, 'You'll kill the people, as always. Oh, won't everyone be surprised! It certainly is great seeing you all again. This'll be fun.'

Lyla got them settled and returned to her guests, flushed with excitement. It was going to be a perfect evening. She spied Stella and Brian Manchester holding court for a dozen people. Brian's evening companion for the past two years had been a pert little dental technician whom he kept in a charming apartment not five blocks from the store. But on glittering nights such as this, Brian was trotted out as Stella's husband to reinforce her always impeccable image. On these occasions he drank little and his party manners were letter perfect. It was an ideal tableau of wedded bliss. Lyla joined the group and confided in a stage whisper, 'They've arrived, Stell.'

'Marvelous. Brian and I can hardly wait.'

'Right after Gamin finishes, Lanny will announce them. Must dash. See you at dinner,' she said backing away.

Stella and Brian excused themselves and moved away to join another group. He decided to use this lull to begin the discussion he'd started so many times during the past years.

'Stella, you look exceptional tonight.'

'Why thank you, Brian.'

'You are more self-sufficient than ever. It's a wonder how you do it all.'

'It's simple, really. Classify your priorities and stick to your schedule.'

'And where does our farce of a marriage appear on that list?'

'Please, Brian, don't start that again tonight.'

'Stella, I want a divorce. In fact, I must insist on it.'

'Never.'

'I can't accept that. If I have to, I'll sue you for one.'

'Not in this state, you won't.'

'Then I'll establish residence in Nevada.'

'Lyla's friends will see that your residency is dangerous.'

'But why? Why in the hell must we continue this disgusting charade?'

'There are certain events taking place in my life that necessitate the status quo. In addition, divorce is against my Judaic tradition.'

'Your what? Christ, Stella, you're the least Jewish woman in America.'

'Not when it comes to this, I'm not. Besides, a divorce would destroy my father.'

'Be realistic if you can't be fair. Mr. Abe cannot live the year out, not that he'd ever know.'

They were passing a group which included Quentin Kimball, who, though he resembled a thyroidal pussy with tiny yellowed teeth, possessed the true reporter's instinct for a story as well as an uncanny range of eavesdrop. Kimball's eyes remained fixed on Mae Ritz, but he shifted his ears toward the Manchesters' discussion.

Stella's venom and hatred showed as she answered, 'You poor, miserable, drunken excuse for a man. Do you really think I'd expose my biggest mistake by letting you go? How do you think *I* would look . . . the store would look . . . after you married some hundred-dollar-a-week nurse who doesn't even have enough taste to buy her clothing at Lehson's? No, Brian, 'til death do us part. Now start mingling and try to keep your consumption of Bourbon down so as not to embarrass Lehson's any further.'

'But, Stella . . .'

'This discussion is over.' She waved towards a cluster of people. 'Lady Vidal . . . and Mrs. De Soto, I'll be right over.' All smiles, she turned and under her breath told Brian, 'I don't know what the stupid little tramp sees in you, Brian. You always were the lousiest lay in the Southwest.'

Brian swallowed hard, turned away from her and headed to the bar.

Kimball, sipping through the fourth layer of his pousse-café, volunteered to Mae, 'Oh, she is a strong woman, that one! Sent him off quick and clean; he's swallowed his pride; she's digesting his balls. Formidable, Miss Stella, quite formidable.'

Stella, a benign smile set upon her lips, passed C.Z. standing against a pillar, sipping and observing the party.

'Having fun, Carl?'

'As Tina Bethel would say, "I'm as happy as a sow in . . ."'

'I know what Mrs. Bethel says. Lovely party, don't you think?'

'Stella, if I thought at all I wouldn't be here.'

'Don't be rude, darling.'

'Not at all. Reflective. I should have been a female impersonator in Saudi Arabia, but I got stuck at an early age in this misbegotten milieu of fashion. I had just entered my teens when I was brought to shame by a Puerto Rican window trimmer. My destiny was sealed in the Thirty-fourth Street windows of B. Altman and Co. Fortunately, the shades were drawn.'

Stella, enjoying his self-analysis, half-mocked his candor. 'Carl dear, one mustn't bite the hand that feeds one.' But her amusement was apparent.

'You are not, I deeply pray, referring to those perfumed harpies who make all this possible—our customers?'

'Of course, dear, and our guests.'

'Perish the thought! Mister Guest sold out long ago and is quite content with his lot. But let us at least be honest among ourselves. . . . You know that I know the facades of fashion are transparent to anyone who looks.'

'We live in a disposable society.'

'Disposable? Trashy is more like it. Such a waste . . . such a pitiable waste. This constant parade of vulgar veneer.'

'Is that why you drink so much, Carl?'

'I drink, Miss Stella, because I like the taste. It is the only taste I completely agree with. Cheers!'

Stella smiled and left this voice in the wilderness of modern retailing to his martini. She joined the circle of people that included Lyla and Heymano.

'Ah, Miss Stella, such a *magnifico soirée*.'

'Thank you, Mano. Is Lyla taking good care of you?'

'Oh yes! She takes fine care of me. It is beautiful.'

'Lyla, you should never wear anything but Mano clothes. That gown is stunning on you.'

'Why thank you, dear.'

'What time did you arrange for dinner to be served?'

'Not for another forty-five minutes or so.'

'I hope they don't drink too much. May I steal Mano away from you for a moment?'

'Of course, I've been too selfish with him.'

'Mano, he . . . I like to receive such attention. Two Lehsons fighting over me . . . lovely.'

Lyla excused herself from the cluster and wended her way through the other guests. Have they enough wine? Canapes? Are they excited at the surprise in store? Alone in the large crowd, Lyla's thoughts left the party and tried to establish some eligible gentleman who might be available to climax the evening's regularly scheduled entertainment. Some of the waiters looked especially promising, but that would be bad form. She knew that was Stella's domain. The unattached male guests were not inclined towards heterosexuality . . . except, perhaps that one.

Lyla's practiced eyes settled on the tall, athletic, clean-cut young man in the white dinner jacket who stood, bored to death, with Michelle De Soto and her entourage. That must be her favorite nephew—the one in college here—the young man she sent so many expensive presents to. Yes, he was very well constructed and looked like he could handle himself. If she worked quickly, she could introduce this stalwart newcomer to the pleasures she so expertly dispensed. Lyla managed to catch his eye across the room. She smiled and beckoned him over. The young man looked around to see if it was really him she wanted. Lyla nodded it was. Bewildered, but happy to break away from his aunt's monologue on tax-exempt bonds and her distended pancreas, he excused himself and walked over to Lyla.

'You're Mrs. De Soto's nephew, aren't you?'

'Yes, ma'am. Chris Flake. Sophomore at Oklahoma U.'

'How divinely clever of you, Chris. I'll bet you a double burger you haven't seen anything like the simply super gymnasium this club has.'

'I might have. I'm a Physical Education major, you know.'

She took his arm and started to lead him away. 'No, I didn't,' she said.

'But ma'am, I shouldn't leave my aunt.'

'Don't be silly, darling, she'd want you to see all the fun things they have here. The wrestling mat we had imported from Yokohama . . . it's absolutely divine.'

SUNDAY, OCTOBER 9

Stella sat in the damp heat waiting for her father, in the oxygen tent, to return to that half-conscious state where she could communicate to him. The waiting was terrible, watching a great man sink slowly and steadily towards death. Stella thought about the temporal reality of power—even though it was as mighty as that which she wielded; the frustration of trying to overcome the inevitable; replacing hard facts with wishful hopes—cynicism with prayer. Mr. Abe's tissue-thin eyelids trembled for an instant, then jerkily and tentatively opened—almost as if he were afraid that he would waken to the end.

'Good morning, Poppa. I'm so happy to hear how much you've improved.'

Behind the cataracts, his eyes answered her lie with a flicker of unseen hope, then receded back to their semiglazed existence, waiting for the ritual of her weekly report.

'Oh, Poppa, I can't wait to tell you about the fabulous week we've had. Everyone at the store is working harder than ever before as a tribute to you and the amazing progress you're making. You see how much they miss you and want you back.'

He tried to smile and Stella gently wiped away the resultant spittle that was the only evidence of his feeble effort.

'And, as proof that your presence still scares us all, the first week of the fortnight was an enormous success. Sales are up sixty-eight percent from last year!'

His mind calculated quickly and his soul was pleased. The increase was amazing.

'Honestly, they're buying everything in sight. We've had to reorder in almost every department. This is going to be your biggest year. We're all so proud of you, Poppa.'

The emotion of being needed and dreaming of that lost vitality showed for a moment in the clouded eyes.

'And this year's customers! Princess Judith has been invaluable, an enormous boon to the business. Oh, and Poppa, she jumped at the sable coat—just like you knew she would, you foxy old thing. But it honestly does look beautiful on her. Imagine, paying all that money to be a walking advertisement for your store.'

His head shook almost unnoticeably, trembling more than shaking. Stella knew what he meant and picked up the glass of water next to the bed. She put in a flex-straw and placed it between his lips. With great effort, he managed to induce a few drops and, satisfied, she returned it to the table and continued.

Stella told him everything that had occurred during the week. The promise of the ambassadorship. The trouble with Culbertson. Morgan Moore going over to the competition. The business problems seemed to excite him more than the good news. Mr. Abe dropped back into his wheezing stupor from time to time, but her presence brought him back again.

When two hours had elapsed, he finally fell into a deep sleep that would last through the day. Stella knew the aged man was content. He had felt every nuance and detail of the fortnight's first week, but Stella was disturbed. As desperately ill as Mr. Abe had been, she still could see that he was a little less responsive, a little more distant than usual. She held no illusions as she rose to leave, but his worsened condition perturbed Stella.

She battled with her emotions as she left the plant-filled solarium. She held in check the overwhelming sense of loss, but the unwanted thought forced its way into her brain: 'Please God, don't let him die until the fortnight is over.'

The ever-present Martin, sitting sentinel outside the sick room, got up as she came towards him.

'Oh Martin, he seems a little weaker today.'

'Ah know, Miss Stella, ah noticed. But them doctors are doing wonders. We'll watch him extra close, ah promise.'

It wasn't much, but it was done with such selfless love and devotion that Stella went from the house feeling better than when she had come.

It was as if Lehson's even controlled the weather. While the rest of the nation shivered in a chilling early winter cold front, a pocket of Indian summer protected Oklahoma. The eye of this marvelous climate was Tulsa City. Nowhere was the balmy warmth more ideal than at the Circle 'O' on barbecue and rodeo day.

C.Z., his crew from the store and the ranch hands had done their best. Not even Busby Berkeley could have conjured up a better Hollywood version of what was expected at a ranch. Edna, still filled with memory of the erotic sensations discovered from Ceil Bordon's Rhythmizer, was outfitted in a lemon-yellow poplin jean and jacket suit studded with chalk white beads, her handsome head capped with a white fur ten-gallon hat. Even her boots were lemon and white. Thus costumed, Edna greeted the busloads of guests as they poured into the Circle 'O' with an energetic wave and smile. The pre-rehearsed ranch hands, uniformed in new blue jeans and checkered shirts, waved their hats and shouted 'Yippee' and 'Yahoo' for the delighted visitors. Each guest wore his own version of eclectic Western gear—all purchased at considerable expense from Lehson's. This was roughing it, with style.

The busses had been outfitted with portable bars, and taped music played all the traditional Western songs. Thus primed, the people arrived ready to enter the spirit of this well-arranged rough-and-tumble festivity. Ceil Bordon leaped joyfully from the first bus. The Western hoedown band, playing on the veranda underneath the welcoming banner—'LEHSON'S RODEO AND BAR-BE-CUE. ENJOY!'—struck up a merry reel and the party began. Ceil ambled up to Edna and was greeted with a warm hug.

'Welcome to the Circle 'O'. '

'Dang nice o' you to invite us, pard,' parodied Ceil.

'Listen, Ceil, before the others arrive, I've got to tell you what a miracle that massager is. Honey, it'll sweep the country.'

'Aw shucks, Miss Edna, t'warn't nothin'.'

They both laughed raucously, while the place began swarming with visitors anxious to see everything.

Today's guest list had been limited to two hundred people and was, therefore, overly impressed with itself after last night's much larger group. These were the ultimate consumers—the wasteful wealthy who pamper and preen themselves to the exclusion of all else. Wars raged, subcontinents exhausted themselves with paralyzing famine, in-humanity was the order of the day; yet, these were the chosen few, the elitists who corrupted corporations and governments for personal gain, solidified their dynamic egos through tax shelters and legal avoidances unavailable to the ordinary man. These were Lehson's customers and guests. The store would see that they did, in fact, enjoy!

Lady Vidal, resplendent in a frilly version of a cowgirl's dream, elbowed over to Edna and apologized for the absence of her lord. 'Too much smoke at last night's wingding for the old codger. Hadda pop him back into the oxygen tent as soon as we got back to the hotel. Hey, Edna! All right if I ride a horse?'

Young Chris Flake, looking both vacuumed and drained, tried to help his aunt from the bus. Since he appeared to need more assistance than his aged relative, a blithely accommodating Lyla did the helping. She cooed over Michelle De Soto's unusual Western outfit—a baby-blue silk slack suit with rhinestone appliques, a Western hat to match, and better than four hundred thousand dollars' worth of sapphires and diamonds around her neck, ears and wrists.

'That boy is dead to the world! Chris! Get back on the bus and sleep for God's sake.' He dutifully obeyed, nervously smiling at Lyla as he took his leave.

'Don't know what's come over the kids today. They just can't take it like we did. Right, Lyla?'

'The poor baby's just done in after last night's party. Even though he's in training, I feel it's good for a boy his age to see what society is like, don't you, Michelle? It helped him. Did you notice his skin blemishes have cleared up?'

Lyla turned Michelle over to Edna and joined Heymano and Pepe, both magnificently turned out as Basque cowboys, which suited their Latin looks perfectly.

'Well, Mano, Pepe, what do you think of the Old West?'

'One never ceases to be amazed at what happens here.'

'Mano and I are continually impressed, Lyla.'

Heymano looked around the crowd. 'I do not see Señor Bethel. Is his arm bothering him?'

Lyla confided to her friend, 'More likely his wife. There was a terrible scene earlier in the week. She wouldn't dare show her face here today and I imagine Bill's staying home to try to calm her down.'

'So your Señor Bethel has domestic woes. It is a shame. He is so jolly.'

'Say, fellows, have you ever had a mint julep?'

They both answered no.

'Then let's initiate you to another unique American experience.'

Lyla hailed a passing waiter carrying a tray filled with frosty silver glasses. They all took one, tasted and enjoyed the crisp, biting chill of the julep.

Heymano got up and excused himself to join some others who were going to get in a little riding before the lunch began. Pepe smiled coldly as he left them. Lyla said, 'He's such a dear man, your Mano. And so talented. I'm thrilled that he's this year's awardee.'

'He is quite the charmer, our Heymano. So smooth. You also notice he has been exceptionally well behaved, too.'

'Yes, we all see that. Thank you so much, Pepe, for your help. Some of the executives were a trifle worried.'

'Needless, Miss Lyla. I have everything under control.'

There was almost an hour left before lunch. Some of the fitter guests had changed to swim suits and tennis togs, and were in the pool and on the courts. Others rode horses around the training track, while still others cheered them on. Many strolled through the wide expanses of lawn, garden, groves and fields, enjoying this manufactured nature. These native Oklahomans who lived in the area merely sat around the grounds under umbrellas and drank.

Quentin Kimball arrived alone. He wore a garish, almost neon pink satin Western shirt, a panama hat and grey flannel slacks. He mingled, accepting the customary plaudits and compliments at his great literary abilities. Spying Edna alone for a moment he waddled towards her and inquired as to Mr. Abe's condition.

'How's the patriarch, dear?' His high shrill voice grated with the question.

'Oh, he's going to be right as rain, honey. We expect him to be up and around before the month's over.'

Eugene and Mary Boardman strolled across to them with Ceil Bordon in tow.

'Mr. Kimball, I don't think you've met Ceil Bordon.'

'No, but I use her astringent. It works wonders, my dear.'

'Quentin, what you did with *Lysistrata* was fantastic.'

'In a time of careless superlatives, I accept your comment.'

'Do you really use my products?'

'Of course, and to let you in on an inside secret . . . do you know what I call you?'

'What?' Ceil asked tentatively.

'The Powder Puff Pasha. Cute?'

'Great!'

'But, if you'd like to know the real reason for my heavenly skin....?'

'I sure would.'

'Well, it's two high colonics each day ... one in the morning and the other just before I say my prayers. Cleanse away those internal impurities and radiate outside.'

'You are what you eat.'

'You are what you get rid of! Oh, there's that diabolic-looking Pepe de Santos. I simply must corner him. Ta ta, see you at lunch.'

Ceil picked up immediately and turned to Boardman.

'Has Edna told you what she thinks about the Rhythmizer?'

Edna interjected, 'Careful Ceil, it was a personal reaction. I leave the merchandising to the experts.'

'No, Miss Edna, Ceil is right. The personal reaction is just what we want.'

'Okay, Gene. Properly promoted—and Della has some great ideas on that—I don't think the store will be able to keep up with the demand. For what it's worth, that's my opinion.'

'Which I respect. Ceil, let's get down to an order first thing tomorrow.' Then, to his wife, 'Mary, Miss Bordon really surprised us all with this one.'

'Why wait until tomorrow?' interrupted Ceil. 'Paris is eight hours ahead of us. Let's find a nice quiet spot and work out the quantities; I can call the factory at midnight. If Lehson's wants to be first, they'll have to act quick.'

'All right,' said Boardman, 'I'll place the order.'

'Cold, hard Boardman, acting as buyer?' amusedly queried Edna.

'Certainly,' he replied, 'this is something mechanical, something I can understand.' Eugene smiled and turned to his wife. 'Dear, you're going to have to enjoy the barbecue for the two of us.'

'Don't worry, Mary'll have plenty of company. Go on and protect Lehson's interests.'

Boardman and Ceil walked over to a small, secluded grove of eucalyptus. 'Okay, Eugene, how many will you want?' asked Ceil.

'Well,' thought Boardman aloud, 'it's too late for inclusion in the Christmas catalogue, but the item is certainly worth a promotional mailing and advertisements. It's a first, and an exclusive. Let's see ... at fifteen dollars apiece, retail, we'll need twenty-five hundred within two weeks . . . and we want a back-up of five thousand available on demand.'

'Whew!' Ceil said admiringly. 'How did you figure that out so fast?'

'Simple, dear, it's very simple. It's all basic mathematics and percentile projections. Buying is so simple, in fact, that I'm convinced the days of the individual buyer are truly numbered.'

'What?' asked Ceil.

'Certainly,' he replied. 'The whole thing can be done with computers. All you do is feed total information into the computer about the last three years' business. Say that Christmas for those years has seen an abundance of bright colors, the computer will know exactly when the buying public is ready for a change to darks or pastels. It'll also tell you what the public will want in terms of fabric, length, cut and all the other variables of style. A buyer will merely receive a computer printout detailing colors, styling, quantities and price range of what he or she is to buy; then they can shop for the manufacturer of their choice. Finally we can put an end to the costly luxury of human guessing.'

'Sounds insane, Gene. When are you going to get this miracle worker?'

'Probably not until the end of the decade. Till that time we'll have to continue operating as techno-primitives. But when we get our procedures transferred to the new system, watch out for soaring profits!'

'Of course I'll be able to lease time on this oracle?' asked Ceil with a lilt.

'Dear Ceil, don't worry, we'll let you know exactly what to create. Lehson's has always been willing to share the wealth with family.'

They all queued up for lunch—the ladies thrilled at this simple form of rural life. It was all so new to them . . . lining up at long tables to personally select their barbecue. Back to nature, so to speak. Good for you, once in a while.

As the immaculate white-coated chefs dispensed aromatic ladles of chili, and helped the guests to platters heaped with succulent fried chickens, roasted wild ducks, venison steaks and baby spareribs, there were whole suckling pigs, entire sides of prime beef and lambs turning aromatically on electric spits over oak fires. Kegs of draft beer and cases of French wine were dispensed by other white-hatted attendants. The twin thirty-foot-long tables groaned under the weight of myriad of trays and platters of steaming corn, stuffed green peppers, hot fresh biscuits, jams, jellies and honeys, salads, twelve different vegetables, five kinds of rice and potatoes, pies, cakes, breads, as well as ice cream, sherbet, fresh fruits and mousses, custards and flans. A typical Lehson cookout.

In addition to the square dance hoedown band, two troupes of strolling musicians, one Mexican and the other Country and Western, wended their way through the guests at this simple culinary orgy. Everyone was seated around tables set for six and the enjoyment of this rustic gourmet cornucopia lulled the diners into a full feeling of content, which the mini-rodeo would help wear off.

Gari Reichman and Nicky ate alone, sitting on the grass beneath an old shade tree on a small rise. There, they nibbled at as spartan a fare as one could select from all that food. They were the only guests who made no attempt to dress the part. They wore identical zippered figure-following coveralls of a lightweight synthetic material. Nicky picked at a shredded carrot and raisin salad, and Gari slowly drank his apple juice and observed the gorging guests in the distance. Like most visionaries, he became depressed when forced to venture outside the existence of his vision. As he marveled at the conspicuous waste beyond him, the realities of a society light-years behind him brought on a wave of morose, down feelings. It was impossible for Gari to join in the fun and frolic of this hedonistic milieu. He had been perfectly content to preach his brand of quiet evangelism during store hours, but on this empty Sunday he had no alternative than to attend and suffer. He confided to Nicky, 'I hate coming to this part of America, you know. I feel terribly uneasy here; it's too raucous, too vital and physical for me. How's the salad?'

'I don't think it's organic.'

'Oh.' He sipped the cool juice and continued. 'These people are so filled with a fake emotion they believe is a zest for living, they're burning out.'

'I've heard they yell 'yippee' when they climax.'

'Probably true. That's it, I think, the thing that bothers me about the Southwest. . . . Everything they do has the urgency of a climax. That's completely unnatural.'

'Climaxing all the time?'

'Climax at any time. Honestly, Nicky, and this is the truth, I can't remember ever experiencing anything other than a sense of lost vitality on those few occasions when I've ejaculated.'

'Really, Gari? I never knew you came.'

'Sure, several times. It was a bore . . . no different, as far as I'm concerned, than urinating.'

'I think it's better than taking a pee.'

'We're different.'

'Yeah.'

'It's the same, disposing of excess fluids to keep the body functioning properly.'

'I guess it's just how you look at it.'

'I guess so.'

Edna made her way to the public address system and, after the music stopped, made an announcement.

'We're giving you another ten minutes to finish lunch and then we're starting the rodeo, so eat up. Here's the schedule for the rest of the day . . . three hours of rodeo, including roping, tying, branding and breaking Brahmin bulls. We've got a greased pig race, followed by a hog-calling contest, the whole kit and caboodle. The rodeo will end at sunset, then back to the house for cocktails and the most stupendous fireworks display you've ever seen!'

Lyla's table included Belle and Sal. The other sisters were allocated around in order to spread the glamour. Belle had been the expected sensation last night and she chatted away about all the clothes she was going to buy when the store opened tomorrow. Edna interrupted this female banter.

'Sorry, Belle, but duty calls.'

'Honestly, Edna, what do you want from Belle now?'

'Hey, Lyla, she volunteered.'

'For what?'

'To sing 'The Star Spangled Banner', of course.'

Sal choked on a piece of beef. 'You sing the anthem at a private party?'

'Sal, honey, you're in Oklahoma now.'

The rodeo was all one could expect from such an event, even more. Belle's rendition of 'The Star Spangled Banner' brought tears to many an eye. One cowboy was horribly gored in the groin and whisked off to the hospital in town. Jewels sparkled in the audience and even the foreign visitors got into the swing of things, whooping and hollering with the locals at the quasi-Roman spectacle of man against beast. In the end, man won. Gari became nauseated when the cowboy was ripped open, so he was driven back to the hotel. Chris Flake woke up and joined his aunt, to her delight. Sal took bets on all the events, just for something constructive to do. It was an excellent Lehson diversion.

The rodeo ended with a final mass shout and extended applause for all those hardy participants. Edna announced over the loudspeaker, 'Cocktails in the main house for you thirsty critters and I'm conducting a guided tour of the stables for those of you with enough sense to appreciate the finest array of championship horse flesh in the state.'

Forty guests still had enough energy to follow Edna, while the others retired gratefully to the cool shade of the main house to await the fireworks. Of the forty on tour, only three were women—Lyla, Belle and Lady Vidal. Heymano and Pepe were the only representatives from the fashion world to follow Edna into the showplace stables. Eugene Boardman came along for he was investigating the possibilities of using horses as the same tax shelter that cattle afford.

During the tour, Heymano descended from his usual happy state. He became quickly and visibly nervous and anxious. His speech became jittery. He was definitely on edge. He extricated himself from the group and started chatting with a somewhat bewildered stable boy. To Pepe's practiced eye, Heymano had started to cruise the ranch hand. Boardman glanced over when Pepe went to join Heymano and saw the two in a heated discussion in Spanish. Pepe managed, using more physical force than gentle persuasion, to lead Mano into a nearby bathroom. Boardman watched until they emerged five minutes later and was satisfied that Heymano seemed to be back to his old self. He was happier and gayer than before. The only thing different, and Boardman didn't seem to notice, was the slight cast to Mano's eyes. They rejoined the others on tour.

Boardman gently took Pepe to one side. 'Too much excitement for Señor Heymano?'

'Ah, but no, he is fine.'

'Do excuse me, but I'm a little concerned that he might . . . well, he just might precipitate some embarrassment or trouble for himself.'

'Mr. Boardman, there is nothing to worry about in the least. All will be fine, I assure you. Do not have a concern. I have Mano perfectly and totally under control.'

Everyone had returned to the comfort and cocktails of the main house. It was exactly seven and the setting sun had produced a technicolor miracle against the clouds and sky. Edna blew a whistle to signal the start of the pyrotechnic display and as the first salvo of brilliant explosions burst against the deep wine red sky, the two hundred guests ohhhhed and ahhhhed. It was a fittingly spectacular closing to an eventful day. Lyla, knowing the fireworks would last forty-five minutes, had found her way back to the stable where two of Edna's youngest and handsomest cowboys awaited her. As she entered the nearly deserted barn, one hand whispered to the other, 'Wish t'hell there was more pussy around this ranch. Miss Lyla don't come 'round more'n twice a year.'

'Yeah, but she's got enough to last any man for quite a spell.'

Lyla reached the anxious pair.

'Evening, boys.'

'Evenin', Miss Lyla, you sure look swell.'

'Thanks, kid. Well, let's get at it. You've had a hard day.'

She turned and led them to an empty stall. As the three of them entered and locked the gate behind them, the taller of the two men whispered to the other, 'Yeah, and even harder evening, looks like.'

Outside, the dazzling sprays of colored fire exploded and cascaded. Inside the stable. Lyla led the two young men in their own private eruptive display. As the three flailed about, moaning, biting, flinging hay up into the air and groaning with release after release of unlocked lust, the pure-bred Arabian horses looked down haughtily, as though wondering what made mortals such primitive animals.

Twenty-four miles away in suburban Tulsa City, in the most exclusive residential area, all the lights were burning in the huge Tudor mansion of Abraham Lehson.

Just moments ago, all had been quiet and calm. The nurse on night duty had been relaxing and reading to the steady pacing of Mr. Abe's forced but sure breathing. Suddenly, amidst gasps, groans and struggles the electrocardiogram plunged violently back and forth, then flicked lightly at a level indicating the barest presence of life.

Now, gathered around the stricken man's bedside, the three doctors confirmed their earlier suspicions. Mr. Abraham Lehson had suffered a massive stroke. An electroencephalogram had been ordered from the hospital to determine the actual extent of brain damage.

The family must be notified. He might not live through the night.

'I'm sorry Mr. Preston, she's not taking any calls right now. No sir, not even yours.'

'What is it, Eleanor? Please tell me.'

'Well, sir, it's Mr. Abe.'

'Oh, my God! He hasn't . . . ?'

'No, not yet. But it seems extremely serious.'

'How will this affect the fortnight?'

'As of right now, everything continues as planned.'

'That's a relief, at least. What's the prognosis?'

'He's critical. A massive stroke early this morning.'

'Tell Miss Stella I phoned. Extend my deepest sympathies, and, should she want me in Tulsa City, I can catch the next plane.'

'Thank you, Mr. Preston. I'll tell her the minute she's free.'

They sat around Stella's desk. Edna, fully alert but pale, toyed with a cup of now-cold coffee. Lyla was the most visibly upset, her eyes swollen, her hair slightly mussed. Stella was noticeably shaken, but still operating.

They had met in the Lehson mansion at four that morning and had been together ever since. It had been terrible, watching as the three doctors tried everything humanly possible to prolong a life that resisted their ministrations. Martin had broken down completely and had to be sedated and put to bed. It was seven a.m. when the chief physician told them that Mr. Abe had just barely passed the crisis. His condition was critical, perhaps even terminal, but the end was not in immediate sight. They must go to their homes and get some rest. Nothing they could do at the house would matter.

Instead, they drove back to the store in the early morning and went up to Stella's office to talk again and to wait. They decided that no word of the severity of Mr. Abe's stroke should be released.

Stella looked around at her two so dissimilar sisters. The three of them were cut from the same cloth yet each was so different. Three childless, lonely women faced at last the reality of how impermanent mortality is—knowing that their father's dream of dynasty would die with him: so much done, so much to leave and so barren the eventual legacy for some foundation or trust. The drive that consumed them dissipated as they waited for news of the dreamer and his final dream. Mr. Abe's presence had never been stronger than on this morning.

'He is such a strong man, Daddy is,' said Stella. 'The doctors say that the stroke was severe enough to kill anyone, and his brain was without oxygen for nearly a full minute.'

'I don't want to hear this!' cried out Lyla. 'He's going to die, he's going to die soon!'

Lyla's agitated emotions upset them. Stella fought tears, and Edna spoke. 'We can't expect him to live out the month, Lyla. We must face this situation.'

'Well, don't go through the details of a premature autopsy,' said Lyla. 'I'm having enough trouble dealing with this, let alone handling the specifics. Damn his strength! If he's going to die, he should have done it yesterday.'

'Calm down, Lyla,' exhaled Stella. 'We have all known this time was coming . . . death is never easy to confront. We must pull together and attend to these realities. How are we going to do the funeral? Rabbi Allenberg will officiate, of course. I, for one, think that Mr. Adler should be allowed to coordinate it. He is impeccably perfect and will insure that Daddy is laid to rest with the utmost res . . . pect.' Stella swallowed the sob that welled up inside.

Lyla became even more upset. 'Can't you shut up, you cold calculating bitch! Fine, fine, let Adler handle it. Allenberg can spew out his hypocrisies. But I don't want to know about the arrangements; just have them do it.'

Stella shook her head and turned quizzically to Edna.

'All right,' said Edna, 'Adler it is. And I'd like to close the store, in memoriam, on the day of the funeral, despite the costs and difficulties involved.'

Stella and Lyla nodded their agreement.

The sisters talked on, working out the broad details of the inevitable. Lyla was more relaxed now. Edna would handle the store's closure. Della would make up the memorial announcement. Stella would be in close contact with the mortician, Adler. The mournfully anticipated death of Mr. Abe would be met.

Now that the logistics had been dealt with, the girls bared their private feelings. Stella broke down and sobbed openly. 'I can't accept it, Daddy can't die, he can't die . . . damn ! . . . He can't . . .'

'There, there, Stella,' comforted Edna. 'It's for the best. He'll be released from his pain, he'll rest peacefully.'

Lyla felt the same way. 'As sad as it is, he'll be better off when his suffering is over.'

The sisters shared their pain. They were as close now as they had ever been, united fully by impending grief.

Aaron Seton's designing star was on the wane. The once-famous milliner turned Manhattan couturier had been a Lehson awardee in the past, but the zenith of his career had long ago been reached. Still, his highly theatrical gowns maintained a loyal coterie of customers and Lehson's continued to feature them. They were extremely expensive and their lush vulgarity returned a handsome profit for the store.

Physically, Seton wasn't very much. Short, flabby, weak in courage and spirit, and outrageous. He was embarrassingly effeminate. He hadn't descended to wearing full make up, but he was not above using a little pancake to erase the hollow cheeks and a subtle touch of eye shadow to accentuate his haddocklike expression. He was bitchy and petulant, and his high-pitched voice often trembled and cracked. Seton fought a losing battle with his perpetual weight problem, was Jewish, and hailed from the improbable state of Wyoming. His creative forte was based upon the opulent fabrics he designed and used for his line—quilted velvets, heavy embroideries and thick laces studded with colored stones. His flamboyance was barely compensation for his monumentally obnoxious personality. This was the not quite has-been who arrived alone at the Tulsa City airport to be met by Sonia Angelini.

'Where is everyone?' he asked in a whiny tone.

'I'm everyone,' Sonia curtly replied.

'I expected Miss Lyla, and the press. . . . Weren't they notified of my arrival?'

'Aaron,' sighed Sonia, 'where are your baggage checks? Give them to the chauffeur and let's get back to the store, all right?'

Confused and bewildered by this lack of fanfare, Seton meekly went through the motions and reluctantly shuffled over to the limousine. Sonia made no attempt to pamper this self-assuming baby. Her disgust at his immature pouting was obvious. Seton's hand involuntarily found its way to his mouth. Sonia said, 'Aaron, try not to suck your thumb. You're in Oklahoma now.'

'Oh, Belle, that looks marvelous on you.'

'Gee, Lyla, everything's so gorgeous I can't decide what to take.'

Sal, sitting back comfortably in the couture department, beamed with the pride of a man who can afford a famous mistress and keep her in a Bourbon's style. 'Then take them all!' he grandiosely suggested.

'Now that's what I call a fiancé.'

'Hell, it's only money. Ya like 'em? We take 'em.'

'Sal, honey, this Heymano's fifteen hundred.'

'Can ya wear it at the club?'

'Can I ever.'

'Then it's deductible.' He turned to the delighted salesgirl. 'Can ya send 'em to Vegas?'

'Of course, Mr. A'Patico.'

'Good, that way we don't have to carry 'em back. What else y'got that Belle'll look good in, Lyla?'

'Sal, this kid looks smashing in everything. Wait! There is one more thing you've got to see . . . just one, I promise.'

'Okay, let's see it.'

'It's a slinky gown that Juan Felipe did just for us. More of a second skin than a dress. You'll knock them out in it. It's emerald green.'

Belle dropped her eyes coyly. 'Ah Lyla, maybe we'd better pass that little job.'

'Why? With your figure . . .'

'That's just it,' she said, turning to Sal, 'Can I tell her, honey?'

'She's yer best friend, ain't she?'

'That she is.'

'Then tell,' he said and sat back to await the shock.

'Lyla, not a word to anyone . . . and I mean it. But in about four months from now you're going to be showing me maternity clothes.'

'Belle! Sal! What simply wonderful news. Oh, if you only knew how thrilled and delighted I am . . . oh Belle!' and Lyla took out her handkerchief and started to cry.

'Hey, Lyla, cut that out,' said Sal, but he, too, had misty eyes. His pride was overflowing, his manhood secure. He might even marry her.

Lyla hugged Belle and they both started crying from the sheer joy of the announcement. Sal, getting a little embarrassed, interrupted. 'Y'say that slinky number is sexy, huh?'

'Oh, Sal, it's a walking wet dream.'

'Yeah? She'll take it. After all, four months is a long time.'

The salesgirl who had been helping them went to the stock room to bring out the Felipe gown. Lyla finally sat down and, drying her eyes, realized how much she liked this warm, open singer in spite of her questionable taste in selecting such an unsavoury man for a mate. Lyla also felt that old void in her stomach that appeared whenever any of her friends became pregnant. But this time, she was so thrilled for Belle that the sadness was transient. The emerald green dress was a knockout and Sal settled up the bill in cash, $9,850 worth. He even tipped the salesgirl a hundred for her time—a momentous day for the Padrone from Palermo.

Upstairs in the Blue Grotto Restaurant, Ann was having lunch with her father, Adam Hadley Carter, city editor of the *Tulsa City News*. He was a wise, gentle man of innate wisdom and excellent at his job, but his philosopher's mind traveled beyond the confines of the city desk, Tulsa City, and even the United States. An advocate of reason, Adam accepted the long view of a situation. He had been widowed for almost a quarter of a century and positively doted on his only daughter. The adoration was reciprocal.

'I'm convinced, Ann, that in my next incarnation I shall be called upon to create the architecture of an Eden-like society. Failing that, I should prefer the cloistered universe of an Oriental lamasery.'

'Daddy, you'd look cute in saffron robes.'

'You are not taking this seriously enough,' he laughed. 'Besides, you look absolutely radiant this afternoon. I have a hunch you'd rather talk about something other than my celestial destiny.'

'My, aren't we the crafty reporter today. Very well, Snoopy, if you must know—I've gone and met that certain man. I'm in love.'

'Congratulations! If memory serves me correctly it's an admirable condition. Who is this worthy?'

'Name's Josh Frankel. From New York. And ... well ... he's married.'

'That's not too good. Go on.'

'Will you believe me if I tell you it's all right?'

'I trust you, daughter.'

'He feels as strongly as I do. He's insisting on divorce so we can marry.'

'Honorable.'

'I won't have any of that. Not yet. I've only known him a few days, you see.'

'How can you be so positive?'

'How long did it take you to fall in love with Mom?'

'That, as you very well know, is not the same thing. Your mother and I kept company for nine months before we became engaged. We were engaged for six months before we married.'

'That was in the Stone Age. You still haven't told me about how you felt.'

'Well, you were born exactly nine months after the ceremony.'

'All that proves is potency.'

'You are a fresh young lady, young lady. I worshiped your mother from the first day we met. Satisfied?'

'I knew it all along. The only thing about Josh and me is the way we met. The store fixed up our date. He took me to one of Miss Stella's dinner parties. I think they expected me to seduce him.'

'Why in God's name would you entertain such devious thoughts?'

'You don't understand Lehson's, Daddy. They want him to quit his job in New York and come out here to work. They want him very much.'

'And you honestly imagine that by offering you up as a tasty morsel that'd influence his decision?'

'When you say it that way, no. Still, I'm not totally convinced that the executives of this store do anything casually. Why me, for heaven's sake?'

'Why not? You're certainly pretty enough. You're bright. Fun. You sometimes even amaze me with an original thought. I'd say they exercised sound judgment . . . and good taste.'

'You may be right.'

'You two did fall in love, didn't you?'

'Yes.'

'Then I am right. Darling, you are everything to me—my life. If you've finally found the man you want, then do everything possible to maintain the relationship. I'm not advocating being promiscuous, I just feel that one has to grasp onto each moment of joy—hold on to it with dear life. I have you plus the memory of those two years of bliss with your mother. We didn't waste a single second of the months we had together. I miss her desperately, still love her, but I know nothing was wasted when we were together.'

'I've told you, Josh is in New York.'

'Well now, daughter, if I were the buyer for a hot-shot junior department, I know I'd need to get myself back to Manhattan and see how all my manufacturers were doing on my reorders, or something.'

Ann reached over and took his hand in hers. This special man who loved her, her father, had stamped his approval on her love.

'I'll arrange for a two-day trip this afternoon. And sir, I love you.'

'Nonsense. Finish your salad.'

The classic Greek portico of the Tulsa City Museum of Fine Art was awash with gleaming light as the rich and influential of the state's establishment made their way up the broad steps to Lehson's party inside. Everyone knew that it was the store's influence and not the museum's strictly second-rate position that had managed to arrange for the visiting exhibition of ancient Mediterranean statuary and artifacts currently on loan.

In this Lehson's once again reaffirmed its position of dominance in Tulsa City. The icing had taken over the cake, for what started as a public relations assignment many years ago had actually become a fact. The public image of Lehson's, the total taste-maker and arbiter of all things cultural, was now a reality. The store accepted this unique responsibility with the ever-increasing prestige and profits that came along with it. In no city in America, perhaps the world, was a department store so influential. Virtually anything Lehson's wished to use, be it public or private, was at the store's disposal. It was not considered a favor to give Lehson's what it wanted, rather, a civic honor.

With Princess Judith absent, it was Heymano who received the spotlight. The white stone statues were a perfect backdrop for the elegant couturier, whose plum-colored evening suit would be a costume on a lesser person, but on him, it was a stunning second skin. The museum boasted one minor Goya painting and Heymano wisely decided that this was where he should stand during the evening—the colors and Spanish grandeur completed the ideal setting he desired.

Stella was official hostess tonight. Her deep concern for Mr. Abe's condition was hidden by the polish of her obligation to the guests. The reason for tonight's function was ostensibly to launch the new loan exhibit for the museum, but the reality was another tax-deductible charity party for Lehson's customers and friends; a good time in this otherwise dull community. Edna was at the old man's bedside representing the family. As Stella greeted the same familiar faces once again, her thoughts (for the first time in years) went beyond the peacock preening and showing off of the store's clientele. Her father's impending death erased much of what she had so strongly believed for years. These people and their little vanities were so terribly unimportant. This huge promotion, all this culture and art, seemed so transient. The handsome Heymano, glistening in importance and favor, would grow old, wither and become dust. Only the ancient statuary frozen in time had any chance of some permanence—and it was visibly chipped and mutilated. It was all so useless, so why not enjoy the moment. That's all there really was.

Everyone had arrived and Stella was free to mingle among the formally attired hundreds who were devouring the canapés and downing the champagne in the name of sweet charity. As she wandered, paying noticeable attention to the exhibits, she chatted, laughed and gossiped with them all. She saw C. Z. standing alone against a massive Roman pillar with that perpetual extension of his hand, a martini.

'Carl, you're not very social tonight.'

'Ah, sweet lady. You have found me out—I'm secretly a closet hermit. The only reason I'm here is to admire this phallic monument from a nobler time,' he said as he patted the pillar.

'Then I shall commandeer you for a little work.'

'I refuse.'

'This is Seton's first public exposure and he's starting to drink. Take him in hand, dear. I want this to be a nice evening.'

'Me? Chaperone him? Never!'

'Carl, please?'

'The things I do for Lehson's. Very well, I suppose it's better than dancing with Lady Vidal—she always wants me to lead.'

C.Z. found the pouting also-ran listening to Michelle De Soto and Quentin Kimball as they discussed the relative equality of the nation's blacks.

'But Michelle, what about Dr. Bunche?'

'Say what you will, Quentin. As far as I'm concerned, they all jumped outta a palm tree and into a Cadillac, and I, for one, won't integrate! Waiter, more champagne!'

'If I may interrupt this merry ménage, I've come to whisk dear Seton away from you. His fans are anxious to see him. Come Aaron, your public cries.'

They left and C.Z. steered Seton towards the deserted atrium garden in the center of the building.

'Why're we going there? There's nobody out there.'

'Fear not, Aaron, I shall not seduce you.'

'Well, I should hope not.'

'It's just that I need a smidge of fresh air to clear away the cobwebs and I'm afraid to go alone.'

'Honestly! What about my fans?'

'You'll dance later, darling. . . . We both need the air.'

'No! I'm an honored guest.' Seton turned and headed back to the crowds. He scooped up a glass of wine from a passing waiter, downed it too quickly, took another, and before C.Z. could reach him scurried over to where Heymano was holding court. Pepe, knowing that his partner was totally at ease, was away from Mano, enjoying the festivities and basking in the reflected glory of his associate.

'Hi there, Mano, don't blame you for getting hung up under the Goya. It's to die over.'

Heymano, sublime in his assurance, deigned to respond to the wobbly designer.

'In Spain, an important household may contain several Goyas. It is unfortunately true that here in America when you get one, it is necessary to erect a museum around it.'

'Whassa madder with America, Senyore?'

'Nothing, señor. It is my favorite nation.'

'You aliens are all alike . . . disrespectful. At least I'm not hung up under a picture.'

'Ah, that is true, but it is sometimes better to be pinned here during *my* party, than to be mired in faded glory like others less fortunate.'

C.Z. averted any continuation of the verbal tiff. He whisked Seton off towards the buffet.

'Guess I told that fella a thing or two. Where we goin' now?'

'A table filled with goodies. You must eat, darling.'

'My diet.'

'Forget all that tonight and live recklessly. Oh, isn't that smoked salmon divine looking?'

'Don' want any.'

'Aaron precious, you must force yourself. It contains vitamins that simply melt the fat away.'

'I'm not fat!'

'Pudgy, a trifle pudgy is all.'

'You eat the damned lox, I'm on caviar,' he said, and he scooped up a plateful.

'How chic of you, Aaron—and how butch.'

'Wha . . . ? What did you say?'

'I said . . . you are the most incredibly dull bore it has ever been my misfortune to meet. Now start behaving yourself or I shall have you taken home.'

'How dare you . . . you display thing! I'm Seton!'

'Bartender, bring Miss Seton some tablets. For his digestion, that is . . . all these rich goodies play havoc on sensitive Wyoming stomachs.'

Stella, with Eugene Boardman and his wife, arrived just as Seton was about to fling his caviar at C.Z. She quickly had the Boardmans take Seton away.

'Honestly, Carl, he is our guest.'

'Well, I'm not sorry. I loathe that ridiculous excuse for a man.'

'Well, that is no reason for rudeness.'

'Miss Stella, Aaron Seton is the kind of person who gives bestiality a bad name.'

TUESDAY, OCTOBER 11

Whenever Lehson's presented a fashion show to its customers, the entire showing was previewed at 8.30 a.m. to the sales staff of the department involved. It was both a run-through for Sonia and the models who wore the clothes, as well as a reindoctrination for the saleswomen on the fine points of the collection shown. Today was Seton's turn.

The average saleslady on the couture floor of Lehson's earned twelve thousand dollars a year in commissions. One or two of the really top women, like Claudia Wright, hit the twenty thousand dollar mark. They were all understated, knowledgeable and professional. They knew their customers and their taste was consistent with their earnings.

Clothes like Morgan Moore's they understood and valued. The more mass-market area of designers, like Felipe, they also knew, and their more attractive price accounted for the bulk of their sales. The specialists, and Seton was that, were another matter. They couldn't understand how any woman who wasn't going to a costume ball or appearing on the stage could possibly encase herself in his outlandish creations.

Instead of fine taste, Seton blatantly trumpeted extravagance. For the understatement of line and craftsmanship, he substituted flaunting cost. Yet, they never failed to be amazed at how well this chinless fairy's gowns appealed to a small, very rich group of nondiscerning women. Mind you, they had absolutely no prejudice against sexual deviation. Mr. Morgan Moore was both a talent and a gentleman, and whatever they thought about his bedroom habits, it was seldom if ever that anyone thought of him as a homosexual. With Seton, when one heard his name, the image of a mincing queer loomed large.

And so it was that the ladies of Lehson's couture floor came in, chatted quietly and took their places for the morning run-through of that afternoon's select showing of the fall Seton collection.

Sonia welcomed them. She began with an apology: 'We are extremely sorry, ladies, that Mr. Seton isn't with us this morning. Please believe me when I tell you his absence is unavoidable. His suite is on the sixteenth floor of the Hotel Royal. There was an electrical power failure there this morning, very early, and the elevators are simply not running. We are assured the situation will be corrected within the hour.'

Claudia Wright, sixty, proud, and with her lovely white hair done in the best of all possible taste, looked up from her seat in the second row. Her opinion on matters of elegance and propriety was unassailable. In a low-keyed, Southern belle voice she asked the fashion director, 'Really, Miss Angelini, why didn't he simply fly down?'

The day had begun at Lehson's.

'Eleanor, would you please ring Mr. Abe's home. I'd like to speak with the doctor.'

In less than a minute, Dr. Gregg was on the phone.

'Yes, Mrs. Manchester.'

'How is it this morning, doctor?'

'I'm going to be perfectly candid, but please don't expect any miracles. . . . We've tested your father thoroughly and, frankly, we're amazed at the lack of permanent damage caused by the stroke. Considering his age and condition, it's medically unique. None of us have seen anything like this before; neither has the cardiologist.'

'Are you telling me he's better?'

'I'm telling you that there do not seem to be any serious effects present.'

'But isn't that promising?'

'Yes, but you must remember that his condition prior to the attack was a very serious one.'

'Is your prognosis hopeful?'

'I'd have to say it is.'

'Oh, Dr. Gregg, this is wonderful. Truly wonderful. Thank you so very much.'

'Your father is an amazing man.'

'Yes, he is that.'

'And physicians, like the family, always hope, too.'

'Thank you again. I must tell my sisters.'

'Let me add a personal note of guarded optimism. . . . It's apparent

Mr. Lehson is gaining some strength, and, between you and me, I wouldn't be too surprised if there were a positive reversal in his condition toward the end of the week. Now you can call your sisters. Good morning.'

Stella replaced the receiver with trembling hands, the tears streaming down her face. What glorious news! She had Eleanor hook up a conference call between the three Lehson women and related the news. The relief they all felt poured out in a huge wave. There was hope. They could dare to dream again.

Stella was finishing her second cup of tea as Eugene Boardman went over receipts from the previous day's sales.

'We are consistently reaching record figures, Stella. This is by far the most successful to date.'

'That's fine, Eugene. Any indications as to a trend?'

'Umm, nothing to speak of . . . except that Culbertson's sales are skyrocketing. The edge is now heavily weighted toward volume prices.'

'I find that slightly depressing.'

'We've got to accept reality. We're cashing in on all those years of building the store's reputation.'

'I suppose you're right. Any figures yet from the Christmas catalogue?'

'Yes, and that too is excellent. We're way up over last year. . . . Let's see . . . here it is, a twenty-eight per cent increase. Again, the bulk is from sales under twenty dollars.'

'Next year we'll have to increase the price of the gift wrapping if this continues.'

'Check.'

'Now Eugene,' said Stella, turning to an unusually playful mood and buoyed by the news from Dr. Gregg, 'about my successor? Do you have any idea who's going to sit in my chair, or do we have to determine leadership by measuring behinds?'

Boardman remained unruffled, cool and efficient.

'Miss Stella, you, more than anyone else, know what is best for the store. Your decision will be correct. We have many top people in the higher ranks of management. Several could fill your chair for a while. After all, an appointment such as your ambassadorship will be over in a few years, and then you will return.'

She turned serious again. 'No, Eugene, I think not. I am Lehson's and Lehson's is me. The family. I've had my turn and if we are to grow, then someone must succeed me. Someone who feels about the store as I do. I'd like to hear your evaluations, please.'

'Bethel would be fine, but I'm afraid the store would consistently look better than it actually operated. Miss Lyla, if she could settle down, would do an excellent job, but she seems to have some inner vulnerability and I do doubt her strength in times of crisis. Culbertson could produce record profits in all departments, but I'd be afraid of what he could do to our standing in the retail community. Josh Frankel seems ideal for grooming, but he's about ten years away from the top level experience and maturity we need. And there's always Frank Preston . . .'

Stella looked at him for a moment and smiled. 'Which brings us finally to you. From a coldly analytical business reasoning, you are the number one choice. But, dear Eugene, a fashion store is also built on intuition and emotion. You are, as you must readily admit, not the most emotional man we know.'

'A balance sheet is bloodless, Miss Stella, unless it contains an unusual amount of red.'

'Well put. The point is taken. The Lehson family has developed a rather high level of expensive maintenance. We appreciate your concern for its continuation. Now, if you'll excuse me, I've got to see Aaron Seton.'

Manny Berns disembarked from his plane from Los Angeles, alone. Manny had only a compact piece of hand luggage, but it was still a weighty baton to hail a waiting taxi. He used the luggage, as he did everything in life, as a stage prop. The cab slid up and the redcap opened the door.

Manny slithered into the back and sat nervously against the stained leather of the cab, watching the countryside turn into the outskirts of Tulsa City with unseeing eyes. Manny consistently acted instinctively, professionally and lethally. Nothing he ever did was without a reason. No act, no matter how inconsequential, was not part of his master design. He had a direction, an avenue to travel, and he did it directly, alone and at great speed. By innuendo, threat, cajolery, flattery and stark blackmail he controlled the destinies of many of the top dress buyers across the country. Bribery, both tangible and emotional, were his top trumps and he played them well.

Berns had to act fast to solidify his position with Juan Felipe. A Felipe boutique in major stores was really a natural, and Juan wanted it badly. Juan was getting edgy about dissipated profits, too, and Manny had to do some fancy side-stepping to explain where the money had gone. Felipe had been blunt with him: 'Boutiques or else.'

Manny had locked himself in his den for a series of telephone conversations that, in two days, had lined up six important stores behind the concept. But Manny needed Lehson's if the plan was to work. If Lehson's went along (he had lied to the six that Lyla suggested the idea) then Manny owned the world as well as Juan Felipe. It was clever of him to have managed those shocking photographs of Lyla and the two sailors he'd hired last summer. Clever, indeed, that such revealing pornography was starring a Lehson in poses and positions that did little to help the store's usual public image. If necessary, the snapshots (poor Lyla was so busy balling she never noticed the photographer secreted in the folds of the drapes snapping away to his heart's content) were all the insurance he needed. Still, this was the most dangerous ground he'd ever covered. Blackmailing some poor lonely lady buyer in the Midwest was a very far cry from using this blatant tactic with a Lehson and the couture director of America's most prestigious store.

They were different sizes, shapes and ages, but the fifty-three women seated comfortably in the private salon at Lehson's had the common denominator of being a 'Seton customer' (and common is the right adjective). Seton clothes were extravagant, sensational even; but when these women wore them, the clothes seemed to be wearing the women and the effect was cheap. Aaron Seton felt nothing of the sort; and the sight of so much buying power in the elegant salon, with Miss Stella herself in attendance, brought him back to those giddy days when he won the coveted Lehson award. The noon of his career.

As was the custom, almost all the customers wore a Seton dress or suit. Seton was in nirvana as the parade of portly mannequins eddied and flowed around him. These were his women . . . his little darlings . . . his rich, adoring public . . . the bitches. . . . Why were there only fifty-three? . . . Ah well . . .

Sonia was outside the salon, chatting with Heymano. She glanced at her watch.

'*Mon Dieu*, I'm five minutes late. Mano, dear, do excuse me, a showing. I'm commentating.'

'I shall go with you, *cara mia*. I have nothing for an hour. It will be nice to view someone else's things for a change.'

'I think not, Mano. You will be bored. Let me have one of the girls take you down to the men's department for a little shopping.'

He smiled charmingly. 'No, I go with you.' He opened the door to the salon. 'Please, *après vous*.'

Heymano froze when he saw the owlish Seton preening next to Stella, reveling in the glory of his little showing. Rage swept over him for an instant, but he quashed it and turned gallantly to Sonia. 'I see what you mean, it's not to my liking. It is bad enough that his clothes are atrocious; but he is a disgusting sow. I am more than shocked that Lehson's would honor him with even this small a showing when Heymano is here. Inform Miss Stella, we must speak later.'

He turned and left Sonia to enter alone. Her back was to the people in the room and she did not see Aaron Seton spy Heymano and deliberately stick his tongue out at the couturier.

Lyla sat edgily across the desk from a confident Manny Berns. He used all his wiles to try and convince her that setting up a Juan Felipe boutique (with a minimum guarantee of $100,000 wholesale) was perfect Lehson merchandising.

'Now look, Lyla darling, you know that Juan's clothes draw customers like nothing else. We'll set aside a space, not excessively large, and have the total line on display.'

'Manny, you know Lehson policy as well as anyone. Lehson's sells Lehson's. We're not going to give up floor space for something as temporary as a Felipe boutique.'

'Whaddya mean temporary? Juan's got at least a full decade of fine designing ahead of him. He's one of the greats, you know that. His power's just beginning to be felt. If Lehson's were to get the jump on the other retailers here, it'd show a million times over in profits. Just imagine it, darling, imagine how impressive it'll be: we'll call it the "Juan Felipe Collection for Manny Berns, Ltd."'

'Manny! How pretentious can you get?'

'Oow wait a minute, darling it was my idea—*that's the name*.'

'I'm sorry, Manny, but I totally reject the concept. It won't happen here at Lehson's.'

The usual charm fell from Berns and he slid the photographs across the desk to her. Nervously, she looked at them. Her inner reaction was panic. She tried to keep control, but was obviously aghast—not so much at the blackmailing shots, but at the fact for the first time in her life, her position as a Lehson daughter was being threatened.

Berns was reduced to pure evil as he laid his cards on the table. 'Lyla, there isn't anything I won't do to get what I want. If you don't convince Stella to agree to the boutique idea, and agree right away, I'm sending copies of this pornography to every Lehson employee, and to every manufacturer, salesman, press editor and fashion reporter in the country. Nothing will appear in the papers, of course, but you *and* the store will suffer a taint that'll destroy your image in the wholesale community. I don't want to have to do this . . .'

Lyla's nymphomania had never really hurt anyone, and she had almost enjoyed the illness, but now with this driven man ready to make good such threats, she was starkly terrified.

Manny, secure in his triumph, rose and tossed a set of the pictures to her, saying, 'Keep these, dear. I have the negatives.' He turned to leave, saying, 'Oh, by the way, darling, let's make it a one hundred and fifty thousand dollar annual guarantee—so much more impressive to other fine merchants. I'll be at the Tulsa City Royal, waiting for your call. I want to be on the ten o'clock plane tonight.'

Alone, trembling with a fear she never knew was possible, Lyla telephoned Belle O'Hara at her hotel.

'Belle? Thank God. I must see you right away. No, I'll drive over to you. Yes, right away. Oh please, honey, can Sal be there? I'm in terrible trouble, Sal's kind of trouble.'

Manny Berns sat alone in his room at the Tulsa City Royal, watching 'Crusader Rabbit' on the children's early show. The phone rang and he checked his watch—five thirty. It was Lyla.

'Manny.'

'Lyla, darling.'

'I've met with Stella and she agrees with me that the concept of a Juan Felipe boutique would be excellent. We have drawn up a letter of agreement, which you will find satisfactory.'

'Divine, darling, simply divine. I'll dash over and collect it.'

'No, Manny. I'll send it around with a messenger. He'll be there in half an hour.'

'Precious. How considerate. Bless you, darling, and I meant what I said about the entertainment I have lined up for you on the coast. This is marvelous for all concerned and I'm sure we're all going to be terribly happy together. How about a drink later, before my plane leaves?'

'Sorry, Manny, impossible.'

'Pity. Okay, Lyla, see you in Los Angeles.'

He returned the receiver to its cradle and leaned back with a satisfied purr. He'd done it. Juan Felipe was securely in his pocket and there was nowhere to go but up. He snuggled back in his chair and chuckled at the animation on the screen. He called room service and ordered a bottle of their best champagne and four ounces of caviar.

Six thirty. Manny was on the telephone to Juan in Los Angeles and was regaling him with the happy news. A large brandy snifter filled with champagne was in one hand. The jar of caviar was empty. He was delirious.

There was a knock at the door.

'Juan, it's here now. Must dash, darling. My plane gets in around ten your time and I'll see you at the office tomorrow. Bye.' He hung up and, glass still in hand, sidled to the door. He opened it and saw a dark young man in a conservative business suit.

'Yes?'

'Mr. Berns?'

'In the flesh, darling, come in. Do come in.'

The young man was polite and entered the room, walking toward the desk next to the television set. Manny surveyed him up and down, brazenly and unashamedly. He was feeling particularly omnipotent at this moment.

'I must say, Lehson's even has good taste in messengers.'

'Mr. Berns, I was told to deliver something to you.'

'Ohh and am I ever waiting for it. Hand it over and I'll give you a glass of wine.'

'Of course, sir.'

The young man reached inside his jacket pocket and took out a revolver with a silencer attachment.

'For God's sake! What the fuck are you doing?'

'With the compliments of the management, Mr. Berns.'

Three short, muffled blasts and Berns fell, eyes popping in bewilderment and fear, in a crumpled heap of flab and flannel. Berns's toupee slid off and the young man picked it up. It was greasy so he promptly dropped it and entered the bathroom to wash his hands.

The polite young man ransacked the room, found the negatives in an envelope in Berns's briefcase. He put the gun away and the film in his pocket. As he left the room, he took the 'Do Not Disturb' sign and hung it around the door handle on the outside. He closed the door quietly and left.

WEDNESDAY, OCTOBER 12

Alice Short, possibly the smallest of the better dress manufacturers in stature, was also one of the largest and most successful in output. Her refined, ladylike clothes were worn by the Washington elite, and smart older women everywhere built their wardrobes around her elegant dresses. Alice Short was a good, sharp, no-nonsense business-woman. She was dynamic and often demanding, but her demands were usually reasonable and justified. Alice Short was a designer with a long, solid history. Her clothes had been an important label at Lehson's for two decades, and she was one of Stella's genuine friends in the business. Behind her back—and because of her diminutive size —she was often referred to as 'Tiny Alice,' but never by Stella.

She had been honored many times in the past by the store. When the plane bringing her in from Manhattan arrived, Stella was at the airport to meet her.

'Alice, dear, how was the flight?'

'Just fine, Stella, though I sat next to one of your more talkative Tulsa City matrons and could use a little time at the hotel to freshen up.'

The steel-grey Rolls-Royce sped along the parkway towards central Tulsa City. Stella Lehson was relaxed and chatty with her old friend.

'Got a problem, Alice. Mind if I bounce it off you?'

'Shoot.'

'Our star of the year has finally started to act up.'

'Figures. Mano can only be good for so long.'

'The crux of it is Seton. He's insulted Mano, plus, Mano went on an ego trip when he saw Seton's clothes being shown privately during the week he was to be honored.'

'I wish sometimes we girls could be as feminine as they are. Doesn't Mano know it's all business?'

'He doesn't want to know. He hates Seton—really—and has focused all his temperament in that direction.'

'Too bad. You'll have to dump Seton. That's all.'

'I knew as much, just wanted to hear it from someone else.'

'Fine thing, when a manufacturer has to give confirmation to a merchant.'

Stella laughed easily. It was settled. Aaron Seton had to be told to leave.

Gene Zeller was in his usual quandary. Claudia Wright was top sales-lady in his department and this morning she was adamant.

'Mr. Zeller, Maybeth Griffith *is* one of the store's most valued customers.'

'Yes, Claudia, I know, but we can't pack up the entire Alice Short collection and cart it out to her house.'

'Why can't we? Mrs. Griffith doesn't ask for unusual service very often. I'll only be gone a few hours.'

'I know that, but Miss Short is due in the store today. How will it look if none of her clothes are in stock?'

'I'm only taking the models, Mr. Zeller.'

Zeller was exasperated. He found it difficult to cope with the sales-women. He found it difficult to cope with the store executives as well as most manufacturers. If only his wife would stop pushing him. He was a nice guy—he knew that. This just wasn't his line of work, yet he seemed to be doing a good job.

'Claudia, the stock of Alice Shorts is being marked in the receiving room. They'll be up on the floor late this afternoon. Can't Mrs. Griffith wait until tomorrow? I can't release the only samples we have.'

'Mrs. Maybeth Griffith doesn't have to wait, Mr. Zeller, and I for one am not ready to ask her. It seems to me that store policy puts the customer ahead of all else.'

Why couldn't he ever win an argument? He knew before he began that Claudia would get her way.

'All right, Claudia, take the damn things, but for Christ's sake try to be quick about it.'

'Mr. Zeller, profanity is quite unnecessary.'

Stella dropped Alice Short off at her hotel and returned to the store. She had her driver leave her off at the front entrance and made her way leisurely through the early-morning shoppers, stopping to chat with a familiar face or caution a salesperson on the way their stock was displayed. It was a mother hen-ish routine and Stella enjoyed the ritual. Even if business was better than ever, it was business as usual.

She thought again, as she had all through these last days, of the embassy she would occupy. Madame Ambassador is quite a mouthful. Not your Perle Mesta type of paid political appointment to some obscure postage stamp kingdom, but a major assignment to an important nation, the Clare Boothe Luce variety. Stella had worked very hard for the President—monies raised, image shined—so that her influence was stronger than the tacit rubber stamp so usual with a President and his home state. She's seen something, all those years back, in the lanky junior congressman and attached herself to his rising star. Not only was the reward earned, but he knew damned well she would be one of the better representatives from the United States.

Yes, it had all worked out so perfectly—quietly, efficiently, with a set goal in mind. The Lehson way. Stella had the bulk of her estate wrapped up in the store and it represented several million. She had a liquid cash position to maintain the ambassadorship for five or six years. Stella Lehson would be the first nonpolitical American representative to a major power. She would become an international power herself. It was sweet, this morning. Yes, Stella had every reason to be in top spirits.

As she walked into Eleanor Long's office, she knew it would remain a fine day.

'Good morning, Eleanor.'

'Good morning, Miss Stella.'

'Come into my office please. Oh, Eleanor? Call Aaron Seton, he's probably somewhere in the store, and ask him to drop in and see me.'

'Yes, Miss Stella.'

'But before you do, get me Dr. Gregg.'

Eleanor beamed. 'Oh, Miss Stella—he called not more than ten minutes ago. Mr. Abe's condition has stabilized. He's getting better, Miss Stella, Mr. Abe is going to get well.'

Lehson's executive station wagon drove up the long drive to the Griffith mansion. The twenty-seven Alice Short originals were hanging on a portable rack in the back. Zack Peach drove carefully and Claudia Wright felt it was going to be a profitable day. The Griffith place was set back half a mile from the road—a neo-Colonial plantation with wide, rolling lawns and perfectly attended flowers.

Maybeth's husband was old Oklahoma money; he brought in his first gusher before World War I. At last count there were more than two hundred wells pumping a tax depletion income into the Griffith family that simply couldn't all be spent. Maybeth was a simple lady who knew what she liked and didn't like. Her values and ideas were neatly catalogued and she could turn to any page for the orderly answer to any and all problems. God—the real Baptist one, of course—America, her family, friends and home were the corners of her tight little world. Maybeth Griffith liked Alice Short dresses as well.

'Ah mean, after all, honey . . . if they're good enough for the First Lady, they sure are good enough for this little gal.'

Zack carefully carried in the dresses, sheathed in their clear plastic covers, behind Claudia Wright. The butler knew they were expected and led the two with their precious cargo into the kitchen.

'Mrs. Griffith, she's makin' fudge.'

It would have been an incongruous caricature anywhere else but Tulsa City: a twenty-thousand-dollar-a-year salesgirl, a uniformed chauffeur with an armful of ladies' dresses, being led by a liveried black butler through a transplanted lush plantation in the parched wasteland of a Southwestern dust bowl to a grandmotherly millionairess in an electrified country kitchen who was making fudge. In Tulsa City, it was simply routine.

Maybeth Griffith looked up as the kitchen door swung open to announce the party. She was wearing a two-hundred-fifty-dollar cotton print dress, with a ruffled apron to protect its delicate purity; her wrists, earlobes, fingers and throat were covered with more than three-quarters of a million dollars in diamonds and she was, indeed, making chocolate fudge.

'There you are now, Claudia honey. Come in and sit. Your boy can jus' hang them dresses on the rack over there while we sit and chat a spell. Oh my, Claudia, don't you ever look smart!'

Claudia sat, assumed an Oklahoma accent reserved for customers like Maybeth, and answered. 'You look real cute yourself.'

'Cuppa coffee, Claudia? Y'all help yourself, y'hear. Ah'm up to my elbows in fudge.'

Claudia went to the twelve-burner range and poured herself a cup of steaming coffee—poured it into a Royal Worcester mug that had been specially commissioned by Lehson's for the Griffith house.

'Mah menfolks just love a big cuppa coffee, doncha know?'

And there they stayed, chatted and looked at the dresses. Maybeth oohed and aaahed as Claudia brought out each new creation. She made her fudge and gossiped and purchased more than forty-five hundred dollars' worth of Alice Short's line.

'Why honey, ah really wish ah could wear a dress more than once, but ah cain't. It's a pity, truly is, as ah do get to like some of them so much. Tell me truth, Claudia. Do y'all think maybe ah should buy two of the ones ah like best?'

'Now Maybeth, that would be downright extravagant and you know it.'

'Yes, ah guess it would. Ah mean, with the nation in such a state as it is, we all gotta do our share to conserve.'

The fudge had cooled and Maybeth sat with Claudia having a last mug of coffee. The two women reminisced.

'Ah swear, Claudia, those two zebras are the cutest things ever.'

The Griffith children had bought their mother a 'fun' gift from last year's Lehson's Christmas catalogue—a pair of zebras.

'But they did make a sight of the backyard. Mr. Griffith, he wanted to shoot them and put them in his trophy room, but ah wouldn't hear of it. We got enough heads stuffed now to open a zoo.'

'Isn't that the truth, Maybeth.'

'So we all just had the lawn removed in the back where the zebras were—y'all know ah call 'em Amos and Andy—and we laid down an acre of that synthetic turf. Them zebras are happy as bedbugs now and it does look ever so much better.'

Claudia glanced at the clock on the wall. It was almost one. If she were too late, even she couldn't browbeat poor Mr. Zeller.

'Well, Maybeth honey, I've really got to be running along. I've taken much too much of your time as it is.'

'Never a care, Claudia. It's always such a real treat when you stop by. Now you remember, all the dresses in that pretty shade of pink.'

'It's all written down.'

'Mr. Griffith does like me in pink, y'know?'

'Maybeth, that *is* your color and those dresses are really *you*.'

'Claudia, the way you do carry on.'

Mrs. Griffith rose and went over to where the fudge was cooling. Claudia called for Zack and they packed the samples.

'Claudia?'

'Yes, Maybeth?'

'Ah read where Miz Alice Short is in Tulsa City for your big do . . .'

'She arrives today.'

'Well now, I've cut some fudge—ah mean the grandchildren can't eat all this—and ah want you to take it back to her with mah compliments, y'hear?'

'Maybeth Griffith, if you aren't the nicest sort.'

'Just a little Oklahoma welcome to the lady who designs all these pretty clothes.'

Claudia accepted the brown paper bag, kissed Maybeth on the cheek and left. Her percentage commission on the two hours' work came to $285.83. And Mr. Zeller didn't want to let the dresses out of the store.

Aaron Seton sat pouting in front of Stella's desk. She was on the telephone with an out-of-town customer.

'Elizabeth, when I saw the skins, even before they were made up into the rug, I thought of your bathroom. This piece is too unique to be flaunted. Imagine dear, an Oriental rug—a Tabriz pattern, of course—in the finest mink skins you've ever seen. Of course it's extravagant, but in perfect taste. Just try to duplicate the sheer luxury —honestly, Liz, it's almost decadent. Think of getting out of your tub and stepping down on hundreds of silky mink pelts. All right, stepping out of your shower. It's the only one of its kind in the world and nobody will see it but you. Liz, that's aristocracy. Of course it's expensive. Singular things are always dear. One hundred thousand dollars. No, there's no tax. You live out of state. No, don't tell him. Surprise the dear man. We'll fly it in to Beverly Hills over the weekend. That's perfect. What a surprise when you get back from the Springs. Liz, I promise you'll take ten showers a day. 'Bye dear, see you soon.'

She replaced the receiver and rang the intercom.

'Eleanor. Have them put a "sold" sticker on the mink Tabriz and hold my calls, please.'

Seton's pout had given way to petulance. He took baths. He would have really appreciated such a rug. But he couldn't afford such outrageous prices. He wondered if Stella would consider trading some of his clothes for such a rug. No, no she wouldn't. The store didn't buy anywhere near that amount from him, hadn't in a few years. Still, it wasn't fair.

'Aaron dear, how nice of you to drop by.'

'You asked for me, didn't you?'

'I'm always asking for you, Aaron. How is your business, dear? We seem to be getting the same clientele over and over again for your things.'

'Well, they are unique, you know. Singular. Almost aristocratic.'

'Indeed they are. Are you enjoying your visit?'

'*No!* I've never been so insulted in my life as I was just moments ago in your men's department.'

'Someone in this store insulted you. . . . I find that impossible to believe.'

'Well, it's true.'

'Where exactly were you when this disgraceful incident occurred?'

'Like I said, in the men's department . . . actually, in the young men's department. I was just shopping around, you know, and honestly, some of the things there were to die over. This cheeky salesman—couldn't have been over twenty—came up and asked if he could help me. I asked him what there was in my size.'

'Yes?'

'And he looked straight at me and said, "Ties." Just like that! I've never . . . such cheek!'

Stella stifled a laugh and made a mental note to reprimand the salesman and give him a ten-dollar bonus for such adroit thinking.

'I shall attend to him myself. Now, is there anything else?'

'Well, it was much nicer when I got the award.'

'Aaron, that was six years ago. The established designers must make way for the newer talents.'

'Some established. . . . My business is off twenty per cent this year.'

'You'll get back in your stride, dear. Soon. Next season for certain. I think I know what the problem is, you've been working too hard.'

'Nothing comes easy, Miss Stella. It's a bitch.'

'Yes, you need a vacation. A nice, relaxed holiday so those creative juices can start flowing again. Oh, Aaron, I can't wait to see the next line. I'm excited already.'

'Honestly, Miss Stella, you do know how to inspire an artist. You are so right that it's to die over!'

'Don't wait for the weekend, leave now. Dash off before the inspiration leaves you.'

'Oh, I couldn't do that. Miss your beautiful gala ball. Why, I'd never think of that.'

'Dear Aaron, do think of it. It is best that you leave today.'

'Oh no, I see what you're up to. It's that disgusting spick and his understated drags. He's jealous.'

'It has nothing to do with anyone but me, Aaron. I think you know by now that I can't be influenced.'

'Oh, you know what I mean.'

'No, I'm afraid I don't. This little chat has taken a rather waspish turn. Yes, you'd better leave today.'

'Well, I won't.'

Her grey eyes turned steely. 'Yes you will. The ride is over, Aaron. I want you on the next plane to New York. The office will arrange everything for you.'

'But, but my clientele. Those women want me to help them.'

'Lehson's is more than able to accommodate the few customers who still wear your things.'

'I . . . Miss Stella . . . I don't believe my ears. You're throwing Seton out of Lehson's!'

'I wouldn't put it exactly that way, Aaron, but in essence you're correct.'

He began to tremble. The color beneath his makeup paled. He managed to rise.

'After all I've done for you. For the store. You can't do this to me. Please . . . Stella . . .'

'Aaron, stop being a bore and act your age. We shall buy your line next season and for as many seasons after as they continue to sell. But, and I must be brutally frank, dear, you are over the hill.'

'I'm going to faint.'

'Kindly do it somewhere else, Aaron. I don't want to be cruel, but you must start realizing what's happening. We're entering an era of good, understated, refined taste and you don't fit anymore. . . . Aaron! Oh, for God's sake.'

She pressed the intercom. 'Eleanor, call the nurse's office. Seton has fainted.'

Eugene and Mary Boardman hosted a small, select party at their substantial brick mansion just four blocks away from Mr. Abe's huge estate. Like the house and its occupants, the affair was proper, correct and dull.

As they dressed prior to receiving their guests, Boardman confided to his wife, 'Yes, I think tonight is the time to start consolidating my position.'

'That's nice, Eugene.'

'I now have enough to eliminate Culbertson and if everything works out as planned, Bill Bethel will not only be out of contention but out of the store.'

'Would you hook my pearls, dear?'

'Certainly. Yes, this will be a productive evening.'

Dinner was over and most of the fifty guests sat in the large living room listening to the Tulsa City Chamber Music Quintet play Scarlatti surprisingly well. It had been a big, heavy, rich meal and the music was well-suited to the leaden feeling that had enveloped the visitors to Boardman's house. When Stella slipped unobtrusively out of the room to make her phone call, Boardman discreetly followed. He stayed at a polite distance until she finished and then joined her.

'Mr. Abe?'

'Yes. Oh Eugene, it's difficult to believe, but it appears he's getting better.'

'He wouldn't miss your installation, Madame Ambassador.'

'You can be sweet, Eugene. Shall we rejoin the others?'

'In a moment, if you don't mind.'

'Not if you have something important.'

'I think it may be. . . . It's about Walter.'

'What has he done now?'

'Leonard Justin rang me from Los Angeles.'

'The coat man?'

'Yes. Until this year, he was Culbertson's biggest resource. I checked and found in 1962 we did a little over two hundred thousand with his things. The maintained markup was excellent. Good record, but for some reason Walter's cut him way down. Now Justin learns that we're returning close to a hundred fur-trimmed coats. Lehson's was the backbone of his operation and he's hurting very badly.'

'Sorry to hear that, but so far I can't see anything we can do. If Walter decides his buyers should pass, well . . .'

'Wait, I haven't come to the crunch yet. In '62 Justin paid off the Culbertson's house mortgage.'

'He did what?'

'Eighteen thousand dollars in cash. Seems that our Mr. Culbertson was getting a nine per cent kickback. Justin must be extremely frantic and scared to tell me that now.'

'This is unthinkable. What do you suggest we do regarding this Justin?'

'I did some checking. The return of the coats has some justification.'

'Then they stay returned, of course.'

'Naturally, but on the matter of the pay off, well, that's up to you, Stella.'

'Retailing is a lot like politics, Eugene. You do what you have to for power, but you never get caught. No matter how profitable an operation Walter runs for us, we cannot tolerate his getting caught.'

'And I'm not in the least satisfied with his flip explanation of the Moore fiasco. I've done some calculating and was astounded to discover what a substantial business we have done with Moore over the years. The future profits Lehson's has lost by his leaving are very large, not to mention the prestige.'

'I'll see him the first thing in the morning.'

'Good. He's definitely not Lehson caliber.'

'I couldn't agree more. Now may we rejoin the others?'

'Let's.'

When the musicale had finished and the guests started to take their leave, Boardman managed to be alone with Ceil Bordon for one last cognac.

'Enjoy your evening, Ceil?'

'A pleasant relaxation in a hectic week. Yes, I did.'

'Good. Any problems with delivering the Rhythmizers on time?'

'None at all.'

'Excellent. Sorry Bill and Tina couldn't make it tonight. He always manages to add luster to any party.'

'That he does. You've got a wonder in that boy, Gene.'

'Indeed we have . . . only, sometimes I worry about Bill.'

'About Bill? Nonsense.'

'No, I do. No matter what we say and do, this is still Tulsa City.

There's a big world out there and lately he's been seeming to eye its opportunities.'

'Bill Bethel would never leave Lehson's.' She paused, sipped the cognac and asked, 'Would he?'

'I doubt it, but we'd better come up with something pretty stimulating to sap those creative juices or he's going to get bored. That's the worst thing with a mind like his . . . if it's not kept active, it tends to wander. It would hurt the store terribly should he ever leave.'

'Well, I'll never steal him, so don't worry about that!'

'Not worrying, Ceil, merely musing. Your drink all right?'

'Fine, just fine,' she said, and her mind raced ahead to exactly how she could lure the restless Bill Bethel to her worldwide operation.

Heymano and Pepe occupied the finest suite in the hotel. Every luxury had been provided and their apartment was in the finest, subdued taste. They returned from Boardman's party and it was apparent that Heymano was edgy and nervous.

He entered the sitting room and slouched down on a sofa. Pepe undid his tie and poured himself a cognac from the bar.

'It was a disgusting party. Dull and stupid. Why did I ever let you talk me into coming here? Why?'

'Calm down, my angel. Pepe will soon fix things right again.'

'Fix things up! I'm bored. I want to go back to Paris.'

'You're letting that little Seton unnerve you, my angel. They did send him away, you know.'

'*Merde.*'

Pepe removed his dinner jacket and laid it carefully across the back of a chair. He placed his black velvet bow tie neatly on the shoulders of the jacket and unbuttoned his shirt—exposing a broad, muscular chest covered in black hair. Drink in hand, he walked over and sat on the arm of the sofa. He sipped from the glass, put it down and picked up Heymano's hand. Heymano refused to look at him and gazed straight ahead. Pepe smiled and placed Heymano's hand inside the open shirt. Heymano's mouth was twitching, but not from sex. Some inner nerve was acting uncontrolled. Heymano withdrew his hand and suffered a slight, involuntary shudder.

'My angel is depressed.'

No answer.

'Well, Pepe knows how to take him quickly back to the clouds.'

Pepe, the smile never leaving his face, got up and headed for the bathroom. Heymano was nervous and anxious.

'I wish to God you had never started me on that shit.'

Pepe, in the bathroom, was untaping something from beneath the basin. 'But you love it, my angel. And you love me. Don't you?'

'Love you? I detest you. I detest what you are turning me into. Why can't you leave me alone? Why, Pepe?'

'Ah, but we are intertwined. In business and in sex, my angel. We need each other. That is beautiful, no?'

'You are too strong for me. Too demanding. I am tired. I wish I was back in Madrid. Alone.'

'Ah, but I can never let you be alone, can I? You would get into trouble without Pepe. Like when I first found you . . .' He came out of the bathroom, the hypodermic filled and ready.

'Do not remind me of that! You swore you would never bring that up again. Oh, how I loathe you.'

Pepe studied the syringe professionally and crossed to a now-sweating Heymano. 'I must bring up unpleasantries, my angel. Imagine, you arrested for such a crime against nature. In the garden behind the Prado, of all places. Such indiscretion. You need Pepe to protect and take care of you. Here, my angel, your ticket to the clouds.'

Heymano scrunched himself up deep in the sofa.

'Go away. I do not need that shit. I am never going to use that again. Go away . . . please, Pepe.'

'Pepe knows what is best for you. Roll up your sleeve. Now!'

Meekly, the shivering, perspiring man obeyed. Pepe found a place on the vein that was not yet scarred and expertly plunged the needle into the pale arm.

'And as soon as the cloud starts to come, I am going to stick you with another needle. My big, fat hard needle. Stick you until you scream with pain while you float in ecstasy. That is what you want. That is what you always want. My poor, sick, stupid angel. I own you, Heymano. Own your body, soul and business.' The empty needle was withdrawn. 'Now take off your clothes, pig. It is my turn to abuse you!'

As Heymano slowly undressed, and as the warm euphoric drug coursed through his body, he murmured, 'Oh, Pepe, to think that you were the policeman.'

Down the hall from the Heymano suite, Alice Short was getting ready for bed. She was burning mad over the discovery on arriving at Lehson's that her samples were gone. That idiot Zeller had tried to explain, but what explanation would hold water when the store was packed with customers and not one Short dress was represented. Inefficiency and stupidity. What were all the things doing down in the marking room when the customers were up on the floor? How dare they remove original samples from the selling area and take them out to some hick in the suburbs? The lunacy of the situation was unfathomable to Alice. Imagine. The customer even had the audacity to send her a brown paper bag full of sticky chocolate fudge. Tulsa City was something else.

Alice creamed her face and made ready for bed. Tomorrow she'd talk to Stella and that Zeller's ass would be in the chopper. She turned off the bathroom light and walked into the bedroom, passing a full-length mirror on the way. 'You know,' she mused to herself, 'I am a little runt, aren't I?' and made her way to the bed.

The bag of fudge was sitting on the night table. 'I shouldn't. Put on weight like a balloon. Oh hell, one little piece can't hurt me.' Alice took out a square of fudge. 'God, it looks good,' she said, and popped it into her mouth. As she bit down, there was a loud crunching noise. 'Oh God, I've broken my bridge!' She spat out the candy along with the dislodged molar, then noticed a foreign object in the lump of moist candy. She picked it up and took out the reason for her cracked denture.

'Sweet Jesus! Isn't this typical of Tulsa City?'

She held a fudge-covered diamond solitaire weighing more than twenty karats.

THURSDAY, OCTOBER 13

Alice Short was hopping mad.

'The wife of the President of the United States can come to me for her clothes, but some nouveau riche Oklahoma matron gets the collection—the entire collection—driven out for her inspection! It is totally unfathomable, Stella, and I'm sorry but I just won't stand for it.'

'I'm afraid I have to agree with you, Alice. I'm terribly sorry and don't know what to say.'

'To begin with, you'd better get rid of Zeller.' She took the diamond ring from her purse and tossed it in front of Stella. 'And after that, return this bauble to your Mrs. Griffith.'

Stella picked up the solitaire. 'What is this?'

'As incredulous as it sounds, that little trinket was inside some fudge she'd baked for me. Broke my goddamn teeth on it.'

'That,' said Stella, smiling, 'is something. Even for Lehson's.'

'The ring is too big for me anyway, though for a moment I sure was tempted to keep it.'

'Mrs. Griffith will be delighted to have it returned.'

'I doubt if the lady has even missed it. Now Stella, about Zeller? Do you know what he said to me when I let him have it? That little twit had the nerve to tell me, "Miss Short, this is my department and I shall run it my own way. And, please try to remember that you're the seller and I'm the buyer."'

'That was both uncalled for and rude. Again, I'm terribly sorry.'

Alice relaxed now that the situation was completely under her control.

'Stella, you and I have been friends for more years now than I like to count and I've seen many buyers come and go for many reasons, but Gene Zeller is the weakest, most ineffective buyer you've ever had. Let's put it all out on the table, Stella. As you must know, the Alice Short volume has increased every year in each of the stores we sell throughout the country. But, since this young man has been buying for Lehson's, our business with the store has decreased. I'm sorry, Stella, but I'm afraid I must now reassess our position on confining the collection exclusively to Lehson's.'

'That is unthinkable. We've been friends as well as business associates for too long a time to let our relationship degenerate over something like this. I'd get rid of Gene Zeller in a minute, if I only had someone here who was equipped to take his place.'

'What about Mildred Moss?'

'She's with Sylvia's in San Francisco, isn't she?'

'Yes, and doing a sensational job. Mildred understands my clothes and your kind of customers. On top of that, she's getting a divorce; she's a lady who would fit beautifully into the Lehson family.'

'Alice, I can't thank you enough.'

Bill Bethel was squiring Ceil Bordon through the store.

'Your demonstrators are first rate, Ceil. Business with your line is up thirty-four per cent so far this season.'

'The Bordon cosmetic business is on the edge of becoming a dynasty, Bill.'

'It will be difficult to top this season, but knowing you, it will happen.'

'Is it true that Stella sent Seton packing, to change the subject?'

'Rumor has it that's what happened.'

'Good riddance. Say, Quentin gave me an idea that could revolutionize the industry.'

'Kimball? What was it?'

'He confided to me that the secret of his beautiful skin was his taking two high colonics a day, with fat-free milk.'

Bill laughed and said, 'Don't you think that's more wishful thinking on his part than anything else?'

'Of course it is, but it gave me an idea. The basis of my formulations is milk—and they do work from a cosmetic viewpoint—but cosmetics are for the outside. I want to come up with something that can be used internally. It'll change the whole market and give my firm the impetus to move into number one place.'

'Methinks you are testing me, Ceil.'

'Think anything you like, Bill. I need a zinger for the spring line and am willing to pay for the man who can give it to me. Interested?'

'Always interested, Ceil. Money, when it is coupled with a position that is exciting, makes an ideal pacifier.'

'I don't have to tell you that there is more promotional money in the cosmetic industry than any other segment of the economy ... Detroit included. Let me tell you how it really is, Bill. Beauty is built on bullshit and we pay for the very best.'

'Are you indicating that I've gone as far as I can go here?'

'You figure that out.'

'Gossip has it that our Miss Stella is up for an important governmental position. That could leave the presidency of the store up for grabs.'

'Big deal. What's Tulsa City compared to the whole world?'

'Quite a bit, actually. But don't let me interrupt.'

'How would you squeeze out the bullshit and turn it into money for me? And no hedging.'

'You are nothing if not direct. Indelicate, perhaps, but candid. Okay, Ceil, this is what I'd do. . . . The trend is changing and I feel you know it is. The old concept in cosmetology of covering women's faces with creams and paints is passing. Hell, Ceil, you started the new trend with your milk bath. Today it's the fresh, the clean, bringing out what is natural instead of covering up. Okay, go one step further . . . create a line of youth-giving products all derived from milk. One basic ingredient, one marketable entity that would capture the imagination and the pocketbook. Call it . . . let's see . . . yes! Ceil Bordon's Oil of Milk—just catchy enough to make it memorable. Lotions, essences . . . the lot.'

'Sounds like it might work when you say it.'

'Of course it will work. Away with animal extracts, chemicals and laboratory concoctions. Milk. The essence of youth and the elixir of life. It can't miss and you know it. Well, how does it sound?'

'It sounds like a starting salary of one hundred and fifty thousand dollars a year plus an unlimited expense account.'

'Not bad for openers. What about stock options?'

'Naturally.'

'Madame Bordon, you have just bought yourself the best damned bullshit artist in the entire cosmetic industry.'

Ceil started to laugh, laugh loudly.

'What's so funny?'

'Just thinking of Stella when she finds out I've stolen you away. She'll crap custard!'

'Not custard, Ceil, unless it's made from Bordon's essence of milk.'

There was a ritual—a clock-setting routine that had been going on for years at Lehson's. Every weekday, at exactly high noon, a little old lady walked onto the couture floor and entered the Ladies Powder Room. She was neatly but shabbily dressed and had never been known to speak to anyone, let alone purchase anything. It seems that she had been using the Lehson toilets on this floor forever and no one questioned her right or her routine. Nobody knew her name or who she was, but she had become a fixture and as such was respected.

On this particular Thursday, as on every other day for years, she walked in the rest room as the clock in the Lehson tower chimed twelve. Sam Simmonds had been floor manager of the couture floor as long as she had been using the facilities and automatically checked his wristwatch as she went through the bathroom door. Tall, grey-haired, distinguished Mr. Sam continued his usual activities. At four minutes after twelve, the little old lady emerged. This time she altered her pattern and approached Mr. Sam.

'Sir, I've been meaning to speak to you for some time.'

'Yes, madame?'

'The quality of your tissue simply isn't up to the standards one has come to expect from Lehson's. Good day.'

That afternoon, the toilet tissue in every rest room was changed.

Ceil Bordon spent the afternoon stimulating sales activity in the canvas cabanas erected around the main floor from which her cosmetics were promoted. Ceil effusively preached the gospel of eternal beauty. She was glowing from the triumph of snatching Bill Bethel away from Lehson's and her busy mind was already concocting formulas that would startle and upset the entire industry.

Her talk, in the privacy of one cloistered cabana, was to Lady Vidal and it was evangelical. The peroxided peeress sat mesmerized, her small cigar unlit, as Ceil waxed eloquent over the joys of beauty and the relative inexpensiveness of staying attractive. Lady Vidal, after ordering a complete outfit of all the Bordon preparations, waltzed dreamily out of the little tent, her forearms raised, the arms entwined much like a footballer throwing a block. Lady Vidal was doing her breast exercises as she strolled unperturbed through the astounded Lehson customers.

Walter Culbertson didn't give a damn. Let the old broad preach, threaten and expound her old-fashioned concept of a family store and its responsibilities to the community, its customers, and its suppliers. Ashes from the cigarette dangling from his mouth fell unflicked onto his suit; his wad of gum cracked.

'Mr. Culbertson, must you always be so patently oral?'

He removed the cigarette and tossed it contemptuously into Stella's ashtray. His animal instinct told him after the first two minutes that this was it. He'd never get her chair, no matter how good his sales figures or high his margin of profit. Like any basic creature, he didn't fret. If she fired him, which she couldn't do and maintain his business, big deal. The largest stores would grab him like a drowning man clutching at a life preserver. Still, it would be too bad. This was the best job he'd had. All the prestige of Lehson's was behind him as he milked the lousy manufacturers dry of every penny and then came back to pick the bones. In a big city department store, everyone was ruthless. At Lehson's, Walter Culbertson was unique.

'Walter, I'm appalled by your tactics and nearly more shaken by the way you smugly justify them. You force me to act in a way that I'd rather not. . . . There will be a monthly review of your transactions, for the time being, and I strongly warn you not to pursue profits at the expense of store policy.'

Stella knew she couldn't fire him. He was the backbone of Lehson's earnings. This forced accountability should hopefully keep Culbertson from tarnishing the Lehson image, while keeping his profits high as they were. Stella hated the way he operated, but loved the results.

'Okay, Miss Stella, I'll do as you wish.'

'Good day, Walter.'

It was an hour later in New York City, four in the afternoon. The little French restaurant in the East Sixties was deserted, except for Ann Carter and Josh Frankel. She had flown in that morning, taken care of the store business and was due to return to Tulsa City the next morning. Josh had stolen away on the pretext of meeting with a new coat and suit designer. They held hands and their eyes saw only each other.

A bottle of Montrachet idled in a silver bucket. The two crystal tulip glasses stood half-filled. It was all so romantic, so special. They didn't even notice the bartender reading *Playboy*.

'It might have been better, you know, if you hadn't come in this week.'

'I just couldn't stay away. How's everything at home?'

'Rotten. As long as there was no one else, my wife looked pretty good to me. I work hard and when I get home, it's pretty routine. She nags a lot, but I never minded. The kids are great, but down deep I know they'll grow up confused. Still, I overlooked. How about you?'

'Like you, Josh, my job takes up most of my time. I've got my father. Oh, Josh, you would love him. What a fine man. Really. A rare person. He advised me to come back.'

'Troublemaker.'

'Philosopher and newspaperman.'

'Dangerous combo, but I guess I'll like him anyway. Your mom?'

'Died. Years ago. Just Dad and I.'

'And Joshua. Don't forget Joshua.'

She held his hand a little tighter. It felt right. Marvelous.

'And Joshua. You know, darling, you have about the sexiest, most beautiful name I've ever heard.'

'All us biblical cats are super groovy.'

'My father told me something once, and I feel it applies to us in this time. . . . He said that what we call reality is the myth that modern man worships. He feels that ancient man was closer to the real truth of magic. He believes that dreams are the only reality.'

'Pretty heavy thinking. I'll have to run that through a few times.'

'He was talking to me about "things" and how we spend our life in pursuit of material objects. My whole life has been spent buying and selling the objects of attraction to other women. I'm a little cynical.'

'Ann. I can tell you this. You're a dream and that's one reality I can buy. Will you marry me?'

'No.'

'Will you be my mistress?'

'Yes, yes . . .'

'I've decided to accept the Lehson offer.'

'Oh, Josh!'

'You decided me. I'll get a divorce. . . . It's all pretty unfair to my wife, you know, I've turned her into an object, I'm afraid. She's young enough to try again and I'll be able to take care of her and the kids financially now.'

'Give her everything. I make a pretty good salary.'

'I've been found out. A gigolo from South Philadelphia.'

'No, I mean it.'

'I'll sort things out. Don't worry. After the divorce, I'm going to ask you to marry me again, not that it will make any difference.'

'All you biblical types are always so anxious to make honest women of their strumpets.'

'Strumpets? What an old-fashioned word for such a swinging kid.'

'Didn't you know, sir, I'm just an old-fashioned girl. Let's go to my hotel and make love.'

In Tulsa City, there was no formal party on Thursday. A night's respite would give everyone a chance to relax before the rigors of the last two days of the Mediterranean gala began.

Bill Bethel had phoned his wife that he wouldn't be home for dinner, and while she knew his time was more often than not spent in entertaining and this was the most entertaining time of the year, she slammed the receiver down in a jealous rage. Bill shrugged and turned back to Ceil. They were seated in her suite at the Tulsa City Royal, sipping Chivas Regal and milk. It was a little after seven.

'Ceil, when I finish this I'm afraid I've got to run. The little woman is throwing a fit and if I don't get home soon, she might burn down the house.'

'She's an incredibly beautiful woman, Bill, but unstable. She might have a problem fitting into your new life in New York.'

'Well, dear, let me worry about that. She's a fabulous model—just watch her on Saturday night—and I think Manhattan just might be the stimulus she needs.'

'Fair enough. Just thought I'd comment.'

'No offense taken, we have to be honest with each other.'

'Check. The con's for the customers.'

'Ceil, I think I've hit on the one new item we need to really turn the industry on its ass.'

'We've been working together for three hours. What took you so long?'

'No, Ceil, serious. Your remark about getting inside for beauty.

I've been thinking . . . what about a flavored douche? From a milk base, of course.'

She sat up. 'A flavored douche? You've got to be putting me on!'

'Not at all. It sounds disgusting when you say it that way, but let me romance it a little. A garden . . . a beautiful garden with all its freshness, its wondrous scents, perfumes and delicious tastes. Nature's way to cleanliness, to purity, to beauty, youth and life.'

'*Veyizmir*. It could work. Wouldn't that be something! Christ, Bill, you are really! . . . Wait, wait a minute . . . how about four flavors. Let's give them a little pizazz . . . can you market, say . . . Sparkling Champagne? Or Fruit Ambrosia? Lime Rickey . . .?'

'Wow, baby, what a team we make. How about this one, just for laughs . . . Ceil Bordon's latest flavored douche for the he-man in your life—Planter's Punch!'

'I like it! Honest to God, I really like it!!'

Bill gave Ceil a brotherly kiss and left her to dream up sanitary cleansers to tempt the vaginal taste buds. He was walking down the hall toward the elevator when he was stopped by Heymano, just putting the key into the lock of his rooms.

'Señor Bethel, do come in for a drink. Please?'

Bill wanted to get home and this guy looked stoned, but he couldn't insult the star of Lehson's gala.

'Nice of you to ask, Mano. Don't mind if I do.'

'It is all quite exciting, a simple man from Spain and all this attention, this great event. I am much overwhelmed.'

Bill's fractured arm was beginning to ache under the light cast and he wished he could get home and just go to bed. Instead, he accepted the drink Heymano poured and noticed that the Spaniard's hands were trembling somewhat. He signaled a small toast to him.

'*Salud*.'

'*Gracias*, Señor Bill.'

Bill took a drink. Heymano drained his glass in one pull and refilled it again. Yes, he was getting quite smashed. Haymano sat down on the Chesterfield next to Bill and casually put his arm across the back of the settee, where it promptly fell on Bill's shoulder. Bill moved away.

'Sorry, old man, this fracture seems to be acting up.'

Mano felt the frenzy rise up in him. The frustration of the past few days. The anguish over Pepe. The constant good behavior towards the idiotic women who crowded him all the time. Enough, he felt. He must have some release from all the tension. He plopped his hand in Bill's lap and genuinely startled him. Bill got up.

'Look, Mano, please don't take any offense, but it's simply not my scene.'

Heymano's head wobbled on his neck. He was having a difficult time focusing his eyes and a small trickle of saliva started to run from his lips.

'I am your guest, Señor Bill. It would make me happy to make you happy.'

Bill Bethel was worried. He couldn't hit the man. He wasn't ready to accommodate him. Why couldn't he just be home in bed? He hoped these kinds of problems were minimal in the cosmetic industry, but doubted it.

'Look, Mano, why don't I ring up some chaps who don't have broken arms?'

'No. It is you I must have. Now.'

He made a drunken lunge toward Bill, who stepped aside, and the designer fell forward spread-eagled on the carpet.

'Then I'd better be going. We all have a big day tomorrow.'

Heymano propped himself up on one elbow and started to rise.

'Let Heymano make love to you. He is quite good. He will make you feel beautiful.'

'Oh, God. Look, Mano, I'm leaving and you'd better go to bed.'

Heymano was up, unsteady but with purpose. He went for Bill.

'Hey, fella, cut that out!'

'No.'

The drunken Heymano chased a worried Bill Bethel around the furniture, across the rug, behind the bar, into the bedroom, out of the bedroom, back again around the sofa. All the while, Bill used his plastered arm to fend the amorous Iberian off. Both were sweating profusely. Finally, Heymano made a lunge for Bill and managed to barely grasp him around the ankles. Bill fell, trying to keep his bad arm from getting the impact.

'Aha, I have you. No one play hard to get with Heymano.'

Bill was almost resigned to letting the man do what he had to do, getting the whole thing over with and getting out, when the door opened and Pepe came in. His face went dark and he stared down at the two of them on the floor. Heymano didn't seem to notice him and was trying with heavy fingers to unzip Bill's trousers. Bill merely looked up, shrugged nervously and said, 'I just came in for a night-cap, honest.'

'I apologize for my drunken friend. Here, let me help you up.' Pepe went over and assisted Bill, while a sotted Heymano sat on the carpet and started to weep.

'Thanks, old sport. Not my scene, you know.'

'Please, Señor Bethel. It is we who must ask your excuse.' He led Bill to the door and let him out. Pepe shut the door, stood for a moment and then turned slowly toward the man on the floor, who was babbling now.

'Pig! You stupid little pig! I leave you alone for half an hour and you embarrass me this despicable way. I'm going to thrash you so you remember good.' He started to remove his wide leather belt. Heymano looked up and the fear in his eyes was quickly replaced by rage.

'No! No more from you.' He was up like a shot. 'I do what I want. I am the star. I am the creator. It is I who am being honored,' and before Pepe could stop him, he was out of the door and running down the hall. Pepe, his belt still half hanging from his trousers, started after him, but by the time he made it to the elevators, they had closed and Heymano was on his way down to the lobby.

The streets of downtown Tulsa City were practically deserted as he raced down the block and away from the hotel. He was looking, searching for someone who could release the turmoil that now over-powered him. With the radarlike instincts of a wanderer who has ferreted out all those places of illicit sex in cities around the world, Heymano made his way to the bus depot. It was quiet and the few people who were sitting idly about were all waiting for buses. He shook his head to try and clear away the drink and made his way to the men's room. He opened the door and stood against the wall. Yes, this was familiar. The dull tiled walls, the antiseptic stink that never quite disguises the thick rancid smell of human refuse. No one was occupying the toilets. No one was even washing their hands. At the urinals, a huge black laborer was emptying his bladder. He didn't turn to see Heymano. The drunken eyes grew wide with anticipation as he walked over to the urinal next to the black and blatantly stared down at the other man's organ. It was enormous. The black man finished, gave it a shake and turned to Heymano.

'See somethin' ya like?' he asked.

Heymano shuddered with delight and dropped to his knees. He was oblivious to everything as he greedily accepted the big man's gift. Oblivious even when the door to the rest room opened and two uniformed Tulsa City policemen entered and stared disgustedly before marching up to arrest the two men.

'Mr. Preston, from New York, Miss Stella.'

Stella put down the morning paper and accepted the telephone from her maid.

'Thank you, Martha. Good morning Frank.'

'Sorry to break in on your breakfast, but I just got word the President wants to see me first thing tomorrow morning.'

'Is that good or bad for Oklahoma ladies?'

'I'd say damned good. Amos reads it the same way, too. He feels it's merely a question of which country you'll be given.'

'I'll be perfectly candid, Frank . . . I'm terribly nervous. You know how much this means to me and I don't want anything to stand in the way of the appointment, but you do appreciate that it must be an important nation.'

'The White House knows that.'

'And there won't be any trouble?'

'None. Amos feels it's a toss-up between Spain and Italy, but not to exclude Portugal.'

'I prefer Italy, but any one of the three . . .'

'I know, Stella. In any event, we'll find out tomorrow. The President of the United States hasn't asked me to Washington to discuss hemlines.'

'If he should, inform him they're still above the knee.'

'Who's getting the nod for your chair, if I may be so bold to ask?'

'The field is narrowing, Frank. I haven't made any decision yet, but Culbertson is definitely out. Tell me truthfully, Frank, would you like the job?'

'Not on your tintype. I'm a big city man and New York suits me just fine. I'll accept a raise in salary though.'

'When the ambassadorship is announced, consider yourself ten thousand a year richer.'

'You're a considerate boss lady, boss lady. Anything else?'

'No, not that I can think of.'

'I'll call you the minute I leave the President.'

'Thanks, and be sure to give him my best regards and deep appreciation.'

'You've earned it, Stella. He's only doing what's right. Until tomorrow then.'

'Until tomorrow.'

Stella allowed herself a contented stretch, pushed the half-eaten breakfast away and left the table. Back in her bedroom, she let her eyes wander over the twelve Chagall paintings that ringed the room. The bold, Byzantine colors—the broad, yet sensitive strokes of black, like stained-glass paning—what a comfort and pleasure this room was to her. She felt better, more content, surer than she had in years.

Tonight, after the final party before the gala ball tomorrow, she must select a particularly virile young man to cap the evening. Yes, Italy would be ideal. The power of the past, the delight of Roman life. And those superb young Italian men, so willing, so accommodating. If they pleased her so as a mere store owner, think of the favors they'd bestow on the person of a United States ambassador.

Feeling warmly about the many fine things she anticipated during the next twenty-four hours, Stella dialed her father's residence and asked for Dr. Gregg, who was now living in Mr. Abe's home around the clock.

'Good morning, doctor.'

'And to you.'

'How is he?'

'Mr. Lehson, I'm pleased to report, has more than stabilized. Improvement is noticeable in all the tests.'

'I can't get over it, it's all so wonderful.'

'My cautious optimism seems to be justified.'

'How can we ever thank you, doctor?'

'Well, it's not over yet. He'll need nurses and the oxygen must continue, but . . . well, the worst has passed.'

'Thank God . . . and thank you.'

'Have a good day. We'll speak later.'

'Yes, yes we will.'

Bill Bethel was sleeping troubled and fitfully. He unconsciously fought off the hangover that must accompany awakening. His wife,

Tina, shoved a perfectly manicured finger into his shoulder and rasped, 'The phone. For God's sake, wake up and answer the god-damn phone. Bill. *Bill!*' Again, she grated, 'Bill! Some wop's on the phone for you and he won't get off until you talk to him, fer Christ's sake. . . . *Bill!*'

The finger again into the aching shoulder. It was useless to fight any longer. Bill managed to pry his lids open and stared up at her with red-veined eyes.

'Why don't you bug off. I'm dying.'

'The phone. The dago on the phone. Jeez, can't you leave that lousy store behind you for just one morning. It's only six-forty-five Bill!'

'I'm coming.' As he shifted out of bed, he felt a sharp pang of pain in his arm. 'Shit!' For a moment he thought it would have been better to let Mano blow him and get it over with. Even that little fairy was preferable to Tina's whine in the morning. Sitting on the side of the rumpled bed, he took the phone from her. His mouth felt and tasted like dry, used toilet paper.

'Bethel here.'

'Señor, it is Pepe. We are in big trouble.'

He thought, 'Christ, he's killed him because of me. I'll be named correspondent in a homosexual murder case. Good-bye, Ceil Bordon.'

'What is it, Pepe?'

'The police. They have arrested Heymano.'

'Oh God. What happened?' He was wide awake now.

'I do not know. They will tell me nothing. They allow him one telephone call and he call me. He is crazy with fear. I can do nothing. You, señor, must do something or all will be ruined.'

'Okay, I'm counting on you to remain calm. They'll be holding Mano at Central Division. I'm on my way over there now. Don't worry and don't talk to anyone. Stay in the hotel and I'll come and get you. *Comprende?*'

'Si, señor Bethel. I do what you say. Only hurry. I know what Mano is like when something like this happens.'

Eugene Boardman's breakfast never varied. One three-minute egg, one slice of dry toast, Sanka with fat-free milk. No sugar. His mousy wife sat opposite him when he took his morning meal and just watched. She would eat later. This was their time together.

Boardman was reading the *Wall Street Journal* and, between checking the closing prices, he listened to his wife.

'Dale wrote us from school and he feels Wharton is best for graduate work. Do you know anyone there?'

'Hmmm? Oh yes, fine institution. Good choice. I'll get on to Dr. Hauser and check into it. What are you wearing to Miss Stella's this evening?'

'The new Alice Short.'

'Which one?'

'The mauve.'

'Like the President's wife has?'

'Same style, but hers is blue.'

'Fine. And the pearls. Go well with mauve. Listen to this, "Federated posted record gains in their third quarter". Aggressive. Very aggressive.'

'How soon after Miss Stella's appointment do you think she'll announce your taking over?'

'Within a week, I imagine.' He put down the paper. 'I've waited a long time for this, Mary. I'm going to initiate some strong, rigid controls at the store and then you watch those profits soar. We'll give Federated a run for their money, I promise you.'

'It's a fine store, Lehson's, but they are a little folksy for this day and age.'

'Stella runs it like a family, which makes for a nice environment, but can wreck hell with the profit picture. But what a base to build from! The accumulated prestige that's been built up will carry through for at least fifteen years. By that time I'll have built it into a chain that will dominate the entire Southwest. Why Mary, I'll have Neiman-Marcus taking a back seat to us before I'm through.'

'As indeed they should. They're getting a little too uppity for their own good.'

'Yes, ma'am, it should be clear sailing from here on in.'

'I'm glad about Culbertson.'

'Yes, so am I. I'm not a vindictive man, but he really got my dander up. Eliminating him was the best thing I ever did for the store.'

'And Bill will be wonderful in New York. He'll make a fortune.'

'Yes, it's all worked out very well, hasn't it? My goodness, look at the time. Must dash now.'

'Call me later.'

'Will do.'

'Have a good day, dear.'

'The best, Mary. See you later.'

Lyla's breakfast with Belle and Sal took place in their rooms at the Tulsa City Royal and she was bubbling over with good cheer.

'My, but they do turn out an elegant egg benedict here. More coffee, Belle?'

'God, Lyla, I'm stuffed.'

'Sal?'

'Yeah, why not.'

'There. Oh Sal, how can I ever thank you for what you've done? I saw my whole life going down the drain.'

'Forget it. What are friends for?'

'Yes, but that wasn't a small favor. I do appreciate it. Well, children, I've got to punch a time clock. Thanks for the feed. Belle, will I see you later in the day?'

'Sure thing, hon. After lunch.'

'Good. Bye then.'

'See ya in the moving pictures, Lyla.'

'Sal! That's not very funny.'

'Hey, I was just kiddin'. Ain't you got no sense of humor?'

'Sorry. I'm still a trifle edgy. I guess. Good-bye again.'

Lyla left, kissing them both on the cheek. Belle wiped up the last remnant of egg with a bit of toast.

'Ummm. That is good. Say Sal, did you give the negatives back to Lyla?'

'Hell no.'

'You destroyed them, didn't you?'

'You crazy?'

'Sal, you promised.'

'Hey, baby, stop worrying.'

'Sal, Lyla is my best friend. I don't want any monkey business.'

His eyes narrowed and took on a dangerous cast.

'Belle, forget it. I keep the pictures. We paid plenty for them.'

'Oh Sal, you wouldn't do anything. Would you?'

'We've decided to investigate the retail business, that's all.'

'Sal!'

'Shut up, baby. Business is business.'

*

'All right, Charley, what do we have to do?'

Bill Bethel, his arm aching and his head splitting, sat across from District Attorney Charles Moran Hayes. Hayes, who had recurring visions of presiding at the governor's mansion, was cool and composed.

'Nothing, Bill. Nothing at all. The law will take its course.'

'Oh, for Christ's sake, Charley. No one was hurt. The poor slob was drunk.'

'Homosexual fellatio carries twenty years to life in this state. Drunkenness is a misdemeanor.'

'I haven't got time to beat around the bush with you. We have to get him off. Fast. The store has a fortune tied up in him.'

'Your dilemma is financial. Mine is legal. No deal. Sorry, Bill, we need a nice juicy case like this. The electorate votes next month.'

'Do you honestly think a blow job will push you into the capitol?'

'My personal feelings have nothing to do with this. It's open and shut. My hands are tied and my duty is clearly defined.'

'You're a pompous prig, Charley.'

'Careful, Bethel.'

'No, buster. I won't be careful. I've got too much at stake myself in this mess to pussyfoot around.'

'You're not threatening me, are you?'

'No, I'm telling you. Now listen very carefully, 'cause I'm not repeating myself. Lehson's department store is the largest advertiser in the state. As such, it has a certain amount of influence in the editorial content of the daily newspapers. We have never, I repeat, never used any of that influence. But we will now. Believe me, Charley boy, we'll pull out all the stops. Destroying the economic growth and prestige of the entire state over a foreign guest who happens to be very, very emotionally disturbed. Miss Stella and Frank Preston have both ears of the President and I can guarantee you that he won't take this well. Not at all. Also, Lehson's political contributions to your party, as well as the opposition, are as large and as consistent as the oil interests, and in politics the only thing that talks to the bosses is money. That all adds up to your not only dropping the entire matter, but releasing Señor Heymano with a personal apology. Have I made myself perfectly and completely clear?'

'Hey, Bill, I didn't realize the fellow was emotionally ill. Why kid, that makes all the difference in the world. Hell, I thought he was just some wetback queer compromising an innocent citizen.'

'Then I assume it's all right for me to take our guest back to his hotel?'

'Hell, I'm going with you down to his cell. We can't have our distinguished visitors getting the wrong idea about our fair city, can we?'

'No we can't, governor. Shall I follow you?'

The eve of the gala ball was the year's last private party held by the store. As such, it was the most exclusive and lavish function. The site was Stella's home, which had been transformed into a replica of the Grand Ballroom of Monte Carlo's Hotel de Paris. No detail or expense was spared. The food, the wine, the entertainment was the choicest available. All three Lehson sisters were acting as cohostesses. It would be the most opulent social function the entire Southwest would witness this year—a secluded party for one hundred given by a store for no other purpose than its own self-advertisement and prestige. The women fortunate to be included would all wear their second finest gowns—the best being saved for tomorrow's gala.

Eugene Boardman, secure in his knowledge that all competition for the presidency of Lehson's was out of the running, watched the unaware junior vice-presidents as they tested each other, feisting for position in the impending reorganization. His smile was benevolent, as befitted a corporate vizier. He was positively gallant to one and all as he radiated confidence and unusual charm. Mary Boardman, sharing the secret of their future, came out of her social shell and was a surprising delight to everyone.

Heymano, subdued and visibly shaken, proved the ideal guest. He was never away from Pepe's side and for once retired to allow Pepe the spotlight. Pepe was up to the limelight. He remarked to Stella and Lyla, 'It is time to branch out, we believe. We have decided that I shall personally design a line of superb men's apparel to be introduced for the next fall season. Yes?'

'Pepe dear,' replied Stella, 'I insist that Lehson's be the very first to view the collection.'

'But of course!'

'And it will be under the Heymano label, won't it?' asked Lyla.

'Ah, but naturally.' He was not as secure as he thought.

'Good. I agree with Stella, it will be perfect for the store,' added Lyla.

Stella turned to Mano. 'And as long as we're discussing new ideas, would you mind if I threw one out to you?'

'I would be honored.'

'I've been giving a great deal of serious thought to the immediate future of fashion and ... well, call it a hunch or instinct, but I'm confident that a new trend is about to emerge.'

He became suddenly interested. For a retailer as important as Stella Lehson to divulge her inner thoughts about what would sell next year was a distinct honor. This great designer was also impressed by the size of the orders the store wrote. 'Please, Miss Stella, continue.'

Lyla interrupted, 'Yes, Stella, do.'

'Lyla, I'm particularly interested in your evaluation of my idea ... mind you, it's just a little suggestion.'

'We're all waiting.'

'Well, I believe that freedom in fashion is the next evolution. Freedom and common sense. I don't know exactly what it will be, but in shape it could be a translation of work clothes.'

'Work clothes?' said a surprised Mano.

Lyla volunteered, 'Why not? That cashmere overall you wore off the plane would look smashing on the right woman!'

'Exactly!' agreed Stella, remembering everything Gari Reichman said to her last week. 'And who better than Heymano to usher in the age of the ... of the naturals?'

'Naturals? I do not completely understand ...'

Lyla was caught up in a sense that Stella had hit on something really big. 'Leathers! Natural fabrics ... cottons ... silks ... wool. Oh Stell, this is a sensational concept!'

'Ah ha ... I see, the naturals. It is better than interesting, but how can I with my great expense of manufacture, startle the world with these naturals. They have never been out of the collections of the couture, you know?'

'Not the way I envisage it. . . . From you, Mano, to really capture the imagination of the beautiful people we must have something so new, yet so readily accepted that everyone will wonder why they hadn't thought of it.'

'I'm afraid I still do not see.'

'Well, I can't design your line for you, but how about a ball gown in workman's blue denim?'

'A blue denim gown?' Lyla was a little taken aback.

Mano thought for a second and then his eyes lit up. 'Why not . . . studded with thousands of tiny rivets . . . like the cowboys on Miss Edna's ranch wore. The designs . . . the execution could be fantastic. In fact, a whole collection emerging from the natural American West. Oh, Miss Stella! It is a wonderful idea! Fantastic!'

Lyla agreed with his enthusiasm.

So did Mano. 'It is ideal also for my men's collection. It is, how do you say it in Las Vegas . . . a natural!'

Lyla found Belle and Sal talking with C.Z.

'Belle, that sister of mine never ceases to amaze me. She really is something.'

'What's she done now?'

'Can't tell you, but Heymano will be bigger than ever next year. If he goes public, there's the stock to buy.'

Sal was more than a little bored with all this chic conversation that he could not understand. He reverted to cryptic directness. 'Naw, Lyla, we gonna buy stock in you. You we understand.'

A sliver of ice went through Lyla. Sal's new-found innuendoes since the Berns episode were definitely disturbing, but she dismissed it—the consequences were too frightening to consider.

C.Z. brought her back to the party with his own observation. 'I, for one, am investing heavily in the stock of Beefeater's Gin. It is both a civilized opiate and accessible. I'm selling vermouth short.'

'Who's talking about me?' piped up Alice Short as she and Ceil Bordon joined them.

Across the room Lady Vidal was discussing horseflesh with Edna and Della.

'Pure-blooded Arabians are too damned temperamental for my taste. His lordship introduced the Morgan strain into 'em many years ago, which produced a new ease in their natures.'

'Interesting, but I don't seem to find any trouble with mine.'

'It's different in Britain, though. Our race courses are hilly and uneven, as you know. Much freer running than in France or the States.'

Della tried to change the subject because she was getting bored. 'Buy anything particularly interesting this visit ... at the store, I mean?'

'Naw, the usual. That Ceil Bordon sure wrapped me up for a bundle though. Think she hypnotized me when I wasn't looking. Dropped almost a thousand bucks on stuff I don't even knew what to do with.'

'Wait'll next year. She's coming out with something that is sensational, a real zinger.'

'Really?'

'Definitely.'

'Think I'll need it?'

'Considering Lord Vidal's condition—yes.'

The main gossip of the evening centered around the strange death of Manny Berns. The local guests felt it would be quickly solved. The imports and those who knew Berns felt it would not. Bill Bethel, hopeful that the worst disasters of the fortnight were behind him, spoke for many who shared his thoughts.

'I wouldn't want to speak unkindly of the dead, but in Manny's case we can make an exception.'

'Now, Bill, don't be cruel.'

'Not cruelty at all, merely fact. Berns was a pimple on the asshole of fashion that someone finally popped. No more, no less.'

Sonia looked around the living room for her husband, but he was nowhere in sight. It was becoming exceedingly agitating to her to arrive with this vacuous elegant and then lose him as soon as dinner was over. This marriage was far from idyllic as far as Sonia was concerned. Roger Gregory, with his impeccable family and private fortune, seemed an ideal catch. His preoccupation with his hobby-business consumed most of his energy. After the initial overwhelming passion of the honeymoon, Roger reaffirmed his husbandly duties only occasionally. Everything else remained the same, but Sonia was an inwardly alive woman and needed the sexual side of the marriage bed to remain a whole individual. She decided several months ago to file for divorce and this only heightened her anxiety at missing him this evening.

'Pardon me, Lyla, have you seen Roger?'

'No, can't say that I have.'

'I'm getting a beastly headache and would like to have him take me home.'

'Oh, I'm sorry, Sonia. I can send you along in one of the store cars if you want.'

'Dear me, no. He's around somewhere. I'll find him.'

And finally she did. He was in the family car. In the back seat, to be exact. He was far from alone. Violet, a stunning black maid hired for the evening by the caterer, was spread-eagled and naked, in obvious ecstasy, as the dapper Roger Gregory plowed into her with a might and dedication that Sonia remembered from their wedding night.

Sonia froze at the sight beyond the closed car windows. Violet's legs wound around Roger with a strength found in passion, her eyes rolled back into her head as she came and came again in rapid succession. Roger unloaded mightily into the churning black woman at exactly the same instant that Sonia flung open the door.

'You filthy swine!' she screamed in a voice that shocked the lovers inside. She ran from the sedan and towards Stella's chauffeur, but Roger's reply still rang in her ears.

'It was *your* darkness that first attracted me. But, unlike you, these girls are scrutable!'

Alex, the caterer, had selected truly superior male specimens as waiters and bartenders for tonight's affair. The handsomest Latin types were efficiently and expertly seeing to the guests' needs. Alex mentioned that the young man who visited Stella last time was available this evening as well.

She replied, 'Alex, I should imagine that by now you would know I never entertain the same gentleman twice. That bartender, over there, mixing the martinis, is he Italian?'

'Yes, Miss Stella.'

'Fine. I should like to meet with him later. I may be going to Rome in the near future.'

The guests had all gone, the house was cleaned up from the party and Stella was alone in her Chagall-filled bedroom. The small reflector lights above each painting gave the only illumination in the large room. Stella was laying on top of her huge bed in the nude. She was smoking a cigarette. Soft music wafted from a hidden stereo. The door opened and the Italian bartender entered. He was confident of himself and knew what he had to do.

He moved to the side of the bed and stared down at the naked woman. Stella extinguished her cigarette. The expression on her face didn't change.

The young man got undressed and put his clothes neatly on a chair. He was tall, leanly built and his chest was hairy. His face was handsome in a cruel way and he was obviously enjoying this role of male prostitute. Not a single word was spoken between them. He walked to the bed, his large sex hanging between his legs. Without a sound, he got on the bed and straddled Stella, sitting upright lightly across her stomach. Slowly she reached up with both hands, took his piece and kneaded it expertly into a giant erection. He placed his arms behind him and braced himself in a slightly leaning back position as she massaged him quickly and furiously. His head rolled back. He was almost ready. He began to moan and sigh. Stella's eyes glistened in the half-darkness as she furiously milked his throbbing member with ever increasing tempo. He started a cry in the pit of his gut and it roared up and out into a shattering sob as he ejaculated massive spurts of thick milky fluid over her breasts and throat. When he finished coming, she removed her hands. His head fell exhausted on his chest. He was totally spent.

Quietly, Stella reached down next to the bed and picked up a soft towel which she handed to him. He got up from her and carefully wiped the juices from her and then himself. He took the towel into the bathroom and returned. Stella had not moved.

He put his things on and, without a look back at the immobile woman, left her bedroom. Stella was fast asleep, dreaming of glittering parties at the embassy in Rome.

For the first time in seven years, Stella Lehson spent the morning in bed. She arose well after ten and leisurely relaxed in her sunken tub.

She knew that downtown the display department was working furiously transforming the ballroom of the Tulsa City Royal into a bejeweled fantasy for the gala that evening. The store would be humming with activity already and, before the day was over, would rack up sales that surpassed anything but those happy days that preceded Christmas.

Nothing could possibly disturb the serene tranquillity of this day. And this evening promised to be the most fabulous and exciting of the twenty galas that had preceded it. The highlight of all previous affairs had been the presentation of the Annual Lehson Fashion Award, but tonight she knew an even more memorable moment would occur. Tonight she would humbly announce her appointment as ambassador and gratefully acknowledge her appreciation to the countless friends who had helped make it possible.

Yes, it was a delicious day, one to savor. Stella decided that for once, on a working day, she would not go into the store. They would have to get used to doing without her, so she might as well start now.

Stella had a light breakfast and didn't bother to read the paper, though she did check the Lehson advertisements for the day. A typographical error in one caught her eye and she made a mental note to mention this to Della. She planned to dress, then drive over to her father's around noon. Perhaps today he would be able to recognize her and there might have been another favorable change during the night. This was a day of miracles and—though she held out little hope for any permanent recovery—well, who could tell? He was an amazing old man.

Stella drove herself to the Lehson mansion. There were two cars parked in front. They must belong to Dr. Gregg and the nurse keeping their around-the-clock vigil over Mr. Abe. A forlorn and saddened Martin let her in. He had aged considerably during the last week. His face was etched with new lines and his hair had dulled. The strain of Mr. Abe's illness was affecting Martin as well.

Dr. Gregg came out to meet her.

'Good morning, Miss Stella.'

'Good morning, doctor. How's the patient this morning?'

'Science is constantly amazed at the human spirit. He had a quiet night and continues to remain stabilized.'

'Thank God.'

He led her towards the solarium.

'But remember, he is an extremely ill and old man.'

'Yes, doctor. I am aware and realistic, but hope is a marvelous tonic.'

Stella went in to see her father. His hospital bed had been moved into the sweating chamber. The hiss and wheeze of the oxygen tent was the only sound in the spacious room. She sat for a while next to his bed, listening to the difficult breathing. However, nothing could dim the delight she felt today. His cataract eyes opened for an instant; Stella felt he did see her and they fluttered closed. She kissed her father tenderly and left.

Stella marked the day well: Saturday, October 15, 1964. Today a dedicated Jewish girl from an overgrown cowtown in dusty Oklahoma would fete the most famous names in the entire world of fashion, along with some of the richest customers in the nation. Today this ambitious woman would see her ambition realized with the honor of becoming an American ambassador to a major European nation. She was completely confident that the President would allow her to make the announcement, rather than waiting for it to come from the State Department. Nothing would go wrong on this glorious October Saturday.

Stella had finally made up her mind on who would succeed her as head of the store. No one person could do the job. Instead, there would be a troika, a triumvirate handling the reins of power.

Eugene Boardman would oversee finance and profitability. Lyla, in spite of her curious sexuality, was still a Lehson and must serve the store as arbiter of taste. She would dynamically motivate the whole couture world and maintain the Lehson standard. Finally, Bill Bethel would be given full latitude to continue the outstanding promotional and image-building job he had done so well. Finance, fashion and flourish—the triangle upon which the store was built.

These three would hold the chair of power and Stella felt secure that, when her assignment abroad was over, she could return to Tulsa City and retire with a life well spent and gloriously lived.

The telephone was ringing as she let herself into the house. The maid had almost reached the table where the phone stood as Stella closed the door behind her and said, 'I'll get it, Martha.'

She hurried into the library and picked up the receiver. It was Frank Preston, calling from Washington.

'It's a smashing afternoon in Tulsa City, Frank. How is everything along the Potomac?'

'Cloudy, Stella. Decidedly overcast.'

She sobered and stood erect.

'All right, Frank, let's have it.'

'You didn't make it.'

'But . . . Amos Barron said . . .'

'Amos Barron doesn't know his ass from his clavicle. I'm sorry, the President said, "No." He had me down to the White House to make it as pleasant as possible. He said he knew what a disappointment it was going to be for you and wanted to soften the blow as much as he could.'

'Why didn't I get it?'

'He said the post must be filled by a Catholic. It's just that simple. Your religion is against you for a Mediterranean assignment.'

'Just like that?'

'Yes, just like that. Oh, he did mention the possibility of something in the Balkans or Scandinavia next year, but . . .'

'No, it was this or nothing. This was my time and I guess I'm too far ahead of the necessary ecumenical. We Lehsons have always set the fashion, never followed it.'

'Personally, I think the religious aspect is just an excuse. They couldn't have let it get this far without considering that side of it.'

'Probably, Frank, but whatever the reason, I don't get the job. Too bad. I really wanted it.'

'I'm sorry, Stella, you know that.'

'Of course I do. Stop worrying, Frank dear. It takes more than a disappointment, even one this big, to fell this girl.'

'Good. I knew you . . . oh hell, I'm goddamned sorry.'

'So am I. Oh, and Frank, that raise in salary still goes.'

'I didn't earn it.'

'No, Frank, I'm the one who didn't earn it. It's yours. Thanks for all you've done and all you tried to do. I've still got a gala on my hands. I'll keep busy.'

'All right, Stella. Bye.'

'Good-bye, Frank.'

Stella hesitated for less than a moment, cradled the phone, then took a breath and set off to busy herself about the house, staying to the schedule she had planned for the day.

Lyla was late. Belle and Sal were almost finished with their cocktail when she entered the dark little French restaurant Sal had suggested for their lunch. The Old Provence was just three blocks away from the store and a favorite meeting place for the wealthy to dine in this culinary desert. Wood paneled, tables lit by candles, it was a dark and intimate spot. The food was just passable French, but in Tulsa City that was tantamount to gastronomic triumph.

For some eerie reason, Lyla had felt queasy every time she saw A'Patico. Ever since Bern's dramatic exit from the worldly plane, he had taken on a new, even more sinister cast. He looked at her with different eyes and she saw him for what he might become for the first time.

'Sorry I'm late kids. It's a madhouse today.'

Sal signaled the waiter who took her cocktail order and vanished in the direction of the murky bar.

'The prices in this joint! Jeez, ya gotta be well-heeled to eat here,' grumbled Sal.

'Well-oiled would be more like it. You're in petroleum country.'

Still Lyla was becoming a trifle frightened at his gaze.

'So da store is busy, huh?'

'Outside of Christmas, our biggest time of the year.'

Belle chimed in, 'But Lyla's never too busy to see her friends.'

'Never. Oh Belle, I checked with alterations and your dress for tonight will be ready by four. Shall I send it around to the hotel?'

Sal answered for her. 'Naw, we'll pick it up. O'Hara here might find something else she wants.'

The waiter brought her drink and handed the menus around. They ordered a light lunch, Sal grumbled he couldn't get spaghetti and the waiter left. Sal leaned back and stared at Lyla.

'The store must do better'n thirty million a year, huh?'

'Closer to fifty. Why?'

'Jus' curious. That's big business, like a million a week.'

'It's taken us over a half century to reach that figure. Besides, the dollar isn't worth what it used to be.'

'Yeah, money's gonna be the cheapest thing around in a while.'

Belle questioned Lyla on protocol for the evening's gala and this led to an interchange of woman's talk. The waiter brought their meal and a bottle of Italian Chianti. Sal knifed at his thick blood-rare steak and the girls toyed with their omelets.

'Dis steak's tough. Shit! Whaddya expect in a cowtown?'

'Sal, stop being disagreeable and let Lyla and me chat.'

'Okay, so chat.'

The edge returned to Lyla and she couldn't enjoy her meal. She forced herself to respond to a bubbling Belle, but it was difficult. Sal's eyes kept staring at her as he ate. Whatever he was thinking, she didn't like it. His eyelids half closed for a moment and then he asked quietly, 'How much your business is cash?'

'What?'

'How much cash? Opposed to charge accounts and credit cards.'

'I haven't the faintest idea, Sal.'

'It would be interestin' to know. Could you find out for me?'

'I imagine so, but why?'

'A business that takes in a lotta cash is always interestin'.'

Lyla's temper finally took over her unnamed fear.

'Sal! I'm nervous enough about tonight, without having you badger me with a lot of insane questions. Why the hell are you so interested in Lehson's?'

'Yeah, Sal, cool it,' added Belle. 'Can't you see Lyla's getting up-set?'

'Hey, don't get so excited! I'm the last guy to upset two gorgeous gals. I'm just curious, like I said. I'm a businessman, Lyla, and you got a business. That's all . . . somethin' ta talk about.'

'I'm sorry, Sal, truly sorry. It's just that I'm awfully jittery. Excuse me.'

'Hey, no excuses. I understand. That Berns must've unhinged you real good. But that's all over, honey, so relax.'

Lyla knew what the lingering fear was when Sal mentioned Manny Berns's name. She took a larger than usual drink of wine while Sal continued talking.

'Y'know, we three have always been real happy together. Real happy and friendly like. I gotta feeling that in the future, we're goin' to be even happier. How 'bout that?' He raised his glass in a toast. 'To my beautiful ladies. *Tchin tchin!*'

Lyla joined Belle in the toast, but her heart wasn't in it. Things were taking an odd and unsettling turn and it would be better if she didn't think about it. As they finished the meal, Lyla's unease continued—unexplained. She refused to accept that any real danger was crouched ahead.

Sal had a menacing gleam in his eyes. He looked at her once again—long and hard—then attacked the nearly raw slab of sirloin with obvious relish.

No one who saw her knew that Stella had suffered the biggest single setback of her life. She had coped with her husband, managed the store in good times and bad, and weathered the storms that business and social competition had thrust her into. But, on the one thing she had set out to do, to cap her life's work and give some reason to existence . . . the one thing she really wanted had been denied her. As the chauffeur drove her downtown to the gala, Stella pushed the disappointment out of her thoughts. There was still the evening to get through and, besides, a new plan was formulating in her mind as the car stopped in front of the Tulsa City Royal.

Lehson's Annual Fashion Award Dinner was the commanding event of Tulsa City's vigorous social season. There was no competition.

Tickets were two hundred and fifty dollars a pair and limited to five hundred couples. There was a gourmet dinner, fine wines, a superlative fashion show climaxing with the awarding of the coveted 'AL' golden plaques; then dancing to an orchestra flown in from New York just for the occasion. And all this transpired among the finest and most exclusive assemblage of high fashion's elite from around the globe.

It was all in the name of sweet charity; this year mentally retarded children benefited. (Ann Carter's father was heard wondering aloud in the city room whether this meant unfortunately stricken children or the denizens of fashion.) In any case, the gala was eagerly awaited and tickets were sought-after badges attesting to charity and taste . . . all fully deductible.

Princess Judith had flown back from Boston to share the spotlight with Heymano. *Vogue*, *Harper's Bazaar*, *Town and Country*, and *Women's Wear Daily* had sent editors and photographers. The local Associated Press correspondent covered for the nation's daily newspapers. The wealth of publicity generated by this affair was incalculable to Lehson's.

By seven-thirty, the ballroom was filled with as splendid and opulent an array of magnificent gowns and exquisite jewels as could be found anywhere on earth. Accents of Rue St. Honoré flowed about those of St. James and Tulsa City. The tinkling laughter of Beverly Hills matrons skimmed a melody line to the solid undercurrent of New Yorkese. The 'wshh' of lightly indrawn breath randomly marked the awe first felt at the presence of a pure, radiant, beautiful Princess Judith sheathed in an elegant white Moore gown. It was indeed one of the finest of international affairs.

Just before cocktail hour ended, Stella managed to get Eugene Boardman alone for a minute.

'Gene, I have a special assignment for you. It's top priority and goes no further than the two of us.'

He nodded. 'Understood.'

'I am giving you two years to put Lehson's in the soundest most advantageous cash position of any department store in America.'

'Do I have a free hand?'

'Completely. Do whatever must be done, but two years from tonight we must be the most coveted mercantile property anywhere. Is that understood?'

'Totally. May I ask why? Lehson's has always stood for many things before profitability.'

'That was the past. Tomorrow we start accumulating the dividends of a slightly parochial attitude. In two years I want us in a position to make the most advantageous sale or merger possible.'

Boardman was shocked, but contained his surprise.

'Sell Lehson's? Yes, we could become a very juicy plum indeed. I can do it, Miss Stella, but I'll need carte blanche.'

'I've already told you, it's yours.'

'Some of the things I shall have to do will rub a lot of the employees and executives the wrong way, you know.'

'That is their problem. Yours is to fatten us up for a sale.'

'Thank you, Miss Stella, you can count on me.'

This strange turn of events suited him exactly. For years it stuck in his craw, the inefficiency that prevailed so executive egos could soar. Lehson's wasn't all that different from any other commercial property, it just appeared that way. He regretted foisting Bethel off to Ceil Bordon, but a new man could be quickly found to build a store image more conducive to the *Wall Street Journal* than *Harper's Bazaar*.

'One more thing, Miss Stella?'

'Yes?'

'Will this new change affect Culbertson?'

'Obviously, he stays. In fact, I imagine we should think about enlarging his area.'

'Naturally, I couldn't agree more.'

He was sorry that he wasn't getting the store presidency. She must have lost her ambassadorship. But this was really up his alley. Yes, Eugene Boardman would fatten up the cowtown calf and he had definite thoughts as to which major chain would do the slaughtering. A most pleasant evening all around.

The rickety Lord Vidal, his gouty foot atop a pillow under the dining table, excused his Oklahoma Lady.

'Honey, I just want one dance. You don't mind, do ya?'

'Not at all my dear. Gavotte to your heart's content.'

He turned back to Edna and their heated discussion of the advantages of artificially inseminating brood mares. Lady Vidal watched the happy couples waltzing across the highly polished dance floor. C.Z. sidled up to her, the ever-present martini in evidence.

'Quite a gathering, Lady V. Lehson's does it again.'

'Hi there, Carl. Yep, some shindig. Say, how 'bout a turn around the floor?'

'Sorry, Dotty, I chafe to anything but a minuet. Excuse me, the glass demands refilling.'

Unbeknownst to Bill Bethel, blithely escorting Ceil Bordon around the ballroom, Tina was getting roaring drunk backstage. This was her first appearance since the fiasco of her party and the insecurity it had festered all week erupted this evening. The other models and those stunning society ladies who enjoyed this sort of thing were all being made up and dressed for the grand fashion parade of Heymano's most fabulous gowns that would precede the actual award. Tina sat before the makeup mirror staring at her gorgeous reflection. Her ninth Dr. Pepper and cognac, almost finished, was by her side. Sonia concluded her last-minute briefing of the others and made her way through the chiffon and watered silk to Tina's table.

'The show begins in a few minutes. Are you ready?'

'Why don' you jus' fuck off, honey?' replied Tina, and then slowly, deliberately smeared the lipstick across her face. 'Think ah'll create a new style. Whatcha think, huh?'

'You can't go on,' Sonia sighed. 'You are disgustingly drunk, Tina. Take off the gown, please.'

'You can go straight ta hell. Ah'm modelin' an nothin' y'all do can stop it.'

Sonia turned to a strong, middle-aged alteration lady acting as dresser. 'Get Mrs. Bethel out of that dress. She's not well,' she said.

'Keep yer fuckin' hands off a me!' Tina screamed and collapsed in an alcoholic stupor across the table.

Sonia ordered the dress removed again and made her way from the backstage area to the main floor of the ballroom. She went directly to Stella's table and whispered, 'Sorry, Miss Stella, but Tina can't appear. She's passed out.'

'Ill?'

'Drunk.'

'She was wearing the presentation gown, wasn't she?'

'That's right.'

Stella, her face still hiding the latest trauma, turned to Princess Judith. 'Dear, could I possibly impose upon your good nature once again?'

'What is it, Stella?'

'Our premiere mannequin has been taken suddenly sick . . .'

'Oh, I am sorry,' she said, but she was secretly delighted, as she knew what was to follow.

'It's the girl who was modeling Heymano's royal presentation gown . . . one we've been saving for tonight. If you . . . could you . . . oh dear, this is so embarrassing. . . . You would keep the dress with our compliments and gratitude, of course.'

'To help you out? Of course, Stella dear.'

'Miss Angelini will escort you.' The men at the table rose with the Princess, who followed Sonia to where the women were dressing. As she walked across the floor, knowing that all eyes were following her, she thought of the fun of still commanding such a huge audience. A lot more impressive than the Monteblanco Army, in fact. There were only sixty of them.

Brian Manchester, at the bar, watched the frivolity and foolishness of another Lehson gala. He saw Sonia hurry from the dressing area, whisper something to Stella; saw the Princess rise and leave ,and knew that another possible clinker had been averted. They seemed to thrive on situations that demanded instant solutions. It's almost, he thought, as if they chose this damned masochistic business to satisfy some inner drive. His reverie and mounting disgust at the whole charade was broken by a salutation from Momma Pepper, who was being carried to the ladies room by Blossom,

'Hi ya, Brian. How's yer Maw? Hurry, Blossom, the good Lord won't wait!'

Della was thoroughly enjoying herself, busy seeing that the working press got everything they needed. As she coaxed the more important and better attired guests to pose for even more photographs she thought, 'What a great gala it's been. The best yet. God, this is a great place to be. Great store. Great job. And that Edna . . . best husband a gal ever had.'

Sonia sent word to Bill that someone had to take Tina home. He turned to Ceil.

'Sorry about this. Tina's sick. I'd better see that she gets home. I'll try to come right back.'

'Bill? Just a minute. Mind if I add my two cents?'

'I'd rather you didn't.'

'Well, I'm going to just the same. We both know what's the matter with Tina.'

'She's just nervous, that's all.'

'Not nervous. She doesn't fit in all this. Like so many great hucksters, Bill, you bought the package without bothering to check on what's inside. There's nothing wrong with Tina that a dumb stud of a husband and a bunch of howling kids couldn't cure. Her face is big-time, but her mind's just small town. Sorry kid, that's the truth of it.'

Ceil was right on target and Bill knew it.

'I'll get her a room here at the hotel. Be back in a minute.'

'Thatta boy. You'll see, it'll be much better in New York and Paris with you unencumbered. Glad you see the light.'

'It's sad though, Ceil.'

'It's always sad when your dreams don't stand up in the morning.'

Michelle De Soto, Mae Ritz and Quentin Kimball sat watching the almost theatrical assemblage.

'New York's going to be dull after all this, Quent.'

'So's Chicago,' agreed Mae.

'Ah'm taking a house in Warsaw for the winter.'

'Warsaw?'

'The one in Poland?'

'Thass right.'

'Good God, why?'

'Well, if the Lehson's can do this to Oklahoma, just think what little ol' me can do in Warsaw.'

'You've got a point, Quentin.'

'Ah think so.'

'Gotta guest room?'

'Thirty-two. It's sort of a palace thing.'

'Shit!'

'What's the matter, Michelle?'

'That means I'll have to buy more furs.'

Sonia signaled the orchestra leader that the models were ready. He finished the number and turned to the dancers waiting for the next song.

'Ladies and gentlemen, if you'll kindly return to your tables the event you've all been waiting for will commence.'

The orchestra played some light walking music as the couples strolled back—women smoothing their hair and checking their jewels while the men adjusted their black bow ties.

At the head table, Stella gave Mano a reassuring squeeze and smile, excused herself and made her way to the microphone on the stage.

'Welcome once again to Lehson's Mediterranean gala . . .' and she waxed on for a few minutes about her happiness and the service to charity this splendid occasion fostered. Then she announced that, before the awards, Lehson's was presenting a showing of the most fabulous creations of that exquisite talent from Madrid and Paris . . . Señor Heymano. The first model came out and for the next twenty minutes the women in the crowd were swept away by the sheer luxury and beauty of the magnificent clothes that paraded before them. The applause at the final gown, worn to perfection by a radiant Princess Judith, was tumultuous. The entire assemblage rose to their feet, and cheering followed the heavy applause. Princess Judith stopped, smiled and turned to Heymano sitting below her. She turned to Stella and the two women led their applause directed to Mano. Pepe, beaming, clapped loudly as a stunned and immensely proud young man got up from his seat and walked shyly up the steps to join the Princess and the Queen. This was unquestionably the grandest moment in a life filled with awards and honors. He had peaked tonight, and savoring the excitement was the most delicious feeling he had ever known. More would follow, but nothing would ever reach what he experienced this truly gala evening. Heymano was installed in the firmament of talented gods in the fashion skies. Little Mano walked twenty feet tall as he joined Stella and Princess Judith. Stella said nothing . . . the orchestra leader handed her the golden statuette, which she in turn handed to the Princess.

Hundreds upon hundreds of flashbulbs exploded, a thousand rich and important cheering people stood up and the orchestra played 'Hail to the Chief' as a humbled and appreciative Heymano accepted the 'AL.' He kissed both ladies and, now glowing and supercharged, accepted the electric applause.

Stella led Princess Judith and Heymano down to the dance floor, the orchestra segued into a lively selection as the two most prestigious people in all of Tulsa City began the first dance after the award. It was almost a royal affair.

The floor filled immediately and everyone was having an elegantly marvelous time. The evening and the party were an unqualified smash. Lyla accepted the courtly Brian Manchester's invitation to join the dancers as he easily and gracefully waltzed her around, her eyes focused on the orchestra; then they zeroed in on an appealing and likely candidate for her late-evening romp . . . a lean, handsome trumpet player with incredible moves. The night-cap was chosen and all the dark thoughts of probable problems with Sal A'Patico and his emotional hold over her disappeared. Like another troubled heroine, Lyla would think about that tomorrow. Tonight, it was merry-making as usual. The music played, the guests drank and danced. Flashbulbs popped and another lavish Lehson gala wound into the night, outstanding to the very end.

Stella, alone at last in her bed, gazed absent-mindedly at the protective ring of Chagall. She was more than exhausted from the pressures of the last two weeks, though sleep eluded her. Her eyes stared at the art treasures, but her thoughts caromed sharply and randomly between the pain of her lost ambassadorship, her father's still grave condition and the new future she was plotting for the store. They kaleidoscoped into a bizarre pattern of overlapping mental images: Was she taking the store in the right direction? Would this move for even greater national ascendancy destroy sixty years of growth? Her dear father . . . how much influence did this near-vegetable still exert on her, despite his illness? Did the President really expect her to swallow that trumped-up reason of 'Jewishness' as a reason for letting her down? What did he really want? Find out and get it for him. It's not too late, even now. The troubled thoughts spun and whirled in her brain until she finally forced herself to snap them off.

Stella composed herself, slid across the crisp, clean sheets and leaned over for the telephone, thinking she'd better check on the store. Must make certain that all the decorations and displays would be gone when the store opened as usual on Monday.

The crisp, sharp click of the opening bedroom door cracked through the room, startling Stella. She froze as a man's shadowed outline entered the room and shut the door behind him.

Masking the fear in her voice as best she could, Stella asked, 'Who are you?' The form wordlessly moved to the side of the bed, staring at her from the shadows. Stella was terrified. 'Who are you? What do you want?' she gasped.

A deep voice spoke softly, 'Easy, Stell . . . easy now . . .'

She choked on her question. 'Brian?'

'Yes, Stella,' he replied with a firm sureness in his voice. Brian Manchester undid his shirt, slipped off his shoes and eased out of his pants. He did not wear underwear.

Stella was speechless until he snapped back the covers of the bed. 'No!' she exclaimed. 'Brian get out of here!'

He answered by leaping onto the bed, forcefully grabbing her shoulders and snapping her upper torso into a face-to-face position. He painfully wrenched her body once more and slipped his knees between her thighs, holding her open and down. Stella was immobilized by fear, disbelief and shock.

'Stella. You listen to me. You are not going to manipulate me anymore ... flaunt my freedom like one of your gaudy handbags. You are not going to show me off for your damn image! No more damn parties! No more functions! We are filing for divorce Monday! Do you understand that? We are getting a divorce! Do you understand?'

He shook her roughly. Stella said nothing, her eyes wide and fixated on the surging pulse of his organ.

'You damn Stella!' he cried out as he crashed into her. He continued to shout and yell amidst his thrusting bellows and roars. Stella could not resist, her mind blocking the pain of his ripping friction and floating to focus on one slab of rectangular light above a Chagall.

He savagely pounded out his fury. She was glazed into a trancelike vacuum.

Brian slipped out of the room less than twenty minutes after he had startlingly entered and roughly asserted himself. Stella remained immobilized on the messed bed. She thought of time spent alone on barren plains land. The pleasure. So rare. Not a soul around for miles upon miles. She thought of Lyla, of crazed, obsessed Lyla.

Stella got up and retrieved a towel. She walked about the bedroom directionless, detachedly wiping her body of perspiration and juices.

She reflexively sat at the foot of the bed, thoughts racing without control. Stella was unaware of the soft, hurting sounds that slipped babbling through her pursed lips. She thought again of her father and burst into tears.

The early morning silence that veiled suburban Tulsa City held an eerie tension. In the massive, lonely mansion he had established with a dream, Abraham Lehson unconsciously beat a painful cadence with his slow, laborious breathing. Only the night nurse was witness as the founder of the Lehson dynasty easily, effortlessly slipped from the shell of life to his well-earned rest.

Four a.m. and the store was still not quiet. Construction workers and display people were taking down the last bits of decoration that had metamorphosed Lehson's into a Mediterranean fantasy. The papier mâché whitewashed walls were all piled neatly in the basement. They would be carted away at seven with the tinsel, plaster shells, fisherman's nets and other artifacts and trimmings that had combined to create the mirage.

The Christmas decor was stored on giant shelves, to be brought out the day after Thanksgiving. For the six weeks between these worlds, the store would be as it always had been: a busy, bustling mart of wares carefully and scrupulously selected for the rich and near-rich of the Southwest.

A huge pile of thin lumber, false walls, façades and cardboard trellises stood ready for removal. The large shipping room doors were open, waiting for the trucks that would haul away this year's dream. A warm front had moved into the area and its dry, desert wind spanked the walls outside the store.

The night watchman's phone rang. He left the crew he'd been supervising and hurried downstairs to answer it.

'Lehson's. Watchman here. Oh, good evening . . . I should say, good morning, Miss Stella. Yes, everything's right on schedule.'

He laid his cigar down on the ledge where the telephone sat and reached inside his overalls for a list.

'Yep, just the cobbler's display in the shoe department and we'll be finished. When the store opens, you'll never know we had a Mediterranean gala at all. Thanks, and good morning to you, Miss Stella.'

His crew called down to the basement insistently, 'Hey, give us a hand, will ya?'

'Fer Christ sakes, hold yer horses.'

The watchman climbed the stairs leading up to the main floor, musing to himself, 'Jeez, four in the morning and she's still up and checking on the store. I guess that's the way it has to be when the store's yer life. Beats me, though, she sure must love this old place.'

His forgotten cigar burned down to the lip of the ledge, hesitated precariously and fell to the floor. It landed in a small pile of shredded packing paper, nestled next to the enormous pile of sets and lumber that had just been taken down.

A tiny spark flitted to the edge of a paper streamer and ignited. There was a wisp of smoke, a slight smoldering and then, in the deserted receiving room filled with highly flammable material, the pile of paper ignited.

The flames grew instantly, fanned to frightening heights by the autumn breeze from outside.

The workmen upstairs were suddenly buffeted by the force and roar of combustion, and the surging waves of heat that followed. Smoke poured into the room as they instinctively fled. Nothing could stop this destructive inferno as it raged unchecked. On this early Sunday morning, the mighty store and its legendary founder passed into history.

SICILIAN DEFENCE
John Nicholas Iannuzzi

On a chessboard called New York City, blacks and whites clash in the biggest game in town – with the biggest stakes. A powerful Sicilian Don is snatched from the top of the New York crime scene. His lieutenants move out to snatch him back – with bribery, violence and corruption, the game begins. *50p*

OPERATION CASINO
Leo Rost

"Rost knows the passion and stench of big-time gambling . . . his suspense broods and smoulders and his people breathe and sweat. This is one hell of a yarn." DAVID MARKSON

A tale of corruption in the Bahamas where the stake is survival. *60p*

THE OVERLORDS
William Woolfolk

When the California Governor's plane crashed and one million dollars in cash was found hidden in his home, Steve Gifford, ex-FBI, tough, unrelenting, was given an assignment. A nightmare spreads to involve the two-faced masks of justice, law, even family and friends . . . and the Syndicate's plan becomes a little more specific – *get Gifford.* *75p*

THE TAKEOVER
Niven Busch

The fierce battlefield of politics versus law. Four men, all well on their way to becoming billionaires, pass a death sentence on a fifth – Jed, the President of their Corporation. Soon enough it's the White House itself that needs paying off . . . "As up to date as this morning's headline news. A fast-paced, spellbinding story, Niven Busch's finest book so far." ARTHUR HAILEY *50p*

FIRST DEADLY SIN
Lawrence Sanders

An astounding novel of cops and killers that carves up the neon-lit city streets of New York into the elemental forces of good and evil. A novel that has become a breathtakingly compulsive read throughout the world. *75p*

BRIEF ENCOUNTER
Alec Waugh

One man, one woman, a blitzkrieg of emotion.
A brief yet unrelenting emotional tug-of-war between two
people — Anna, happily married, Alec, trapped in a loveless
marriage — Between them a passion is ignited well beyond
their ordered imaginations. Can they transform their dream
into a lasting love, or must it founder on the rocks of
reality? Now a film starring Richard Burton and Sophia
Loren.   *50p*

CONDUCT UNBECOMING
Rupert Croft-Cooke

The Regiment in the India of 1878 symbolised honour and
courage. But when the legendary Captain Scarlett's widow
is 'raped' the surrounding mystery throws justice and the
Regimental code into the balance putting the life of an
innocent man right on the line. Now a film starring Michael
York, Susannah York, Richard Attenborough, Christopher
Plummer and Stacey Keach.   Illustrated. *50p*

PAPER TIGER
Jack Davies

David Niven, star of the film by the same name says – "This is a book to touch your heart and set your blood racing." A moving story of one man and a boy set against the exotic background of the Far East. To Koichi, the boy, Walter Bradbury is everything a real man should be. But, when they fall victims to a political plot, Bradbury – poseur and inveterate liar – faces a life-and-death situation for the first time. Will Koichi find that his idol has feet of clay?   *50p*

YOUNG FRANKENSTEIN
Gilbert Pearlman

From the Mel Brooks film based on the smash hit successor to BLAZING SADDLES. "Madder, funnier and more inspired than anything being done in movies today." TIME. The book is complete with sixteen pages of pictures taken from the film.   Illustrated. *50p*

PHANTOM OF THE PARADISE
Bjarne Rostaing

He sold his soul for rock 'n' roll. Winslow Leach is a young man who wants to create heavenly music – even if he has to descend to the depths of hell to do it . . .
A fantastic horror rock comedy starring Paul Williams.
Illustrated. *50p*

JANIS JOPLIN: BURIED ALIVE
Myra Friedman

"Brilliant, marvellous, emotionally devastating . . . A beautifully written, terribly important document of the times we live in." NEW YORK NEWS
This is the full tragic story of Janis Joplin, the rock superstar whose suicidal life-style bought her international adulation, wealth and death at twenty-seven. A big film has now been released.   Illustrated. *75p*

STAR BOOKS

are available through all good booksellers but, where difficulty is encountered, titles can usually be obtained *by post* from:

**Star Book Service,
G.P.O. Box 29,
Douglas,
Isle of Man,
British Isles.**

Please send retail price plus 8p per copy.

Customers outside the British Isles should include 10p post/packing per copy.

Book prices are subject to alteration without notice.